Lonesome
You

TITLES IN THE LIBRARY OF KOREAN LITERATURE
AVAILABLE FROM DALKEY ARCHIVE PRESS

LIBRARY OF KOREAN LITERATURE
9

Lonesome You

Park Wan-suh

Translated by
Elizabeth Haejin Yoon

DALKEY ARCHIVE PRESS
CHAMPAIGN / LONDON / DUBLIN

Originally published in Korean as *Nŏmudo ssŭlssŭrhan tangsin* by Ch'angjak kwa
Pip'yŏngsa, Seoul, 1998

Copyright © 1998 by Park Wan-suh
Translation © 2013 by Elizabeth Haejin Yoon

First edition, 2013
All rights reserved

Library of Congress Cataloging-in-Publication Data

Pak, Wan-so, 1931-2011.
[Nomudo ssulssurhan tangsin. English]
Lonesome You / Park Wan-suh ; translated by Elizabeth Haejin Yoon. -- First edition.
pages cm
ISBN 978-1-56478-909-9 (alk. paper)
I. Yoon, Elizabeth Haejin, translator. II. Title.
PL992.62.W34N6513 2013
895.7'34--dc23
2013027221

Partially funded by a grant from the Illinois Arts Council, a state agency

Library of Korean Literature
Published in collaboration with the Literature Translation Institute of Korea

www.dalkeyarchive.com

Cover: design and composition by Mikhail Iliatov

Thanks to Wei-Ling Woo of Epigram Books (Singapore)
for helping with the editing of this book.

Printed on permanent/durable acid-free paper

Table of Contents

Withered Flower

The only thing I saw of him at first was his hand. A hand with a ring on its finger. Right away, I recognized the deep navy stone lodged in the platinum band as an aquamarine. It isn't an expensive stone, but it isn't all that common either. I don't particularly have an eye for gemstones. Far from it. A friend of mine used to own a jewelry shop in the basement of a five-star hotel. Drawn in by her uncanny knack for telling stories, I frequented her shop, but what I learned about precious stones from these visits had nothing to do with the pragmatic business of discerning the faux from the real stuff.

Was the gist of her stories that beauty has a price? Like a beautiful woman who keeps a man under her thumb, a gemstone can meddle with the fate of those who fall under its spell. My friend knew so many fascinating and tragic tales about gems and the insatiable human greed for precious things in life. And she unraveled these stories with such finesse that I lost all sense of time and reality when listening to her. It seemed to me that she was in the business of selling precious stones not because of money or passion but because she was captivated by these stories herself.

How she told the story of the aquamarine differed somewhat from the elaborate manner in which she narrated the romantic legends surrounding other stones. High quality aquamarines—ones displaying the rich hues of the deep, deep sea—are very rare.

The reason for their rarity was explained to me in the following tale. There once was a young man who lost the love of his life to the sea. For the rest of his life, he spent all of his earnings buying up the best aquamarines his money could afford. In his old age, he had enough to fill a huge burlap sack. Instead of plunging into the ocean after his beloved, he exchanged his life and soul for those ocean-hued crystals. For some reason, my friend told this story plainly and indifferently. But now that I think about it, what better tactic was there to maximize dramatic effect? Although I listened to the story with only a passing interest at the time, a second look at the aquamarines' intense navy blue color pierced my heart like a sharp and cold razor, giving me goose bumps all over.

Having missed the last train, I arrived at the bus terminal huffing and puffing, only to be told that all of the seats were sold out. No tickets, with Seoul-bound busses leaving every ten minutes and still two hours left until the last departure! It was a Saturday afternoon. Even at the train station just moments before, what I had lacked was not the time to catch the train, but the time to buy a ticket at the crowded ticket counter.

I was on my way home from attending my nephew's wedding. As a so-called family elder, I was outraged by my nephew's thoughtlessness in not preparing for my safe return home. Perhaps it was my own fault for not having bought a round-trip ticket, but the truth of the matter is that I wasn't expecting to return on the same day. My oldest nephew, who relocated to that city for work five years ago, always extended an invitation to visit him whenever I talked to him on the phone. I naturally assumed that he would have his aunt stay for a night or two after attending his brother's wedding. My family is originally from Seoul, but after my older brother and his wife passed away one after the other, their four children went their separate ways, finding jobs in different cities. The youngest was the only one working in Seoul, but he met a girl from Daegu and was getting married there among all of his bride's clan. If it weren't for my oldest nephew and his wife, I would have felt even more like a fish out of water on the bride's home turf. Actually, it's no accident that the bride is from there. My youngest nephew wasn't overly choosy, but he didn't meet a suitable girl for marriage until his older brother's wife set him up on numerous dates with girls from Daegu.

The reception hall was noisy with everyone speaking in the thick Daegu dialect. That upset me even more, when I was already feeling down after being treated like a second-class citizen by my oldest niece-in-law. I was wearing a traditional *hanbok* for the *pyebaek* ceremony, where the newly wedded couple bows to the elders in the groom's family. But my oldest niece-in-law had told the bride's family not to bother. "We don't really have any elders to disappoint" was her justification for passing over this tradition. What, no elders? So an old aunt on the male's side of the family is not an elder? I was rendered speechless by her audacity to insult me to my face, and I instinctively looked around for an ally.

My, my! If they're going to skip pyebaek, *then why bother with a marriage ceremony? They can just live together. Never in my life have I seen anything like this, especially from such a respectable family. Nope, this is pure madness. What will others say about this family? And what about the bride's family who agreed to this preposterous idea? This is not just a bad reflection on individual families. This is a terrible infraction of our sacred cultural traditions.*

Someone my age, just as offended as I was at my niece-in-law's bogus good intentions, might have been eager to bash her in this manner. But everyone around me was a stranger. Who is a paternal aunt-in-law? I suppose someone who has married out of the family, according to the letter of tradition. It occurred to me that the proper treatment of an elder denied me by my niece-in-law was a calculated move to deal with an outsider. I suddenly lost my nerve. Without the parents around, should *pyebaek* still be performed, or is it okay to omit it? I wasn't sure anymore. What am I sure of? For someone turning sixty the following year, it was depressing as well as baffling to be disregarded as a family elder.

With an ice sculpture of a phoenix hovering over them and artificial fog misting their feet, the happy couple cut their cake and popped open a bottle of champagne amidst much clapping and cheering. From the guest tables all I could hear were the excited, celebratory voices in the regional dialect. After the brush off I got from my nephew and his wife, the accented voices ganging up on me and mocking my isolation added insult to injury. The pink *hanbok* I wore at my daughter's wedding, made of God knows how many yards of fabric, sprawled out uncontrollably, trailing behind me in all its pathetic tackiness. How unbearable it is to be an unimportant person in an ostentatious dress, to suffer so many looks from judgmental people! Aware of every painstaking second that ticked by, I hardly tasted my food.

"By the way, Auntie, what time is your ticket for?" My second niece-in-law, who had been too busy fussing over her kids to mind me, suddenly turned to me, wide-eyed and innocent.

"Ticket, what ticket?

"Your return ticket. Oh, no, you didn't reserve it? But it's Saturday . . ."

Instead of answering, my eyes searched for my eldest niece-in-law, who was busy making rounds among the guests. But my second niece-in-law, who was quicker to find her, made a big fuss to her about how I was still working idly on my slab of steak without a clue as to how I was going to return home.

"It may not be too late, if we hurry now . . ." my eldest niece-in-law said, looking at her watch. I had no choice but to accept that I had to leave that day. I felt crushed as the last thread of expectation that I'd be asked to stay, even out of obligation, disappeared. Lest I spill a tear of disappointment, I kept shoving pieces of cut-up beef into my mouth.

"Oh, please take your time with your food, Auntie. I think we still have some time."

"Actually, we don't. We have to take into account the time it takes to get to the station."

"We can leave a little early and take her with us on our way back. I'm sorry, Elder Sister, but I won't be able to help you clean up here."

"You'd do that? Good thinking. There's nothing to clean up anyway. Taking Auntie with you would be a big help to me. Thanks."

This was the dialogue exchanged in my presence between my eldest niece-in-law and the second eldest, who lives in Woolsan. They must have driven. As it turns out, they had brought their old Excel. Except for the bride and the groom, only the nephews and their wives saw me off. The second niece-in-law sat in the back with her two children while I sat in the passenger seat. I looked at my nephew, who was driving.

"Why are you staring?" he asked.

"Because I think you look the most like your father . . ."

"I think you told me when I was young that I take after my mother's side."

"No, no, I didn't," I firmly denied without any real conviction.

"I haven't seen Hyung-Seok in a while. I thought he'd come down with you."

"Didn't I say that he's on a business trip? His wife works also."

"Honey, when will you be going on a business trip, huh?" an impudent voice chimed in from the backseat.

"Why, you want to be free and single?"

"I just want to be spared from these family events from time to time."

"How is a cousin the same as a sibling? The things you say . . ."

Although the words out of his mouth were disdainful, the

smile on his lips showed that he couldn't get enough of her adorable whining.

"What's so different? I didn't get a single thing from the new bride. Elder Sister told her family not to worry about wedding presents. Humph, when I got married, she made no such exception for me. I don't know what she has against me. Look at me. What's not to like?"

"All right, all right. Why do you even care? The only person you need to find favor with is me."

All the way to the station, they didn't give me the slightest chance to join in their playful banter. At Daegu station, the attendants were blowing their whistles and blocking cars from entering the fully occupied parking lots. Jumping at the chance to make a perfect escape, they left me on the sidewalk like a piece of luggage and took off. It was as if I could hear them going, "Yippee!" as they drove off. Well, the feeling was mutual. The relief of being spared from their sickening exchange was more immediate than my worry over obtaining a ticket home. I also took pride in the fact that my kids, Hyung-Gook and Hyung-Seok, would never behave that way in my presence.

New Village Railway was completely sold out; the Rose of Sharon Express barely had any tickets left, and they were for standing room only. Taking the train was out of the question. If I were to spread out my dress on the ground, at least five or six people could sit on it comfortably without getting a speck of dirt on themselves. Stuffing as much fabric as possible into my hand, I dashed bravely toward the Express Bus Terminal. Fortunately, the bus terminal was not too far from the train station. Discovering upon arrival that bus tickets were also sold out was the last straw.

Jam-packed with people, stale air, and a frenzied din echoing with the Daegu dialect—more than these things, what I couldn't stand was my pink *hanbok*. I had to get home that night just to be liberated from that garish dress. My unspeakable distress must have shown on my face. Someone asked me if I was alone. I just nodded. Then I was told not to just stand there, but to get myself over to the platform. Apparently, it was easier for single travelers to get a hold of a no-show ticket. I guess there's always a way out, even from hellish pandemonium. Though immensely grateful to the stranger who gave me this invaluable piece of information, I ran off toward the platform without thanking him properly.

But I wasn't the only clever one. There was already a line of hopeful people waiting for a chance standby ticket. It was actually better for me that people were patiently waiting for their turn instead of eyeing one another or bickering. In my anxiety, ten-minute intervals seemed to crawl by, although one or two people in line did get to board with each departure. Even so, the hope of ever leaving this town was becoming increasingly bleak. Priority was given to people with reservations who showed up at the last minute over people waiting in line. I didn't have the patience to wait endlessly for such an unpromising endeavor, especially because of the damn silk dress I had on. Silk from the old days hugged your body in warmth, but the newer, supposedly four-season fabric was flimsier, puffing up with the slightest gust of wind. The platform was in the middle of nowhere. As the autumn sun was smothered, I could feel the chill on my skin.

Turning to a young woman behind me, I pretended to be in a hurry to go to the bathroom and asked her to save my spot. It seemed that I'd have to be inside the waiting room for anything to happen. If the bus company had any concern for travelers, they should operate more Seoul-bound busses on Saturday afternoons. Perhaps other people felt the same way and we could voice our opinion in solidarity. With renewed energy, I barged into the waiting room, flapping the train of my *hanbok* like a proud flag. There, as in a dream, a miracle was waiting for me. As soon as I saw the pair of tickets—tickets that I had been praying for—in the waving hands of an elderly man, I knew right away that he was on his way to return them. Before he could reach the ticket counter, I blocked his way and quickly checked the destination on the ticket. It was for a bus leaving for Seoul in thirty minutes.

"Grandpa, sell me this ticket. How much?"

"Well, I can return them for the full price at the counter . . ."

I had meant that I was willing to pay more. My open wallet and the shrewd expression on my face must have scared him into thinking that he might be ripped off, for he tightened his grip on the tickets. When I told him that I would pay him fairly, he said that he wanted to sell both tickets. He obviously didn't want to go back to the ticket counter to return the other. That was not a problem for me; I could return the other one myself. Before I could say so, a hand appeared from nowhere and someone said, "I'll take the other one." It was the hand with the aquamarine ring. I didn't get a look at the face. I didn't have a chance to, nor was I really interested in doing so just then. Having secured a ticket home thrilled me more than winning the lottery.

To prolong this feeling of bliss, I grabbed a cup of coffee from the vending machine. Thirty minutes was just the right amount of time, neither too long nor too short, to do so. I didn't expect to get a seat in the waiting room, but leaning against a wall in a cozy corner felt just as divine. I didn't care that I wasn't dressed appropriately for slouching against the wall. The bittersweet coffee caressed the tip of my tongue. Perhaps what I was savoring was not the coffee, but aquamarine-tinged nostalgia.

I boarded the bus five minutes before the departure time and sat in a window seat. He boarded just before the bus left. I didn't glance in his direction. He took off his khaki-colored trench coat and raised it up to place it on the rack, and as he did so, the coat fabric folded over, revealing the London Fog tag. I must say that his refined and clean-cut appearance pleased me. The worst thing that can happen to you when you travel alone on a train or a bus is to sit next to someone who incessantly munches on pastries, milk, or tangerines while insisting that you have some too. It looked like I didn't have much to worry about with this man. Even up until that point, the aquamarine ring and the London Fog coat roamed separately in my mind. Outside the window, the darkness was changing from a smoky fog color to a deeper shade of ink. Leaving behind the foggy city of Daegu, the bus entered the highway. Opening a newspaper, his arm brushed against my shoulder. "Excuse me," he said politely. Without looking at him, I nodded my head curtly in a gesture of acknowledgment. The ringed finger holding up the paper clearly came into my peripheral vision, bringing together the separate images in my head. The simple but stately metal setting holding the gemstone well suited his thick, manly hand. Someone else's clothing and accessories had never intrigued or titillated me this much. My keen interest in him disconcerted me, so I decided to leave it at that. Reclining in the chair, I closed my eyes and soon drifted in and out of delicious, light sleep. Although the long travels of that day had been exhausting, my curiosity over who he might be held back one stream of my consciousness from more restful sleep. Pretending to awake from deep sleep, I sat up abruptly and looked out the window. But the frosted window was opaque. I was about to wipe the window with the curtain hem when he handed me a small bundle of tissues. Instead of saying "Thank you," I nodded my head again and wiped the window glass with the tissues. The bus was speeding through vast, empty fields. Road signs appearing every half a mile or so indicated the distance left to Seoul, but what I really wanted to know was the amount of time the remaining journey would take. But converting distance to time on a congested Saturday evening was an exercise in futility.

"We'll be stopping shortly at the Keumkang rest stop," he said.

"Oh," I replied tersely, conveying that I understood.

A twenty-minute stopover was announced. I took my time getting off the bus long after he did. The bathroom was not dirty but it was sopping wet. When I was inside the stall, someone hosed down the tiled floor again, flooding the place. I walked out irritably, desperately trying to keep my long *hanbok* skirt hem off the wet floor. Outside, while looking around for my bus, I spotted him some distance away sipping a drink under a streetlamp. He smiled at me. It was the kind of smile that could break a few hearts, so I quickly averted my eyes. Standing there like that, he could have been the male lead in the memorable final scene of a movie. He had on a burgundy sweater over a navy button-down shirt and a chartreuse woolen scarf carelessly knotted over his collarbone—an outfit loud enough for a young pop star but somehow flattering against his silver hair. Pouting, I quickly let go of the skirt hem I was clutching and scurried over to the bus. I was angry and embarrassed that I had my skirt lifted up to my knees on dry land with the slip underneath showing.

Inside the bus, I continued to watch him. I could tell that he was not only stylish but fit as well. He wasn't carrying any weight around his mid section, and his long legs made graceful but powerful strides. I glanced woefully at his neatly folded trench coat on the rack. I, too, own a fairly decent trench coat of a different brand. If it weren't for the cursed *pyebaek*, I might have worn it that day. It would have made me look ten years younger.

Before I knew it, I was imagining myself with him, entering a swanky bar for a drink with the hems of our trench coats flapping against the breeze. This kind of strange behavior on my part probably had something to do with the aquamarine gemstone. Or perhaps it was because I knew of a perfect bar for such an occasion. I was a much younger woman when I frequented my friend's jewelry shop. Well, not that much younger. I had spent many years plodding through the daily grind of taking care of the kids and my husband. Toward the end of it all, I was left with mixed feelings of both fulfillment and emptiness. I was well into my forties. My children had grown up to be decent, well-adjusted young adults and my husband had become a respectable upper-level manager. Once I began feeling empty, however, these successes seemed lackluster. And once things became lackluster, all energy drained from me until the tips of my fingers and toes ached with numbness. When my well-off friend opened the jewelry shop around that time, I visited her day in and day out even though I couldn't afford anything on my tight budget. My visits had a lot to do with the emptiness and listlessness I felt. The inevitability of aging that lay ahead terrified me more than death.

In the hotel basement where the shop was located, there was a bar called Casanova at the corner of a corridor lined with restaurants. We used to go there once in a while to have a glass of wine or a cocktail. We were drawn to the place not because we liked to drink, but because we liked its elegant atmosphere. At first, we were a little timid about going to a bar by ourselves, worried that our husbands might frown upon the idea. So we got them to join us a couple of times. Coincidentally, they were alumni of the same school. But neither man felt obliged to consent every time we asked them to take us out for drinks. If they had lectured us about going out so often, we may have gone straight home like good little housewives. Instead, they claimed to be otherwise engaged and magnanimously suggested that we go by ourselves. Middle age for men appeared to be far less miserable than for women, making our own experiences infinitely worse. Being dismissed by our husbands did nothing to uplift our crushed spirits. I knew that going to an elegant bar to sip pricey drinks paid for by my friend was as pathetic as going to a fancy ball decked out in borrowed jewelry, but it was a comforting and pleasurable diversion I could not turn down at the time.

More than the wine or the whiskey, it was the ambience of the place that kept us returning. And one thing that could not be discounted when it came to creating such an ambience was an older couple who were regulars there. This classy, sophisticated couple always sat on stools across from the bartender, and the long-legged, backless bar stools added to their elegance, like high-end accessories. There were other more private, dimly lit seating areas in the bar, but ironically, their usual place in the spotlight at the bar seemed more romantic. When they were there, other customers who also preferred the bar area steered clear. It must have been because their intimacy exuded a peaceful calm that no one wanted to disturb. We secretly liked to assume that they were elderly lovers instead of a married couple. That idea stemmed purely from our overactive imaginations, and we never did find out the truth about their relationship. From the dark nook where we sat, we delighted in observing them. When the good-looking bartender added ice to their pumpkin-colored whiskey or served them simple hors d'oeuvres like cheese or pickled treats, we devoured their every move like captivating scenes from a famous movie. The couple always nursed their drinks slowly, savoring each drop with every lick, but they clinked their glasses quite often. Though we were not privy to their conversations or facial expressions, their seemingly fulfilled lives provided us with much-needed hope and consolation. Watching them, a new realization hit me that a true connection between two people would be possible only at that age.

Although my middle-age, middle-class life was becoming more stable, relationship issues with my family and relatives were beginning to annoy me like an early onset of rheumatism. In retrospect, those problems were mere trifles, but they seemed serious enough for me at the time. My friend often said that she didn't know what she lived for anymore, and I'd heave a deep sigh in reply. Idealizing the old couple was our way of coping with these feelings of futility and the fear of impending deterioration in old age.

The final curtain fell on our bar-going days when my friend went out of business. Curtains are supposed to come down slowly and dramatically, but this was not the case for us, because losing one's wealth can happen in the blink of an eye. My friend's husband defaulted on his debts and fled overseas. The creditors claimed the store and my friend was left alone and penniless. Then one day she left without a word to join her husband. That was all the wake-up call I needed. I quickly came to my senses and returned to my domestic duties, grateful that my family fended well for themselves during my emotional absence.

How long has it been since I stopped going to that hotel? It could easily have been yesterday or a lifetime ago. I wondered if Casanova was still there. Casanova and the elderly couple may both have been gone by then, but my memory lived on. Like someone who had finally found the right person to carry out a long-lived fantasy, I dreamed of clinking crystal glasses with him in a fancy, exotic bar. He boarded the bus and handed me a paper cup. It was Job's tears tea. I finally looked him in the eye and thanked him properly. His face was devoid of excess flab and the chiseled features hinted at a fine moral character. Warmth radiated from his eyes. My heart skipped a beat. Who would believe that one could have such feelings at this age?

After the bus left the rest area, we began to encounter traffic. Without notifying the passengers, the bus driver took the liberty of getting off the highway, so I no longer saw the road signs with the remaining mileage to Seoul. The bus sped through the darkness on what seemed to be a national parkway or a shortcut known only to the driver. Whenever lights appeared as the bus went past a small village, I peered out the window to get an idea of where we were. Each time I did this, he handed me tissues to wipe the window. After long stretches of dark fields or mountains, I welcomed the occasional appearance of store lights, but they proved to be quite unhelpful. These days, even rural towns are fraught with misleading store signs like Seoul Hair Salon, Myeongdong Boutique, or German Bakery, so of course it was impossible for me to guess where we were. Instead of moving forward, it felt like the bus was forever meandering through a dark void. At almost ten o'clock, we suddenly came upon a bustling city. Vehicle plate numbers indicated it was Daejeon.

"We're in Daejeon. So I guess we were headed to Seoul after all." This time, I made the first move.

"Did you think that we were headed somewhere else?"

"It made me nervous to go off the highway. I thought maybe I was in for an all-night bus ride headed nowhere."

"A bus headed nowhere . . . That's interesting. You have quite an imagination, more poetic than mine."

"Why, what were you thinking of?"

"I was thinking that a person with an important mission or loads of money was on board being kidnapped along with the other innocent passengers."

"If the driver hears us, we may offend him. I'm sure he was just trying to get us home faster by taking a shortcut."

"I'm sure we offended him just by being awake. Look around, everyone's sleeping. They wouldn't be sleeping so soundly if they didn't trust the driver to take them safely to their destination."

I looked around and it was true that we were the only two passengers awake. For some reason, that fact exhilarated me.

"Do you live in Seoul or Daegu?" he asked.

"I'm on my way back from my nephew's wedding in Daegu."

"Ah, that's why you're dressed so nicely."

"Yes, I thought it'd be fitting to wear a *hanbok* as an elder, with the *pyebaek* ceremony and all." I conveniently left out the part about not having received the formal bows. But what a relief it was to be able to explain my ostentatious dress that was obviously inappropriate for a long bus ride.

The traffic was very slow all the way from Daejeon, and the bus arrived in Seoul well past midnight. The other passengers continued to sleep, and the two of us remained awake, acting like a couple of hip, young kids. We didn't bring up stuffy topics like the Korean War, how old we were when it happened, where we'd fled to, or how we endured the hardship. Instead, we talked about old movies, actors, music, good restaurants, and current events. I never realized before that I was such a chatty and cheerful conversation partner, well-versed and quite witty on various subjects. It felt good to know that. Incidentally, we didn't share the same opinion on all of the subjects we discussed. Of course we passionately agreed that it was tough to live through the oppressive Yushin reforms and the military regimes. But when he mentioned that he owned a pet Jindo whom he considered family, I reacted vehemently, as if I had a strong allergic reaction to the mere mention of a dog. All these trivial exchanges provided endless merriment for us. It was past midnight but I couldn't believe how quickly we arrived in Seoul.

The subway had already closed and only a few city buses were in operation. Most of the passengers headed toward the taxi stand once they got off the bus. The night air was frigid. He took off his coat and put it over me. I complied willingly, curling up inside his coat. No longer was I conscious of, or acting, my age.

"Where do you live?" he asked. "Near Goduk," I replied. What were the chances of us living in the same area? It's an ordinary neighborhood, but how can it still be ordinary now that I know he lives there? I immediately remembered that there were many beautiful wooded areas and hiking trails in the outskirts of our town. My heart fluttered like a smitten schoolgirl. Naturally, we shared a cab. Although in the same town, his apartment was quite a distance away from my house. Before dropping me off first, he gave me his business card.

The light from the student's room in the second story was a welcoming sight. Not that I knew what the student looked like. His mother had pleasant manners, and I had on occasion asked her to pay my utility bill on her way to the bank. Once I heard her mutter after comparing our electricity bills, "A high school senior sure can run up the bill . . ."

My house is a three-story house built to bring in rental income. As the property owner, I live on the top floor. Unlike the other floors, each accommodating two separate units, I have more than a thousand square feet of living space all to myself. One might expect me to feel depressed about returning to my big, empty house in the middle of the night, but it felt good instead. Although I live by myself, I know that a fourteen-member family portrait is waiting for me. The photograph is half the size of my front door and was taken before my eldest son's family moved to the United States for his work. My husband and I, our two sons and a daughter, all with spouses and two children each, make fourteen. My husband passed away after the photograph was taken, but I gained a grandchild around that same time so the number remained the same. I have yet to see my new grandchild because he was born in the States. My son is undeterred by the expense of international calls and checks in on me at least once a week. Sometimes he puts his newborn child on the phone and lets me listen to the sweet baby talk. My daughter lives nearby, and my other son's family is also not too far away in Bundang. They both call me every day without fail. In this way, the telephone lines in my home empower me by keeping me closely and constantly connected to my loved ones. As I stepped in, the lights in the foyer automatically went on, and before they went off I quickly stepped into the living room and turned on the lights there. As usual, I greeted the family portrait and breathed in the stale air that was as familiar to me as worn clothing left on the floor. I looked at his business card. It was a simple card with neither a title nor a company name—just the three characters of his name and a home and an office number. I rather liked the simplicity of the card because I thought it suited him well. Funny I should think that because I really didn't know much about him. At any rate, I was not too curious about where he worked.

In a few days the weather turned colder. The view outside my third-floor window showed autumn at its peak with leaves in splendid colors. Already, the foliage in the Seorak Mountains was said to be past its prime. What time of the day does he walk his Jindo, I wondered. His apartment was too small to keep such a big and active dog, so it went to and from his place and his second son's house, which had a yard. He said that up until then, he had never broken a single rule in his life, but he had to make an exception to keep his Jindo in the building. He also said that he walked on eggshells with his neighbors, especially the women, who might take issue with the dog being there. From our conversations it was evident to me that he was a kind and educated person of means. That's all I really needed to know. I placed his card neatly next to the telephone. I never gave him my number, but I often thought of him when answering the phone. Of course, the person with the number should call first, but I couldn't. I never even considered calling. The fact that he knew where I lived was quite useless in my hopes of seeing him again because his going there unannounced would be so out of his gentlemanly character. If anything were to happen, I needed to initiate it. This opportunity presented itself sooner rather than later.

An in-law passed away. It was my younger daughter-in-law's mother, who lived alone in a rural area. The whole family, including the kids, went down to her hometown, entrusting me with a tiny puppy belonging to my grandchildren. A poodle, I think they said. It was small enough to be a hand-held stuffed animal. Every time it wiggled, it moved like a wind-up spring toy instead of a living thing. Because it felt like a toy, I didn't really raise objections when it was thrust into my care. But I was not properly instructed on what it liked to eat, where it went to the bathroom, and other necessary details. The whole family had left in such a hurry. I left the bathroom door slightly ajar just in case it knew what to do, and to my surprise and delight, it did its business only in there. But the puppy proved to be precocious only in relieving itself; it refused to eat anything. I tried to feed it everything from milk and porridge to pound cake, but it just ran away without even sniffing the food. Left to its own devices, I was sure that it would starve to death. When nothing I tried worked, I sought help from the student's mother on the second floor. She told me that the dog was probably used to store-bought dog food. She was planning to go into the city tomorrow, so she offered to stop by a pet store and bring some for me. That evening, I poured soup broth over some leftovers and pushed the bowl under the puppy's nose. I knew it would turn away in refusal, but I had nothing to lose. Instead, the dog madly bolted to the bowl and started lapping up the broth, flashing its red tongue in and out. *That's right*, I thought. *Even the almighty gods kneel before hunger. A small thing like you is in no position to be so picky, right?* Before I could complete my self-congratulatory smile, however, the dog began writhing violently, shrieking in pain. I panicked, thinking that it might roll over and die. I couldn't think straight about what went wrong. How would I face my son and my daughter-in-law, let alone my granddaughter, who was like a mother to this dog? In my frightened state, he was the first person I thought of. I dialed his number with shaky fingers and when his voice came through on the line, I was overcome with tears. I could hardly speak. He must have understood my babble between sobs, because he came over right away and drove us to a nearby veterinarian. When I saw him, tears began pouring out again inexplicably. He drove with one hand on the wheel and the other hand patting my shoulder. The dog cried out even more pitifully when it was being treated, and I sobbed miserably in his arms. I knew that I was being a pathetic damsel in distress, but I couldn't stop the flow of sentimental tears. The veterinarian showed us a fish bone he dug out, commenting that he'd seen plenty of kids crying over their pets but never a grandmother in such distress.

The dog was fine and returned to its home in a few days. I of course felt no grief in parting with it because I hadn't grown to love it. But while the dog was under my care, he and I started contacting each other. What began as an inquiry into the dog's well-being naturally progressed to a get-together for coffee. Then I met him for a morning stroll and on the day of the first snow, we went to an elegant bar much like Casanova and sipped whiskey together. I treated him that time, and he returned the favor by taking me out for rice wine at a traditional pub, a place just as charming as a Western-style bar. When I bought him Korean food, he bought me Western food; when I treated him to something cheap, he treated me to something more expensive. We reciprocated, but not in accordance with any rules or norms. Nothing was set in stone, and we let our moods dictate our actions. I became acquainted with his handsome Jindo, and it sometimes accompanied us on short drives to scenic places near Seoul. On such jaunts, it felt like we were discovering these places for the very first time. All this happened after I stooped low enough to weep over a dog I was babysitting. When visiting beautiful places or savoring good food, I was not above squealing in delight or skipping around like a sixteen-year-old girl. People say nowadays that young celebrities "pop" in their performance or demeanor. I felt something akin to that inside me, a playful and bouncy ping pong ball invigorating my every move. Moreover, I couldn't deny that there were elements of playacting in what we did. The carefree joy I felt inside came from frivolous gestures performed for amusement. This kind of fun was by nature far removed from reality. When fantasies come true as in a dream, the reality bares no difference from the dream itself.

One day I had a rude awakening. I was taking a bath when the phone rang. I have one phone in the bedroom and one in the living room, and neither are cordless phones. The phone in the bedroom is on a chest next to the dressing table. I strutted out of the bathroom into the adjoining bedroom naked—moments like this undoubtedly being one of the perks of living alone. I threw a small towel under my feet to catch the water dripping from my body and reached for the phone. Then I froze in mid-action. Who was that hideous old woman? I almost screamed out loud at the reflection in the mirror. The dressing table is an old piece of furniture that I have kept since my wedding. The dresser mirror is small, and it reflected only the bottom half of my bare body. I had been pregnant three times in my life and have three children, but I had given birth to four. My last pregnancy resulted in twins, but I lost the younger twin within a year. Given that my lower abdomen had accommodated several babies, including twins, it was in dreadful shape. The protruding bulge of wrinkly flesh below the belly button slumped steeply toward the pelvic bone like a wrung-out lump of laundered silk. My flesh obviously hadn't gone saggy overnight, but my shock came from the fact that I usually saw only the upper (and better) half of my nude body in the fogged-up bathroom mirror. I'm sure that my subconscious was selective in what it wanted to see. I quickly picked up the towel under my feet to cover up the unsightly half of my body, swearing to myself that I would never again expose it, not even to a mirror.

For Christmas, I gave him a wool scarf and he gave me a silk one. Both were hip and bold in color and pattern, too young for our age. We obviously thought alike, placing more importance on shock value and fun than on practicality in choosing our gifts. He said that it had been a while since he'd bought a gift for a woman. Three years, he said, casually adding that that was when his wife died. We had had plenty of opportunities to reveal our present situations as a widow and a widower, but that was the first time he mentioned it openly. I showed no interest and changed the topic of our conversation. I didn't feel the need to exchange private information like we'd exchanged scarves.

The New Year marked the year of my *hwangap*, or sixtieth year. That's one complete rotation in the sixty-year Korean calendar cycle. I don't understand why everyone wants to celebrate it when the phrase "spinning through the sexagenarian cycle" is hardly a compliment in Korean. When my oldest son called on New Year's Day, that was the first thing he mentioned. Instead of a big celebration, he wanted me to visit him in the States. He said that a party could be postponed until my seventieth birthday. My three children apparently agreed to go along with this proposition if I were willing.

"I don't know. You shouldn't worry about this. Really, I won't be hurt if you don't throw me a party. And don't think that you have to do something else. Sixty already—that's depressing enough without making a big fuss," I replied in a lukewarm tone. I wasn't being modest. I really felt that way.

"That's why we want you to travel and not mope around. I'll make sure I get enough time off from work. Heck, let's go all the way to Europe, Mother. We only have a year left here. If you miss out on this opportunity, you'll regret it for the rest of your life."

It sounded almost like a threat. I wasn't surprised. He'd been nagging me to visit him ever since his company transferred him overseas. But just as I didn't want a tacky sixtieth birthday bash, I didn't want to become a wide-eyed tourist in another country just because my son was there. I know that most people my age jump at such chances of a lifetime. How often had I seen one huge mob from the wife's side of the family pile onto a plane and another from the man's side follow suit soon thereafter? I hung up the phone without giving my son a definite yes or no. It wasn't unusual for me to hang up first, fretting over the cost of international calls.

I guess my sixtieth birthday was just as much of a nuisance to my children as it was to me. They wondered if they should interpret my reluctance to travel as a preference for a party. Once convinced that I didn't want a party, they then fussed over finding out what I really wanted. It was ridiculous that they wanted to know what I wanted when I didn't even know myself. But their concern and effort warmed my heart. What parent wouldn't be moved by such filial piety? My daughter was entrusted with the task of figuring me out. As the oldest, she was closer to me in age than my other children and some things were easier with her because we were both women. She had always been mature for her age so I often considered her as a friend. Her younger brothers also treated her with respect and sought her advice on all matters. Thus, not many things happened in the family without her knowledge.

Her officious tendencies kicked in soon enough. She became curious about the mysterious man her mother was dating. Our society is so small that unless you are dropped off from outer space, you can't escape the extensive networks of families, schoolmates, and regional acquaintances. Once Hyung-Sook set her mind on finding out about him, she easily unearthed everything I knew about him as well as everything I didn't. The fact that he was a professor who'd retired the previous year from a regional college, that he and a few other colleagues who taught Korean history now ran a small research office, and that his wife passed away three years before—these things I already knew. What came to light was: that the couple had a very loving relationship; that in addition to their son's house he owned one more residence as well as some land in a rural area; and that his daughter-in-law was a smart, beautiful woman from a wealthy family. There was plenty of information about his daughter-in-law, who turned out to be the same age as Hyung-Sook. Although they never attended the same schools, they were bound to have some connection simply by going through the educational system in Seoul. Having learned much about him, my daughter asked me pointedly what I was going to do with this old fogy. She sounded like a parent trying to steer a daughter away from a bad relationship.

"What do you mean 'an old fogy'?" I protested.

"How can I be nice when he seduced you?" she said, her eyes getting moist. I immediately regretted taking his side without hearing her out. After all, he and I weren't having an illicit love affair that we had to hide from our children.

"No one seduced anyone. That's crude. Someone might hear you and misunderstand," I reprimanded gently.

"Do Hyung-Gook and Hyung-Seok know about him yet?"

"So what if they do?"

"Oh, Mother. What good is there in their knowing? They might not like the idea of you being in a relationship. Don't give away any information that can be used against you later."

"How will they ever find out if you keep quiet?"

"Fine. I'll keep quiet so please be discreet in what you say to them. I'm sure you don't want to make yourself or your children look bad."

Again, she acted like an indulgent mother promising her wayward daughter to keep the father in the dark. My daughter's meddling did not end there. Truthfully, he and I never made any effort to change because we had nothing to hide. But regardless of what we did, my daughter was able to obtain firsthand information from his side of the family. Hyung-Sook's best friend in high school turned out to be his daughter-in-law's college classmate. Furthermore, his daughter-in-law lived in the same apartment complex as Hyung-Sook. Once that connection was formed, nothing was off limits. We were like two families bound by multiple relationships, and no secret could be kept from anyone who made it her business to know. It wasn't inconceivable that the mutual friend acting as a mediator distorted or exaggerated some of the facts. Even so, what the other side brought to the table must have been impressive enough to win over my skeptical daughter. She changed her position to such a degree that she would tease me playfully about my feminine prowess over men.

One day, she asked me with a straight face, "Mother, do you love Dr. Cho?"

I was drinking coffee at that moment, and I almost burned myself. Bursting out laughing, I choked on the sip I was taking and spilled the rest onto my lap. It was funny that an "old fogy" had turned into "Dr. Cho," especially when I knew that he wouldn't care for either moniker. Once when we were together we had run into his former, now middle-aged, student. After warm greetings were exchanged and the student left, he commented that students from long ago used to call him "Teacher," a much more endearing title he preferred. He didn't feel as close to younger students these days because they called him Doctor or Professor. These titles seemed perfectly fine to me, but I guess he did have his own quirks.

"What's so funny?" my daughter asked.

"You don't think it's funny that an old fogy has suddenly become a doctor?"

"I can see that you do love him. You seem so happy," she said, pouting a little. I could tell that she didn't harbor any resentment, but I detected a tinge of loneliness in her voice. I knew then that I must soon make my position clear for everyone involved. I might end up being lonelier than what my daughter was feeling at the moment, but I couldn't let things drag on at the same time.

Soon after the old fogy turned into Dr. Cho, Hyung-Sook met his daughter-in-law in person. The mutual friend introduced them, and Hyung-Sook recognized his daughter-in-law from seeing her at the supermarket and other places around the neighborhood. Without a mediator, I could see that Hyung-Sook was getting to know his family better and developing even more favorable feelings toward them. Seeing her siding with them more and more each day disheartened me for some reason.

"Mother, are you worried about what Hyung-Gook and Hyung-Seok will say about your relationship? Is that why you can't make up your mind? Don't worry. I'll talk to them so they'll understand," my daughter told me.

Were the two younger women up to something we didn't know about? Otherwise, why would Hung-Sook say such a bold and specific thing? I became concerned about him because that would also mean that his daughter-in-law was in a hurry to see this matter through.

"Get to the point. Are you saying that you want to marry off your mother?"

"You love him, right? A second marriage based on love—not because you need to lean on someone financially or because your children won't take care of you—well, how neat is that? I'll be proud of you and defend you, no matter what other people say."

I stared at my daughter, who was babbling on about love. *What does she know about love? Love isn't so grand. It's just life itself.* I wanted to make light of the whole situation, but my heart felt heavier the more I tried to do so.

Before long, his daughter-in-law came up in conversations between him and me. When I asked, "Oh, is that a new jacket? So stylish!" He replied that she'd bought it for him, scratching his head bashfully and adding that he didn't know why she was trying so hard to make him look younger. I've never met his daughter-in-law, but the more prominent she became in our relationship, the more I felt overwhelmed. One day he told me that she wanted to invite me over to her home at my convenience. I almost lost my temper because I was sick and tired of hearing about her. Seeing that I avoided giving an answer, he didn't pursue the subject. Although he smelled of expensive, fragrant lotion, something about him came across as shabby just then. His daughter-in-law conveyed the same message through my daughter. Presuming that I would naturally accept the invitation, Hyung-Sook immediately began fussing over what I should wear to impress his fashionable daughter-in-law.

"She must be such a decent daughter-in-law. A rarity these days, I'm afraid."

"She is, Mother. She's so good to him. Still, it can't be easy taking care of a widower. She says that when things get hard, she just thinks of it as volunteer work for a good cause."

A pang of sorrow seized my heart. But I couldn't let a passing sentiment of anger or compassion rule over an important decision.

"I want you to listen to me, Hyung-Sook. I want to be buried next to your father."

She remained silent upon hearing my declaration. Although we don't own a private family graveyard, my husband's burial ground was designed with room for me to join him upon my death. There is a tombstone with our names on it. Yes, I already have a grave and a tombstone with my name and birth date. Only the date of my death has yet to be engraved. I have always enjoyed visiting the grave site, and my relationship with Dr. Cho did not change that. My feelings for him never once made me feel guilty toward my husband. Nothing I do is so free of any hidden agenda as my impulse to visit my husband's grave. The joys and heartaches of everyday life are nothing but currents that skim the surface of the deep and complete peace I experience there. The peace that I feel is not the peace of death, but of life. There, the grass is greener and the ants, grasshoppers, and snails that live among the grass blades are lovely. I feel one with all living creatures. *His body is feeding them, and one day mine will do the same alongside his.* This thought makes me unafraid of death even though I have no specific convictions of an afterlife. It is my intention to ask my children to cremate the remains of my body after it has nurtured the small creatures at the grave. Then my ashes can be scattered to freely roam the mountains and rivers. Nothing could tempt me away from this kind of peace and freedom promised to me.

My daughter backed down quietly on the day I mentioned my burial, but she soon returned, armed with new feedback from their side.

"Rest assured you'll be buried with Father, so please don't worry. Think about it. He also has a wife to be buried next to," she said.

How could I explain to her that the peace I sought was different in nature than the sordid details she was working out? I didn't feel the need to explain what she couldn't understand.

"Enough. This is an inappropriate conversation for a daughter to have with her mother."

"There's nothing shameful in what I'm saying. Why do you think that Jacqueline was buried next to John F. Kennedy? Leave it to me. Whatever my brothers or our relatives may say, I can make sure they don't go against your wishes. No one has the right to make Father stay alone by himself."

"I don't want to hear it anymore. Why are you like this?"

"Why are you? Everyone knows that you're a passionate person. If there's any fire left in you from the old days, you have nothing to be afraid of," she insisted.

I couldn't believe what I was hearing from my daughter. But I could see where she was coming from. Her blunt words gave me no choice but to reflect upon the matters of my heart. As the eldest, my daughter knew a great deal about my life. She was born into our family when we didn't even have a decent home and witnessed firsthand throughout the years how we struggled to pay the bills. She was also the main audience for my mother's criticism of the difficult life I had chosen. My mother felt sorry for me but still held me accountable for how my life had turned out. Nowadays my in-laws are much better off, but back then, this wasn't the case. Compared to my family's comfortable, middle-class upbringing, they could barely make ends meet. They were also coarse and uncultured, and my husband was the only one to receive a proper education. As a sensitive teenager, my daughter must have wondered about these differences, and I'm sure my mother's grumblings provided her with easy answers.

When I was dating my husband, my mother thought highly of him as a person, for she referred to him as 'a dragon from a bog.' But when I wanted to marry that dragon she opposed it adamantly. She said that marrying a dragon from a bog was not rescuing the dragon but throwing one's self into the bog. But no matter how much she cried over me, I could only see the dragon and not the bog. She was right, of course, and I floundered in that bog up until the time when his youngest sister got married and left home. But I have no regrets. What other people saw as a bog became the fountain of my life, my *raison d'etre*. The blinders I had on kept me focused on one man through all the hardship I endured. My daughter was perhaps referring to the power of that blind devotion as passion. Call it passion, call it devotion, or call it stupidity; it was all the same to me.

That's exactly what I didn't have with Dr. Cho. The romantic sentiment was the same as it was in my youth, but the blind passion was missing. Love based only on romantic sentiment was only a superficial fascination. What I had with him was nothing more than a charming escapade, an illusion of love. Without those blinders on, I could see so clearly what the future held for us, so clearly the deterioration into old age from which no one is exempt, not even a stylish gentleman like him. Sagging flesh and shedding, dry skin flakes exposed when changing into long underwear; deafening snores that could move high mountains; cigarette ashes flicked everywhere; thick phlegm forced up by a protracted, guttural cough; a stream of farts released from raised buttocks; burps reeking of gastric acid; a gluttonous, selfish appetite; incessant nagging based on groundless suspicion and forgetfulness; and stinginess as if saving up for another lifetime—all these visions were crystal clear. Tolerating these sordid idiosyncrasies in each other required more than love. It required sharing many savage years together, raising children and surviving the daily grind. Only now could I fully appreciate how much more beautiful such animalistic devotion was compared to superficial romantic sentiment. There was no reason for me to look back. And certainly I was too old to be deluded by foolish hopes. My daughter continued to prattle on about things that were better left unsaid.

"If you don't marry Dr. Cho I'd feel so sorry for him. His daughter-in-law says that she can't take care of him any longer. She would prefer him to be with someone he loves, but she plans to marry him off soon in any case. She's confident that someone financially stable like him will have no trouble finding an eligible spouse. But she doesn't want anyone too young. It can be awkward with a young mother-in-law, but mostly I guess she doesn't want to be responsible for her later in life. I'm sure she'll have no trouble snatching up someone needy or desperate. Do you really want someone you love to come to that?"

Her impudent, joking manner made me lose my temper.

"What's wrong with being needy or desperate? You have no right to look down on such people. Helping them is holier than any charity work, for sure," I snapped.

Certainly it was holier than an illusion of glamorous love. With those words, I felt the weight lift from my chest. The superimposed image of the face of his daughter-in-law, whom I'd never seen, and my daughter's face, flitted across my mind. I didn't want either of them to meddle in my affairs anymore. The day that I met him for the last time, I told him that I was preparing to go to America for an indefinite length of time. I added that I couldn't commit to a relationship that might make me a widow a second time around. As I said this, I carefully placed my hand over his ringed finger. Although I wanted to let him down gently, I feared that I may have been too harsh nonetheless. I looked into his eyes for any signs of emotion, but they betrayed nothing.

Psychedelic Butterfly

That house gave you a feeling.

The feeling is different from the impression you get of a house based on its scale, the raw materials used, or the owner's upkeep. In a person, such things would be comparable to one's temperament, manners, or fashion sense—factors that can easily and randomly change at a moment's notice. What I'm talking about is an inherent and permanent quality that comes from a deep core, the very essence that exudes from within. Because of this feeling, people were drawn to this house and went out of their way to walk by it. Although the house stood alone, apart from the other houses in the neighborhood, it was strategically located at the crossroads to the local mineral spring as well as the shortcut to the nearest subway station.

Administratively, the house was in a neighborhood inside Y city, a satellite city near Seoul. The Y city residents called that neighborhood the native village. Not that any cottages or tiled-roof houses remained. Slab houses that were fashionable in the 1960s, now decrepit from neglect, and filthy, narrow streets made the place look older than it was.

The children from the newly built apartment buildings in Y city probably took the name of the village literally, believing those slab houses to be our cultural equivalent to the caves or huts of uncivilized tribespeople who have maintained their way of life since prehistoric times in the South Pacific islands or the African wilderness. But the truth of the matter is that the village was no more than thirty years old. Before the new neighborhood was built by landowners in collaboration with developers, the area consisted mostly of open farmland and orchards. With awe and admiration for the then novel homes cut square like tofu blocks and covered with shimmering tiles, the farmers called the new development the Western village. It took less than thirty years for the place to go from Western to native.

That house existed before the neighborhood became the Western village. It remained untouched during the development, like one last drop of flesh and blood preserved out of compunction before the farms were wiped out. Despite obvious signs of numerous remodeling jobs and expansions in the neighborhood, the house alone retained its rustic simplicity, which permeated down to its very frame. The U-shaped floor of the great room was spacious. The columns and rafters holding up the roof were made of pine, but the roof itself was made of gray slate. The contrast between the wooden framework and the slate roof created a peculiar balance with the contrast between the papered shutters with broken slats and the newly installed glass double door. Someone who has lived in the native village for a long time may remember that the roof was once made of corrugated iron. Before that, the roof must have been made of straw or Western-style tiles. But it's impossible to find a witness to these changes in roof styles in this neighborhood, where a five-year resident, let alone thirty years, is a rarity. The term "native" is inappropriate not only for the houses but also for the residents whose turnover rate is greater than apartment dwellers. According to the city's statistics, the average length of a stay in that village is one year and six months shorter than in the apartments. Enticed by rumors of redevelopment, which were probably cooked up by real estate brokers, buyers who moved into the homes there noticed soon enough that there were no plans in place for growth. Real estate developments do not just happen automatically without someone's initiative, and the owners without a take-charge attitude or the industry know-how eventually resold their houses. Others, hesitant to abandon the last shred of hope, rented out their places before leaving. But leave they did, one way or another. Betrayed by the very thing that had hooked them in, it was no wonder that they no longer wanted anything to do with their houses.

If the native village was an island inside Y City, that house was an island within the native village.

The children from the native village and from the apartments attended the same schools. In the eyes of the apartment kids, the native kids were different somehow. Yesterday's enthusiastic talk about computer games instantly turned into a back-stabbing betrayal once an apartment kid realized that his new friend was from the wrong part of town. If a child had lived in that house, he, too, might have been ostracized. But no child ever lived in that house. There may have been when the farms were still around, but those were during the prehistoric times of that house, with no one to bear witness.

2

She was well aware that parking spaces during these hours were scarce, but Young Joo still grumbled about how fed up she was and furiously turned the steering wheel toward the playground located behind the apartment building complex. The oval pavement surrounding the playground and a patch of grass was originally a no parking zone so that children could cycle and rollerblade. Banning cars there, however, was like urinating on frostbitten toes; the lot cleared up briefly before being taken over by cars again. Fortunately, Young Joo found an ideal open spot that would allow her to move her car easily the next morning. Gathering up a pile of stuff from the passenger seat, she again muttered the phrase "fed up." She didn't have many belongings: a jacket, a sac-like purse, and several books—items that she'd been lugging around since her peddling days. Today, she had the addition of two huge pumpkins to deal with. While driving on rural roads, she saw them piled high in beautiful pyramids on the side of the road, and today she finally bought a couple. The street vendor said that they were great in soups and gave her detailed cooking instructions, but she didn't really listen. She was sure that her mother would make sticky pumpkin chunks.

How nice it would be if Mother got excited about making pumpkin chunks. Young Joo's mind wandered off for a minute. Could her mother still make them? She really shouldn't try to test her with things like pumpkins. She should understand. Day after day for more than half a century, her mother had been cleaning the dirt off collard greens to make side dishes, scraping the scales of fish to fry up in soy sauce, and adding pinches of spices to soups and stews. No, no one would expect her mother to perform these chores with much enthusiasm after all these years. After a lifetime of drudgery, her mother had naturally lost interest in the little things in life. So why did she look at her mother askance? Young Joo pushed aside her things and put her forehead on the steering wheel. She knew that her mindless anxiety was directed more at herself. What she earned after six years of door-to-door selling and getting her degree three years ago was a fulltime position at a university. Although the school wasn't in a major city, she was in no position to be choosy. It wasn't that her livelihood was at stake; her sense of urgency had come from age. It certainly wasn't easy to commute to and from Daejeon, but the fact that it was even possible should be considered a blessing. She was now not just a capable but an expert driver. And she had another reason for braving the long distance commute. After her share of used cars, she now had her fingers wrapped around the steering wheel of a brand new car she'd bought two years ago. The car ran like a dream and felt as comfortable as an extension of her body. She was on the verge of turning forty. She expected the next ten years to go by in the blink of an eye, like a quick run down a slide. Anyone in academia with half a brain knew that a woman, especially at her age, should thank her lucky stars for securing a position at a university. During her first semester at the school, she was drunk with her own sense of achievement, and no amount of hard work could burst her bubble. These days, however, she thought with shame that she was the only one blind to the declining merit of doctoral students and professors. Why didn't she realize this earlier? I wouldn't have put myself through that hell if I'd known, she thought, but that line of thinking made her hate herself more because she knew it was the stumbling block of overzealous women in academia who never realized what they were getting themselves into. For her, the deflating value of a PhD had more to do with distinction rather than financial compensation for the time and effort invested in attaining it. A friend had mocked her blatantly one time: "Did you work like a dog so you could end up in a no-name school in the boondocks?"

"I suppose success for someone as shallow as you is to spend your whole life in Seoul enjoying what money can buy while keeping up appearances."

That was how she wanted to retaliate, but somehow she couldn't bring herself to say it. Her friend had touched a nerve, and it made her insides ache with deep-seated hatred. Teaching, that is spreading her knowledge for other people's benefit, was not as rewarding as she thought. She could have blamed the caliber of her students or her lack of pedagogical skills, but she was disillusioned with knowledge itself, which was even more depressing. In short, she was undergoing a completely corny and hackneyed form of disillusionment.

For her dissertation, Young Joo had chosen to study Heo Nanseolheon, a mid-Joseon Dynasty poetess, because she had been drawn to her, profoundly moved by her work and her life, which ended prematurely. She did not need much knowledge to be moved by Heo Nanseolheon. She knew only as much as other people about the poet's family background and social context of that time. Of course, with her limited knowledge of Chinese characters, it was impossible for her to study Nanseolheon's original works. She was enamored not just with the artistry of the poems but with the romanticized vision of the downtrodden female poet whose genius was denied by the myopic society of her time. Writing a doctoral dissertation, however, required not imagination but a concrete, substantiated output of knowledge. Her faculty advisor, who had persuaded her to enroll in graduate studies when she was teaching at a middle school, was very wary of Young Joo's imagination. What she hated hearing the most was his constant advice: don't mistake writing a thesis for writing fiction. While doing research for her thesis, she fell out of love with Nanseolheon. Moreoever, she had just about had it with the whole subject matter. Conducting research was like taking a pair of shears and ripping apart carefully constructed straw effigies of the poetess. In return for mutilating her love of Nanseolheon, she was left with a degree and a heap of straw clippings under her feet.

How long did she stay like that in the car? She lifted her head when she heard her son tapping on the car window. Choong Woo was wearing worn-out sweats and a pair of flip flops.

"Why are you out here? You going for a walk?"

"No, I'm not on a walk. I'm looking for Grandma." Choong Woo spoke casually, but Young Joo felt her heart skip a beat.

"How come you let her out alone? I told you to keep a close eye on her."

"She must be around here somewhere. Go in, Mom. I'll get her."

Then he walked away, swinging his arms. Gathering up her

things hurriedly, Young Joo stepped out of the car and called out to him. The casual way in which he turned his back on her angered her suddenly.

"When did she leave?"

"It hasn't been long," he said hesitantly. She couldn't let that pass.

"Exactly when?"

"If I knew exactly when, would I have let her out?" Choong Woo snapped defiantly at Young Joo's hostile questioning.

"You didn't even see her leave. What were you doing?"

"I was on the phone. She just disappeared."

"On the phone with who? Probably a girl. That's what kept you busy, right?"

Instead of answering, Choong Woo whirled around and left. Young Joo took a few quick steps after him, but changed her mind and turned toward home. She immediately regretted how she'd treated her son. He was a good boy who rarely gave her a hard time, but it was almost her habit to treat him like a rebellious teen. Why am I like this? She sensed something like panic at her slipping self-control. Looking at her reflection in the elevator mirror, she saw a handful of gray hair sprouting from the top of her head like resilient weeds. She instinctively felt ashamed of her doctorate degree, which seemed to hang from her like raggedy clothes. Unlike the mirrors on her dressing table or in her makeup case, the elevator mirror was unforgiving. This was especially true on her way home from work. When her shoulders, the flesh on her cheeks, her eyebrows, and even the hair she had carefully teased into place all drooped from exhaustion, the silver strands pushed their way out mercilessly. This is what her little sister called her "professor look." Gray hair is common enough for people approaching fifty, but her sister constantly teased her about it and she couldn't help but feel insulted every time. No one was home, but the front door was not locked. Inside, the house was messy.

I hope this is not a repeat of last time, thought Young Joo. It had been some time since she was first alarmed by her mother's forgetfulness. It all started long before they'd moved into the apartment the previous year. In their previous residence, her mother occasionally had trouble finding her way back to the right apartment building after walking to the supermarket. But they had lived there for so long that someone eventually recognized her, or the security guard saw her and telephoned them. Then she was perfectly normal for long stretches of time, and refused to believe or became angry when told that she had been experiencing bouts of forgetfulness. But what happened soon after they moved into the current place was not something that could be taken lightly. It happened even before they had finished unpacking. Her mother had left at dawn before anyone else was awake and could not be found until after midnight. Clearly, her running away was not an impulsive but a carefully planned act. To everyone's surprise, she had brought a sack with knick knacks inside and crumpled up money that she had been saving for this purpose. What was even more shocking was that the highway patrol found her at the Euiwang Tunnel. Young Joo's family lived in Dunchon-dong. It was impossible to get her to tell them whether she walked or took some other means of transportation. She only spoke gibberish. After getting the call, the whole family hurried over. Everyone was relieved to see her standing there, tightly clutching her sack to her bosom and staring blankly into space. Kyung-A, who was always loving toward her grandmother, ran to her and cried loudly in her arms, and Choong Woo also hugged her from behind, rubbing his cheek against hers. Young Joo's husband bowed his head many times to the patrol officer in gratitude and then took off his jacket and wrapped it around his mother-in-law, who was shivering in the cold.

Young Joo stood quietly out of everyone's way. She couldn't stop her heart from turning ice cold. When the kids clung to her, her mother's empty face gradually regained an expression. She hugged them back, cooing, "My babies . . . my babies . . . Where have you all been?" Beauty spread over her face as it lit up. Young Joo's two children, Choong Woo and Kyung-A, had often clung to their grandmother like this, ever since they were little. As a fulltime working mother, Young Joo didn't have much time to dote on her children, but they also knew that it was their grandmother who loved to coddle them. They were old enough now to feel awkward about outward displays of affection, but with her, they still maintained their playfulness. When Grandmother's food was especially yummy or when she stayed up late to fix them a snack after they came home, they clung to her freely, as if in compensation or in charity. This is not to say that the children were calculating with their affection; to them and to her, their interaction was no more, no less than happy playfulness, and watching them always brought a smile to Young Joo's lips. She was sometimes secretly jealous of their mutually blissful intimacy, but it never occurred to her to be more like her mother in front of the kids. She had given birth to her children, but it was her mother who had raised them. Call it the special rights of an older person who's accomplished a difficult and admirable feat. Her confidence with the kids could not be imitated or interfered with, as there was something so natural, and almost animalistic, in how she interacted with them. Watching the three of them, Young Joo sometimes felt as though her mother was licking the children with a soft, red tongue as if they were a litter of newborn animals, the three of them wrapped in an aura of soft, furry warmth.

But this time, things were different. Young Joo was upset enough to think that she must keep her aching heart in check. What upset her was the location—the Euiwang Tunnel. The young patrol officer noticed the different attitudes among the family members and presumed Young Joo to be a disgruntled daughter-in-law.

"Why leave home and trouble your good son here? I know things can get upsetting sometimes, but don't let that get to you. It's a different world nowadays. Do you know how lucky you are to have worried family members rush over to find you? I've seen people abandon their elderly parents. So sad, isn't it? People like that don't come running just because we say we've found their mother or father. You may not believe it, but some of them even move so that they can't be contacted."

When Young Joo's eyes met her husband's, she lowered her head in shame. Facing him was worse than being labeled a mean daughter-in-law. Pleased about how things had turned out, the patrol officer continued to prattle on.

"I was so sure that she was one of those abandoned folks. She kept insisting that she had to see her son—like a stubborn child, she was—but didn't even know his phone number or where he lived. Well, we've seen that kind of act too many times from people who've got no place to go except nursing homes. Then your mother finally thought up a phone number, but we didn't expect it to pan out. Sure enough, the person who answered said he had just moved there and didn't know anyone like her. But that number eventually led us to you, thank goodness. It's so nice to see you folks reunited like this."

So that's how it happened. Her mother's destination was as Young Joo had expected. She decided to leave the scene and wait in the car. It seemed a fitting act for a crabby daughter-in-law, but she also wanted keep the truth under wraps. Her husband would certainly understand and faithfully play out the part of a good son. Young Joo smiled bleakly, thinking that her mother would likely approve of the arrangement.

Young Joo and her mother were not in-laws but mother and daughter. Thus, her husband was not a son but a son-in-law. She didn't know exactly when Mother had begun to feel ashamed about living with a daughter, but it must have been soon after her younger brother had gotten married. That's when relatives began wondering why she didn't move in with him. Mother's sisters, especially, fussed and fretted over her situation, even pitying her at times. Clicking their tongues, they'd said, "You eat standing up at your daughter's house but you sit down for a meal at your son's." Young Joo wanted to spit on her aunts when they were condescending like that. Except for their parasitic existence with their sons, they were no better off than her mother. As a young girl, Young Joo dreamed of making it big and giving her mother a life of luxury. She was at her happiest when dreaming those dreams, but things hadn't gone as she wished. Even if they had, Mother's happiness would have been unaffected. That was what was so depressing. She knew her mother better than anyone. Her happiness came from nurturing her children, not from being nurtured by them. The self-assurance that came from a lifetime of hard work caring for them was her only pride, and Young Joo found it difficult to forgive anyone who threatened that pride—even if they were her mother's own siblings.

Young Tak, her younger brother by thirteen years, was born after their father's death. After Young Joo was born, her mother was without child for ten years until her younger sister, Young Sook, came along. Before Young Sook was one, Mother became pregnant again, and before she gave birth, their father passed away. All he left the family was their home. At that time, the house was located in an undeveloped area, but fortunately it was near a university so that Mother could bring in income providing room and board to students. Young Joo was known from that time on as the landlady's daughter, and she fulfilled that role as if she was born to be one. Some chores, like running errands to the supermarket or fetching browned rice broth from the kitchen, she could do in her sleep. She also learned to keep alive the coal briquettes used to heat each of the rooms. In high school, she stayed up late with her mother to record in the household ledger, discuss the next day's menu, set up the next month's budget, and worry about her younger siblings' futures. During the busy months leading up to the college entrance exam, she coaxed and bullied her younger siblings into giving up their rooms so that they could house more students. Even the master bedroom was put up for rent, and the family slept crammed in the small attic. For Mother, Young Joo was more of a partner than a daughter. They worked together and worried together. In her effort to be helpful, Young Joo was just as strict as her mother in dealing with her younger siblings. She never once harbored feelings of sibling rivalry or jealousy. She acted more like a parent than an older sister, so much so that the other two often complained, "Who does she think she is, our father?"

Choong Woo returned alone, dejected. Young Joo half expected this and wasn't too disappointed, but nonetheless something burned inside her and she leapt to her feet.

"I'm sorry, Mom." Startled, Choong Woo apologized, clutching Young Joo's shoulders.

"I'm not mad at you."

Young Joo had a hunch that her mother had gone to Euiwang Tunnel again, and that was what made her mad. Euiwang Tunnel was on the way to her brother's house. Her mother went there only three or four times a year, and Young Joo drove her each time. Previously from Gwacheon and also from their current residence in Doonchon-dong, they had to go through the tunnel. It was the only place that might stand out to Mother en route to her son's house. Both the Gwacheon Tunnel and the Euiwang Tunnel were built a few years after Young Joo's family moved to Gwacheon. Considering that they moved into a small apartment from a spacious house with enough rooms to sublet, Mother adjusted remarkably well. The apartment was only about seven hundred square feet, but it was on the first floor so that Mother could garden in the outside yard. From the yard, her domain continued to expand to the nearby Cheongye Mountain and then to Gwanak Mountain. She hiked several times a day to draw mineral water from springs and was also an expert at picking edible plants growing wild along the hiking trails so that other elderly neighbors, most of them too urbanized to tell an edible shoot from a weed, followed her around like groupies. Mother was a member of an outdoor badminton team, the Gwanak aerobics club, and the Cheongye senior's league. When construction work began on the two tunnels, Mother was highly upset about the changes being made on her turf. She was especially annoyed with the Euiwang Tunnel, mostly because she had trouble pronouncing it. It was during that time that Young Joo's brother moved into a newly developed neighborhood just past the Euiwang Tunnel, so she told her mother that the tunnel was being built as a shortcut to his house. Upon hearing this, Mother would immediately become happy. Construction on the tunnel coincided with Mother's increasing lapses in memory, about the time when she began having trouble finding her way home. So the shortcut story was repeated many times.

"Aye, aye. So you're saying that they blasted open a tunnel so I can get to Young Tak's faster? Goodness gracious! Who'd do such a kind thing for me?"

Such was the conversation exchanged between the mother and the daughter countless times. But the faster route did not result in Mother visiting Young Tak any more often. She knew without being told that it was no longer socially acceptable to invite yourself over, not even to your own son's house.

On the day that Mother went to the Euiwang Tunnel by herself, she never revealed how she ended up there. She probably could not have even if she wanted to. No doubt nothing registered in her mind except for the name of the tunnel. Mother probably did not walk all the way to the tunnel from Doonchon-dong. She must have walked some of the way and been driven the rest.

Young Joo was about to run outside, but she stopped and looked for her car keys.

"Are you going somewhere?" Choong Woo asked.

"The Euiwang Tunnel."

"There? Why, do you think she's there?"

"Your uncle lives beyond the tunnel. Remember that other day? It wasn't coincidence that Grandma was found there."

"I know, but it could also be that the tunnel's close to Gwacheon." Choong Woo eyed his mother cautiously, for whenever that city was mentioned, Young Joo got angry. Her mother's obsession with Gwacheon completely baffled her. Mother's desire to be cared for by her son was understandable. It presented itself rather suddenly, but it was to be expected. If anything, it presented itself much later than it should have, given that it's a long-established belief shared by all of the aging mothers of this land. The family had lived in Gwacheon for over ten years, but considering that much of that time was spent in a tiny apartment, Young Joo could not understand Mother's strange attachment to the place. And what she could not explain, she didn't want to acknowledge.

"If your grandmother likes Gwacheon, that's because it's closer to your uncle's house than here," she said in a cold tone that was unwarranted.

"If she thinks about him so much, why did you make her leave his home and bring her here?"

"Listen to yourself. She's family. You're making her sound like someone who's not."

"Please calm down, Mom. I think it's you who think that. I know you're upset, but this is not like you."

"Maybe I shouldn't have brought her. She's really not better off here. I won't even bat an eyelid this time if I find out that she went back there."

"At any rate, she hasn't been gone an hour. There is no way that she could have gone there in that time."

"I doubt she walked all the way to the tunnel on that other day."

"Don't you remember how her feet looked?" Choong Woo asked, frowning slightly. Young Joo remembered how she cried after soaking her mother's bruised and blistered feet in warm water. How angry she was! To Mother, her son's house must have seemed so far beyond reach. The determination that sent her off on her journey despite that sense of hopelessness was evident on her mercilessly battered toes. Young Joo spent a sleepless night thinking of her mother's feet with both compassion and disgust. In the morning, she called her brother and asked if he could take Mother in. It was more like begging than asking. Before he married, Young Tak talked big about how he was going to take care of Mother in her old age. Young Joo didn't insist then and there that he didn't need to, but she had been very proud of him. She wasn't hoping for him to take Mother off her hands someday; she was just glad that Mother wasn't going to be one of those unwanted elderly parents passed around from one child to another. Surely, Mother was loved and wanted. So why was Young Joo pleading with her brother now? She didn't like the submissive way she came across, but she couldn't readjust it. It was probably due to Young Tak's response, which was completely unexpected. He listened to her quietly without revealing any emotion, and after hesitating for a long time, all he managed to say was, "Elder Sister, I guess you're no different." She didn't understand what those words meant, but there was no mistaking the underlying sarcasm. Although she was offended, she couldn't retaliate. She hated herself for ultimately conceding to the social norm that shoved the care of the elderly in the hands of the son. Perhaps she deserved to be offended.

"I'll let you know after I talk to my wife," said Young Tak.

Given his reaction, she had to say something.

"Tell me what you think. That's what I want to know."

"You know that women actually end up doing most of the caretaking. I can simply order my wife to take care of Mother, but I really don't want to."

Young Tak and his wife had dated for several years and were now happily married with kids. Mother would undoubtedly be a third wheel in their home. Young Joo knew that they needed time to prepare themselves mentally and to make practical arrangements to accept Mother into their household. But with no word from him since he left, Young Joo spent her days seething in resentment. How could he, as her only son, be this insensitive? Inability to forgive her brother overlapped with self-blame for backward thinking, and she couldn't tell exactly where her anger was directed. Mother's behavior made things worse. Whether he was making a real or an empty promise, Young Tak left that day assuring her that he'd return soon to take her with him for good. Mother packed her bags right away, anxious to leave.

"My son said he'll come and get me. I wonder what's keeping him."

Muttering to herself, she'd pace around or stare out the window like someone confined to a waiting room. She even began pushing the other family members away, shutting down emotionally. Young Joo couldn't stand it any longer, so she called her sister-in-law and had her come and take Mother.

Mother lasted less than three months there and returned to Doonchon-dong. It wasn't correct to say that she didn't last, because Mother was losing her will each and every day. Young Joo was the one who didn't last.

After packing off her mother to her brother's, Young Joo called every day to check on her. "I want to go to Gwacheon. Take me there, please," was all Mother said to her each time they talked. She sounded so desperate. Because Gwacheon was where Young Joo's family had lived previously, Young Tak and his wife understood Gwacheon to mean Young Joo's house. But neither of them said anything to her, determined not to be the ones to first suggest that she take Mother back. Young Joo almost hated them for not suggesting it because she was so worried about Mother being there. After her mother left, Young Joo had not spent a single day in peace, and that was because she, too, believed her mother's constant longing for Gwacheon was a plea to return home. She couldn't ignore her mother's plea unless she could undo all those years she shared with her as a daughter and a partner. Still, she did nothing, enduring it like she would torture. If they had begged her to take Mother back, she would have in a heartbeat. But she wasn't going to be the first one to say it. Likewise, now that they'd taken Mother in, Young Tak and his wife weren't about to send her back unless Young Joo begged them. Young Joo's pride and Young Tak's stubbornness seemed polarized, but in actuality, they were one and the same thing. What they wanted to uphold was not Mother, but the notion that it would be a disgrace to entrust an aging parent with a daughter when there was a son present.

Mother either didn't know about or didn't care that the two of her children were engaged in this tug of war. The issue of staying with a son or a daughter was immaterial to her. When she was here, she wanted to be there and when she was there, she wanted to be here. And neither here nor there was Gwacheon. Her mental acuity appeared to be slipping, but perhaps it was actually getting sharper. Instead of going back and forth between her children's homes like an unclaimed package, she was demanding to be sent to Gwacheon, a no man's land that was neither here nor there. Before long, Mother began running away from Young Tak's home. She never got farther than the apartment parking lot because his wife had been so well prepared for such an event. She was an intelligent woman who also had an extensive social network in her building complex as the president of the women's association. She dressed Mother in clothes no one would be caught dead wearing outside the home. In her pajamas or bloomer pants, Mother was easily spotted by children or building security guards. Once found, the nearest security guard was to be notified. With this system in place, Mother probably never got past their building, let alone the neighborhood. As Mother's escape attempts continued, however, a new lock was added to the front door. Most apartment doors open from the inside but not from the outside, but with the new lock, the door could not be opened from the inside without a key. When Young Joo got upset with the new lock, her sister-in-law asked defensively what she should do when no one could be home with Mother. Short of hiring a fulltime caregiver, Young Joo knew that this was a necessary measure. Her sister-in-law certainly took care of everything with impeccable precision, but it was that very precision that so frightened Young Joo. She imagined her mother to be infinitely more frightened, wasting away and screaming for help. Young Joo showed her restraint at least up to that point. In a few days, another lock was presented, and this time, it was to keep Mother inside her room. They said they had no choice. Confined indoors, Mother spent the whole day opening and closing every door in the apartment. Because she kept reopening and reclosing every bathroom and closet door, Mother thought that the house had a countless number of rooms.

"Here's a room. Here's another one! How can a home have this many rooms? All shamefully empty, too. That no good, lazy housewife! Why doesn't she rent them out?"

Muttering to herself like this all day, she'd roam from room to room until the other family members couldn't take it anymore.

"Do you think we wanted to do this? It was too trying on our nerves, and we just couldn't live like that anymore," her sister-in-law had said. Young Joo could see from Mother's haggard and desolate appearance that being locked up had taken a toll on her. The vicious battle of the wills had left both parties bleeding, but her sister-in-law trivialized the matter by describing it as "trying on their nerves." Young Joo was filled with contempt for her sister-in-law. Instead of wishing for things to improve, Young Joo was now hoping for Young Tak and his wife to throw their hands up in defeat. Even that didn't go as she had hoped.

It happened on a day when Young Joo was visiting. As usual, her sister-in-law greeted her impassively, and Young Joo walked in apologetically for coming too often. Long after the tea was brought out, her sister-in-law still had not opened the door to Mother's room.

"Is she taking a nap?" Young Joo asked.

"If you're curious, you can look through the window from the veranda."

"What are you talking about? You don't want to bother opening the door now? How can you be like this?"

"I learned it from Mother," whimpered her sister-in-law, shedding a tear for the very first time. Mother's condition had gotten worse lately. At all times of day and night, Mother escaped the confines of her room by crawling out the window to the veranda. From there, she'd stare into the couple's bedroom window.

"When our eyes meet, she asks me with a straight face, 'Who are you?' Do you know how that makes me feel?"

Her sister-in-law didn't say anything more, but Young Joo could clearly see how weary she was. Anger mixed with humiliation tightened Young Joo's chest. She made her way outside to the veranda and looked through the window into her mother's room. Mother was staring into a wall mirror, glowering at her reflection and stamping her feet in fury.

"Who are you, huh? Move out of the way. I told you to get out!"

Just as her mother didn't recognize the old woman in the mirror, Young Joo could not acknowledge that the old woman trapped inside the room was her mother. She had not become thinner or scruffier. Dressed in clean, comfortable clothes, she looked better than when she had loose trousers or pajamas on. But Young Joo had never seen such fierce defensiveness in her eyes. Her mother, who was always as inviting and comforting as a warm hearth . . . It wasn't just her eyes. Young Joo could see that her small body was tense, with every hair standing up. If someone were to lay a finger on her she would have fought back like a cornered rat. How agonizing it must be for her, fighting alone against the world . . .

Instead of asking for a key to the door, Young Joo climbed in through the window. Mother stood frozen with her back against the wall, neither asking the intruder who she was nor making a move to fight her. She was deathly afraid, as if she had run into a Herculean foe against whom her defense strategies were futile. Young Joo took her in her arms. Mother smelled pleasantly of soap. The room was plain and tidy, with a couple of landscape paintings adorning the bare walls. With an attached bathroom, this was the master bedroom suite in the apartment. Young Joo had been so grateful that her brother and his wife had given up their room for Mother. She needed to maintain a positive attitude now. Her mother's tiny frame fit inside her arms, and Young Joo patted and stroked her back. In doing so, perhaps she was soothing her own anger and licking her own wounds. She knew she had to take Mother home with her, but she didn't want to provoke her brother and sister-in-law. They must not exchange any angry words. She harbored no ill will against her brother, who must have struggled to mediate between his mother and his wife. Young Joo always felt more like a mother to him than an older sister. Not only was she many years older, but she had also shared with her mother the compassion for the fatherless boy and the responsibility of raising him to be a strong, independent man. Young Joo held her mother for a long time until her mother squirmed to get free. It took Young Joo that much time to get ahold of herself.

Thus, Mother returned to Doonchon-dong and began making an incredible recovery, gradually returning to her old self. On the car ride home, her accusing glares and defensive gestures began subsiding so that by the time Young Joo's family greeted her, they had no suspicion of her worsened state. It was as if she was returning from a vacation. Young Joo even doubted herself briefly, wondering if she was too quick to blame her sister-in-law. The risk of Mother wandering away from home remained unchanged, so she could not be left home unattended. This was not an easy task without a fulltime homemaker defending the home front. Excluding Jung-A, a busy high school junior, Young Joo and Choong Woo took turns watching her on the days they didn't have classes. But the two of them could cover only so many hours, so part-time domestic help and the aunts were brought in from time to time. Fortunately, Mother was faring well, even helping with household chores, and their vigilance was beginning to slacken. There wasn't much to the chores—trimming bean sprouts, tearing up balloon flower roots, or determining whether the mushrooms or bracken at hand was Korea- or China-grown. Mother was peeved when she was spared from these chores, saying that she didn't want her body to be idle when one day it would rot underground anyway. Young Joo was thrilled to hear her say those words. Mother used to say them often when she ran the boarding house, and hearing them again brought great relief. It was the same kind of relief she felt during her childhood when, after waiting for hours for her mother to come home, she'd finally see a familiar shape appear out of the fog. She'd then run toward her mother and would be swathed in the abundant pleats of her skirt. Mother's impeccable laundry-folding skills also returned, making Young Joo even happier. Mother always took slightly damp clothes from the line and folded each article of clothing with such love and care that even the long johns looked like they had been ironed. No one else could fold laundry like her.

Young Joo must have become too careless. In fact her mother's memory had never recovered fully, and was still coming and going haphazardly. She left Mother at home alone at times when she couldn't find a helper. She felt bad about asking her aunts every time, but she was also afraid that they might brainwash her mother again into thinking that she must properly live out her days at her son's house. Young Joo didn't believe that idea was completely erased from Mother's mind, but the last thing she wanted was to have the aunts rehash a latent memory and reinforce it over and over.

3

Myriad lotus lanterns hung from the eaves of that house. They appeared a few months after a sign went up with the symbol of a Buddhist temple and the words "Cheon-gae Temple Outreach House." The lanterns on the eaves circled all the way around to the back of the house, and more were hung from a suspended rope above the front yard. It was the first celebration of Buddha's birthday at the house after the temple sign was posted. From the native village, the lanterns looked like pink balloons, filling the villagers with an expectation that the house might lift off the ground and float away. That kind of expectation was silly but joyful, like a warm breeze blowing festive air into the neighborhood. Even before the lanterns were hung, the villagers were happy to see the temple sign go up and looked upon the house with fondness. This is not to say that their fondness translated into patronage. Not a single person from the village decided to attend the new temple. More than half of the neighborhood families considered themselves Buddhists, regularly frequenting temples to pray and seeking out fortunetellers from time to time. But no one patronized *that* temple. The villagers were delighted to see so many lanterns, interpreting that to mean that there were many members at the new temple. They were not the kind of people who easily delighted in other people's successes. Before the house became a temple it had been a fortunetelling outfit, and this upgrade in identity may have factored into their favorable opinion. A temple was certainly a nobler place than a fortunetelling joint, better for a small neighborhood with impressionable children running around. Not that they snubbed the house when it was a fortuneteller's. They didn't have to, because the house was already isolated from the town. When a stranger came into town asking for the lady fortuneteller, they directed him to the old house beyond the empty field. No sign or banner identified the house, but all of the townsfolk knew of its purpose. But they didn't know anything about the person running it. They assumed that a young woman was running the place because strangers asked about her, but they had no way of telling whether she was pretty or homely, a true psychic or a charlatan. Most of the native village residents had had tough breaks in life, so seeking out psychics and fortunetellers was a familiar practice. But even among those who engaged passionately in this activity, not a single soul had gone to see the woman. Apparently, Jesus was not the only one unappreciated in his hometown.

On Buddha's birthday, the neighborhood children could be seen snooping around the house. Just as light objects are the first to be carried away by the wind, the children became excited by the festive mood. The adults did not budge. Families celebrating that day had already taken off on buses or trains to their regular temples far away. The front door of that house was wide open, and sitting on a silk cushion inside the room with sliding doors was a petite golden Buddha with a subtle smile on his face. The courtyard was bustling with visitors looking for the lantern labeled with their family name. The silk *hanboks* they were wearing for the occasion were beautiful to behold with all their colors in full splendor.

The person running the temple was a Buddhist nun. The lady fortuneteller and the Buddhist nun were one and the same person. Even the golden Buddha gracing the new temple was the same one worshipped by the lady fortuneteller. Only, the golden sheen was brighter than before because the figure had been plated again around the time the temple sign had been hung. Most of the temple members were formerly regular customers of the fortuneteller. The few new members were those lured in by the regulars' claim of the temple Buddha's divine powers. These regulars did not think it at all strange that the lady fortuneteller had become a Buddhist nun. As a fortuneteller, she had always worshipped Buddha and claimed him as the source of her psychic powers. So nothing had changed. She and her customers bowed to Buddha before and after each session, and this routine remained unchanged at the temple. Then and now, visitors came to the house to be inspired by her words, usually uttered in a brusque and indifferent manner, relating to the future endeavors of their spouses or the welfare of their children. Because she became spiritual around the same time that the Buddha she worshiped gained divine powers, nothing was strange about her change in status. Everyone had respectfully called her by the honorific title Bosal-nim when she was a fortuneteller, so when she became a Buddhist nun, they had no trouble calling her Jayeon Seu-nim.

If anything had changed, it was that one day a month had been set aside for the reading of the Buddhist scriptures. These sessions were conducted by an elder monk from the Cheongae Temple. He came to the house on red-letter days like Buddha's birthday, New Year's Day, and July seventh of the lunar calendar. He also came to lead the forty-ninth day ceremony following the death of a follower and to hold special prayer sessions requested by members. Oddly, none of the members knew where the main Cheongae Temple was located. Because Jayeon Seu-nim treated him with the utmost respect and because she used the phrase "came down," they assumed that the temple was high up in the mountains in a distant, scenic place. The followers did not think all that highly of the elder monk. Although he commanded a certain presence befitting of someone with his age and position, he really hadn't demonstrated any clairvoyant powers. There were at times persons of high social standing among the followers, and the consensus among the members was that he excelled in recognizing such persons. This particular ability was of no practical help to the followers, and if anything, disrupted the equality of fellowship among them. Thus, they accepted the elder monk simply as part of the change that took place at the house and hoped that Jayeon Seu-nim would soon learn to lead important services. Although she had never said anything to them, the word among the followers was that she was preparing to study Buddhism properly at an institution of higher education.

The elder monk from Cheongae Temple had not yet arrived, but food preparation was in full swing inside the kitchen where a large cauldron hung from a wall. All kinds of fruit, traditional pastries, and rice cakes ordered from a shop were laid out in abundance on tables on a small deck adjoining the kitchen. Since it was Buddha's birthday, lunch as well as supper needed to be served. And there was no shortage of helpers to watch over soups or to season the vegetables. Mageum's mammy, the person orchestrating the whole operation, had a surprisingly effective and commanding voice for someone nearing seventy. Mageum was the secular as well as the legal name of Jayeon Seu-nim. Since Mageum's birth, Mammy had never felt this happy or proud. She was giving orders and her daughters-in-law were scurrying to carry them out. One word from her, and there was even a son-in-law who would run to a wholesale market in Seoul at the drop of a hat. At this rate of business, in two or three years the old house could be torn down to build a bigger one, or a new temple independent of the Cheongae Temple could be established elsewhere. Just thinking of these possibilities made Mammy stand taller. She looked around the house with eyes filled with intensity and desire. She wasn't without her misgivings, though. The atmosphere of the house was transforming from moribund to thriving, as if the spark of change had just caught on fire. Mammy had reservations about touching up the house too soon because doing so might break its lucky streak. But greed often overpowers these feelings of reservation. Today's festivities served as the defining moment in galvanizing the long-time patrons and the elder monk over the issue of building a Buddhist sanctuary on this very spot. It was almost a done deal. Mammy was no expert on spiritual matters of ministering hope and peace. But she clearly understood that this business was a goldmine and that few other enterprises could have such an auspicious beginning and promising outlook.

While sitting on the kitchen patio and yelling out orders, Mammy was busy making mental calculations of the offerings from the lantern lighting and the altar money that would be collected by the end of the day. As she did this, her face displayed conflicting emotions, grinning from ear to ear one moment and scowling in disgust the next. On the one hand, she was thrilled that the temple business was booming, but on the other, she knew that what they made was peanuts compared to how much the bigger temples raked in on days like this.

Mammy glanced at Jayeon Seu-nim, disapproving of her indifferent expression and relaxed attitude. The success of the temple business depended on their teamwork. Never mind teamwork, her daughter was refusing to make eye contact. Putting up with such a behavior was trying Mammy's patience. Who got her to where she was now? Now that she was a big shot, how dare she look down on her mammy? But because her daughter had her reasons for acting that way, Mammy glowered at her in private, but hammed it up when she was around. Mammy hated putting on this act, and perhaps her daughter was avoiding her for the same reason. Avoiding eye contact had become something of a silent agreement between the two. Mammy only set foot in the temple for worship services and prayers, leaving Jayeon Seunim to be by herself at other times. As a fortuneteller and now as a Buddhist nun, her daughter remained the only breadwinner in the family. Mageum usually avoided making conversation as well as eye contact with her mother, but she allowed her to pull the purse strings. In fact, Mageum didn't know how much she actually earned. Knowing would require her to talk to her family, so she ignored money matters in order to avoid her family. This much she knew: she was the sole breadwinner in the family, and her money was Mammy's money; and Mammy's money was always Mammy's money.

Mammy was a true native of the neighborhood, for she was familiar with the prehistoric times of that house. She no longer lived in the native village. From her apartment where she now lived, she looked down at the village with the others, condemning it as an unsightly and unwelcome part of the neighborhood. Before the apartments were built and the native village was formed, the area consisted of vast farmland. Mammy was born somewhere around there, grew up and married someone from around there, and lived a tough, exhausting life. Even back then, the house stood alone, isolated in the middle of the fields. The house Mammy was born into was much worse than that house, and she married into a family whose house was worse than her own. Back then, she had no dealings with the house whatsoever. After the outbreak of the Korean War, she left her hometown for the very first time, and when she returned, she found that the neighborhood had changed greatly. Many people had moved, some leaving behind empty houses. That house had also been left empty and had further deteriorated. The owner was said to have been a cruel master of forced laborers, and one of them had massacred the whole family in revenge. Those who knew about the gruesome deaths went out of their way to avoid the house, believing it to be haunted. So it sometimes served as a den for hobos and vagrants. The house became more and more decrepit. Years passed and the area's residents changed so much that no one who remembered the war remained, but the infamy of the house lived on in exaggerated tales. Mammy had married an orchard day-laborer and had five children. She was unable to break away from the village and lived in squalor without a home to call her own, but she never gave a second thought to the house as a place where her family could get a decent night's sleep. To her and everyone else, that house was haunted, not a livable home.

Thin smoke rose from that haunted house one day. No one bothered to find out if hobos passing through the town had dropped in for a few days. This was before the native village had come into being, and houses were sparsely scattered in open fields or orchards. Although there were clear signs all around that the farms were dying out, no one suspected back then that the land there would become prime real estate. When the façade of that unkempt house suddenly showed signs that it had become a civilized residence, one person took notice: Mammy. She was also the only person around who could recognize the new resident of the house as the younger brother of the deceased slave owner. He was a mere boy during the war when he witnessed the brutal murder of his brother's family. Having no other family to turn to, he lived apart from the world in a remote Buddhist temple for twenty years before returning home. Mammy had no specific intention of bullying him, but she got restless just thinking about his true identity. She had the inexplicable feeling that she could put that knowledge to good use someday. Real estate values began escalating around that time, and day after day, Mammy's gaze toward the house became more and more fixed. For a man who had suddenly abandoned an ascetic's life after spending his entire youth at a Buddhist temple, the new resident didn't appear to have any other means of livelihood waiting for him in the secular world. The house soon donned a sign that read, "Meditation Center." He must have gained quite a useful network of people from the temple because the influx of scholarly types to the house, though not abundant, was steady. Mammy and her husband frequented the house to help with menial chores and learned that most of the visitors came to study Chinese characters or Buddhist scriptures. There were even regular large-scale meetings every month. Mageum, who had recently graduated from elementary school, was sent there as a live-in helper to run errands and do chores. Certainly, times were hard for Mammy's family and having one less mouth to feed was a relief. Unable to send her daughter to middle school, Mammy could have arranged for her to learn a trade. But Mageum had displayed from an early age a flair for the melodramatic and an occasional, uncanny ability to speculate about future events. Mammy thought that it wouldn't hurt for Mageum to stay at the house and pick up some knowledge of the Buddhist teachings.

The native village was beginning to be referred to as the Western village during that time. The Western village residents called the strange man who was neither monk nor layman "Master" and kept a respectful distance from the dilapidated house known as the Meditation Center. No one from the village ever visited the house to offer prayers or to study the scriptures.

Soon after Mageum went to live in the house as a helper, the master violated the fourteen-year-old. Mageum told her mother, hoping to avoid a repeat of the incident, and Mammy went berserk and threatened the master. She also helped him to become the official proprietor of the house and the surrounding fields. Eventually, she extorted the house from him and he was left with the fields—a mutually beneficial resolution at the time. As a result of the incident Mageum came to abhor all men, but she also became more perceptive in reading people's thoughts based on their facial expressions and manner of speech. Mammy tried to maximize these skills by raising her as a shaman, but because Mageum was fickle and not interested in money, the business never flourished as Mammy had hoped. It was just lucrative enough, however, for Mammy to support her other children, who wanted to live off their older sister's gifts. For the house to transform itself from a shaman fortuneteller's pad to a place of worship, synergy and timing was required. The master sold his portion of the property, bought a small temple somewhere remote, and returned to the mountains. More importantly, Mageum willingly endorsed the change, even suggesting that she take up Buddhist studies to further her new career.

But she was too old to begin her studies, which was just as well; she was inherently as uninterested in studying as she was in money. She didn't believe in anything other than her instincts. And her one desire was to take off to another place by any means necessary, to be anywhere but where she was. She wanted to escape not so much the town, but the people. The people she had come into contact with thus far, including her family, thought of nothing but ways to take money or power away from others for their own gain. Her insight into this matter actually served her well in fortunetelling. But she had a vague feeling that not everyone in the world was like that. She didn't have a child of her own, but her mother, by serving as the very antithesis, gave her an inkling of how a good mother should behave. This thought tortured her the most. It was an honest thought that stirred from deep within, and she wanted it to be validated by the silently smiling Buddha she faced when she woke up in middle of the night sometimes.

However much profit was netted from Buddha's birthday, the house afterward became peacefully quiet like a bona fide temple.

The lotus lanterns in the yard needed to be re-hung on the ceiling above the deck. Swaying in the wind, the scene resembled a pond being held upside down. Jayeon Seu-nim looked up at the sky and smiled. Then she went to the garden in the backyard to pick vegetables. So much food had been made, but rice cakes had been sent home with the visitors and other leftovers had all been carried off by her family. Not a single morsel was left to eat. Mammy had never seen her daughter eat anything with a hearty appetite. Instead of getting her to eat better, Mammy was more interested in taking food home, claiming it would go to waste if she didn't. Before taking off with the food, she always warned her daughter sternly to abstain from meat and fish so as not to offend the spirits. As if Mageum had private feasts on her own. Without much knack or interest in cooking, Mageum got by eating whatever food she had on hand that could be prepared quickly. She ate just enough so she didn't starve. She wasn't the one who sowed the vegetable seeds in the backyard, so she knew little about cooking with them. She grabbed a handful of unidentified greens and sat down to sort through them when an elderly woman appeared. It was instantly obvious to Mageum that she was not a temple customer. The woman was wearing clothing that was out of season, but her face was beaming with a curious glow. She smiled and gently chastised Mageum.

"You don't know what to do with curled mallow? You're old enough to know better, tsk-tsk."

She sat down casually across from her and began trimming the greens as if this was the most natural thing in the world to do. Mageum learned for the first time that the skin of the soft stem should be peeled for this particular green.

"You don't know how to trim it, so I guess you don't know how to rinse it either. I'll show you."

She walked over to the faucet and rubbed the vegetable hard under the running water with both hands, crushing it until the water ran green. Doubting that Mageum had saved any starch water, she demanded some uncooked rice. She washed the rice grains in the water also, and after pouring out the first couple of batches of rinse-water, she collected the milky, starchy liquid in a bowl. Looking around the old-fashioned kitchen, she exclaimed repeatedly how nice it was. Then she set the rice pot on the stove and dished out some bean paste from a giant clay jar to make soup. This granny was a veteran homemaker who obviously knew her way around a kitchen. Mageum combed her memory for the strange woman's identity, but nothing came to mind. She knew from experience that unlike the thoughts that hit you right away, a protracted thought becomes less accurate the more it lingers in your head. Mageum wasn't frustrated in the least that she didn't know who the stranger was; instead, she felt the tingling sensation of happiness slithering onto her back. This was the first time in her life that she had felt this way.

The two sat down together at the table the granny had prepared. The bean paste soup with curly mallow was so delicious that Mageum finished off a bowl of rice with it in no time. The granny kept offering her more rice, worried that Mageum was too thin and weak. It was difficult to tell who was the hostess and who was the guest. In fact, ever since she set foot in the house, the granny behaved as if she was in her own home.

"I've got to cook you something good for dinner . . ."

Mageum suddenly longed to be babied by this woman who was already worrying about their next meal. This feeling, too, was a first. Never having been cared for by another, she soaked up every minute of this attention. It seemed too good to be true. In the evening, she picked up some groceries for the granny. She went to a convenience store in the native village and bought tofu, sprouts, and even some dried anchovies. Then she helped Granny prepare dinner in the kitchen, having more fun than she could remember. She was scolded for pouring out too much of the expensive sesame oil. Granny scolded her often for her shortcomings in the kitchen, but not in a scary or hurtful way. Mageum wondered how a person, especially an older person, could act with such ease around her. At night, the two placed futons side by side and lay down. Afraid that Granny might just as easily slip out at night as she had slipped in during the day, Mageum tentatively reached out for her hand. It was small, rough, and doughy.

"Shall I tell you a story?" Granny asked, gently squeezing her hand.

"A long, long time ago, there was a widow living with her young child. She had a lover, and every night, she went to bed fully clothed so that she could sneak out. The child, who caught on to the fact that she left every night, knotted the long strand of the bow on her *hanbok* top to his wrist before falling asleep. After the child fell asleep, the mother snipped off the bow with scissors and took off like the wind."

"That is so sad, Granny," Mageum muttered, drifting off to sleep. It was a deep, restful sleep that healed her body and mind, and when she awoke, it was morning.

Granny was not by her side. But she heard movements outside the room. Granny was sitting on the living room floor folding laundry.

"Aye, I'm losing my mind, for sure. I forgot to bring in the laundry last night." She was smoothing out the wrinkles and patting down the clothes dampened by the morning dew.

"These have to get some more sun later. That's how you get them nice and fluffy soft."

Listening to the rhythm of her words, Mageum wondered how this gem of a person had walked into her life. She had wrung out her clothes the previous day and hung them without shaking out the wrinkles so that they had shriveled up in the sun like dried fish. In Granny's hands, her crumpled clothes looked like they had been neatly pressed and folded into a rectangular stack.

Thus began Mageum's new life with Granny and the days rolled by in peace and comfort. Mageum decided not to question where Granny had come from or where she was headed. She knew nothing of Granny's identity except that Granny was more at home in that house than she was. When it came to her past, Granny made absolutely no sense. Mageum didn't think that she did this on purpose. When pressed for details about something she'd mentioned, she looked confused and tried hard to search her mind. Then she got annoyed and changed the subject. Once, she was staring at the Buddha figure and mumbled that Jesus-lovers were also kind-hearted. She had passed out on the street from sickness and hunger, and when she came to, she was surrounded by Christians praying. When Mageum asked her for more details the next day, she said something completely off topic. Pointing to a greenhouse constructed from vinyl, she said that the reason her back ached was because she had been sleeping there all winter long. Mageum couldn't make heads or tails of that, but she thought there might be some truth to what Granny said. Mageum knew instinctively that Granny's memory came and went randomly. It was clear, however, that Granny was happy with her current situation. She was at ease, like someone lazily stretching out her limbs. Granny sometimes said that it was good for people to return to their roots, just as fish are happy in their home waters. Mageum wondered if Granny had lived in this house long, long ago. This was not at all an unpleasant thought. She imagined herself as her granddaughter from that time gone by, as if she had gone back to another time from her former life. But sometimes when Granny looked into the distant mountains and wondered out loud why her son hadn't come looking for her yet, Mageum's heart skipped a beat. What upset her was not that the son might show up one day and whisk Granny away but that Granny might be one of those old people intentionally abandoned by their families.

4

Young Joo's guess that her mother's destination was the Euiwang Tunnel proved to be incorrect. After a sleepless night, she spent the next day searching in vain all the places her mother might be. Then she filed a missing person's report with the police and the family welfare departments of the village and the district offices. During this process she discovered that there was a national hotline just for missing persons. Despite Young Joo's desperate search for her mother, days passed without much progress. She took out a newspaper ad and pulled some strings with her husband's friend in the broadcasting industry to make radio announcements during peak listening hours. She obtained several leads through these efforts, but none of them got her any results. People claimed to have spotted her mother begging for change at Suwon subway station or some other similar place, and each time a tearful Young Joo ran over there only to be disappointed. She also received prank calls. Once, someone called to say that her mother was eating a bowl of noodle soup that was unpaid for and then hung up without disclosing the location. Distressing incidents continued in other ways. Young Joo had placed a request with the local police for confirmation of accidental death, and consequently, she was called in several times to view the decaying corpses of perfect strangers. Thereafter, her husband and her brother stepped in and spared her from these morbid tasks. Everyone in the family tried anything and everything they could to find Mother, because they couldn't just sit around and wait. Young Joo, especially, couldn't stay still at home for long periods, and soon her home became unkempt and neglected. She drove anywhere she thought her mother might have visited. As a result, she discovered that her mother had gone to Gwacheon once or twice. Having lived there for so long, the family still had acquaintances, and one of them had seen and talked with Mother.

Mother was well-groomed and cheerful, so that person thought Mother was just visiting. She never imagined that Mother had been lost. If she had known, she would have surely held on to her and contacted the family. Young Joo could have kicked herself for letting Mother slip through her fingers. Thinking it was better late than never, she decided to print a flyer to be distributed as a newspaper insert. Choosing Gwacheon as the central search point, she spent several days visiting every newspaper agency in Pyungchon, Sanbon, Anyang, and the area. Still unsure whether the flyer inserts would catch the attention of the readers, she also printed posters. Putting them up within the parameters of Mother's possible whereabouts was no simple task, but it was a blessing to at least be able to do something.

All these tasks required manpower and time beyond what Young Joo or her family alone could afford. To divide up the work and to consult with one another, the three siblings and their families gathered often. And when they gathered, they talked, and these talks sometimes led to finger-pointing, with much of the blame falling on Young Joo. Although Young Tak often said, "I have nothing to say because I'm responsible," he and his family appeared to be the least guilt-ridden. His wife never interfered in family discussions, only watching with cold detachment. But Young Joo could almost see in her silent smile the accusation that door locks, indeed, would have prevented their current plight. Young Sook must have made a similar observation.

"Elder Sister, you should have waited. No, you just had to go and bring Mother back, and now look at them. They're off the hook. I'm sure Sister-in-law is feeling quite smug about the whole thing."

"Do you really think that now is the time to discuss who's right and wrong? We don't even know if Mother's dead or alive. I only wanted to do what was best for Mother. That was my priority. I didn't know things would turn out like this, but I still don't think

I did anything terribly wrong."

"Well, when does my smart PhD sister ever do anything terribly wrong? And Mother's still alive or else the police would have contacted us, right? Didn't you say something about fingerprint matching?"

"What does my PhD have to do with anything?"

"You're the one who got so much out of Mom. After all she did for you, you still kept her working until old age because you just couldn't let go of your ambitions. And now look what's happened."

Her sister couldn't be more different from her mother in her opinion of Young Joo. Who had financed their college educations? Mother had always been proud of Young Joo for taking care of her younger siblings and credited her with half the work of raising them to be responsible adults. Mother often used to say that if only Young Joo weren't a landlady's daughter, she could've made something of herself, that she was smart enough to be a professor. Young Joo would not have had the courage to undertake postgraduate studies at that age if it weren't for Mother's high hopes for her. And like the good daughter of a landlady, she met and married one of their tenants. Because her husband had married her knowing all about her family situation, he had no qualms about living with her family. They say you shouldn't move in with your wife's family even if you have to live on a few scoops of unshelled barley otherwise. But he did so for many years without complaints even after Young Joo became a middle school teacher. When asked, he said that he lived with his mother-in-law with the same kind of dignity that a daughter-in-law might show. It was at those times that Young Joo felt the greatest respect and love for her husband. Mother, too, loved her easygoing son-in-law. Young Joo knew that her husband was deeply distraught over Mother's disappearance and that he missed her more than most of the other family members.

Nevertheless Young Sook was critical of her well-meaning brother-in-law. Days turned warm, easing their fears of Mother sleeping outside with the vagrants. Young Joo's husband mentioned that he missed Mother's fermented bean paste stew and kimchi radish stalks. Everyone knew that Mother could make this dish like no one else. Young Sook happened to be present when he mentioned this, and although he said it ruefully with a quivering voice, Young Sook stormed up from her seat, saying that kinder things would be said of a maid who had gone missing. If what he'd said was insulting, what were her memories of the mother she missed so much? As for Young Joo, the most endearing memory of her mother was, of all things, laundry. Every time she did laundry she was reminded of how Mother folded clothes so neatly that they looked ironed. Mother was present in those small things in her life, so Young Joo understood where her husband was coming from.

Almost six months had passed since Mother had left home. It was now early summer. Young Joo reordered posters numerous times, a thousand sheets at a time, but she was nowhere close to covering all of Seoul and its nearby areas. Leads had stopped coming in long ago. Young Joo routinely visited organizations serving the elderly to put up her posters and inquire about her mother's whereabouts. Scattered throughout various regions, many of these organizations were privately run and were not registered with the local social welfare departments. She had to rely on word of mouth to find them.

Young Joo was returning from a visit to one of these hard-to-find places one day. She came upon a town on the outskirts of Seoul when she felt a sudden urge to stop and take a break. She got out of the car and took a deep breath. There was nothing particularly refreshing about the air in that small, rundown village. She was considering putting up a poster when she spotted a lone house. With so much land development in and around

Seoul, it was amazing that such an old house was still standing. The house wasn't old in a charming, historic sense; it was simply getting on in years, but Young Joo was strangely drawn to it. Not knowing what attracted her, she took a few hesitant steps. She suddenly remembered the room-and-board house of her youth even though the house in front of her did not bear much resemblance to it. As she approached she saw a sign that read "Cheongae Temple Outreach House" and her mother's sweater swinging from a clothesline. She gasped. Still panting from lack of air, Young Joo let herself gravitate toward the house. Lotus lanterns hanging from the wooden ceiling and a golden Buddha were obvious signs that the house was a Buddhist temple. In front of the golden Buddha underneath the lanterns were two women in gray robes intimately chatting away while peeling mountain herb roots. A mystic aura of idyllic serenity enveloped the two women. Perhaps it was the oversized monastic robe hanging from her small frame, but Mother looked like a butterfly resting with its wings neatly folded. No, no, it wasn't just the loose robe. It was the freedom, the lightness of being released from all the things that weighed her down in this life. Has anyone or anything ever made Mother feel this happy and free? Young Joo had never seen such pure innocence in a person well over seventy.

This can't be real. I must be hallucinating. With her mother right before her eyes, Young Joo froze, unable to move a single step toward her. Her feet were grounded in reality. Because no matter how close or transparent the other side may appear, reality and illusion were two disparate worlds that could never be bridged.

An Unbearable Secret

She had waited too long. Was it still daybreak? The translucence of early dawn showed no sign of ebbing. Was she really waiting for the sun to break through the clouds? When she registered at the hotel, Ha Young never gave a thought to the Eastern seaboard sunrise. Even when the front desk receptionist handed over the key and proudly pointed out that the room had a wide open view of the sunrise, she was unappreciative of her good fortune. The dignity of the phrase "Eastern seaboard sunrise" failed to elicit a response from her. But as soon as she opened her eyes, she lay on her side and looked out the window.

With the sky and the sea coming together like ink dissolving in water, the horizon line remained undefined. High above where the horizon should have been, the sky ripped into a long, crimson line. But no light poked through. It was only a celestial wound about to bleed, not at all helpful in pushing out the chalky dawn. It did, however, make Ha Young realize that the sun had risen, but the sky was extremely overcast.

She crawled out of bed as sluggishly as an old person and walked toward the window. The mellow shoreline and the vast, sandy beach came into view. It was a well-known beach that was often featured on television in the summer. The recent late-summer heat wave made it just as hot as the peak of summer, but the beach was empty and quiet. Drawn by its undisturbed serenity, Ha Young dressed herself hurriedly and went outside.

The hotel entrance was just across the road from the beach. Just outside the entrance window was a zinnia plant blooming against the backdrop of a dense bamboo forest. Ha Young trembled. Perhaps because of the bleak weather, the vivid scarlet blooms weighing down the branches of the small sapling seemed so out of place. The riot of color that inundated her vision turned into a bunch of immature girls snickering. *Why did you? . . . Why? . . .* Her meaningless mumbling was only an attempt to control her breathing. She hated immaturity. No, not hate. It was more correct to say that she was afraid of it, of the irresponsibility that comes with immaturity.

The road leading to the beach was a winding slope. The damp shade of the thick trees on both sides of the road made dawn seem just like dusk. The road wrapped around a U-shaped bend and the beach loomed ahead. It was still free of people. Heading toward the beach, she walked down the street with its rows of sushi joints. They were all closed, but squirming fish in tanks meant that they were still in business. What was inside the hearts of the captive fish gazing at the raging ocean in front of them? Did they even have feelings inside their cold hearts?

Ha Young leisurely walked along the shoreline immersed in these choppy, off-the-wall thoughts. She avoided the wet parts of the beach that had been licked by the waves, but with each sinking step, the sand that made its way into her sneakers felt damp.

Just ahead, she saw a ring of people. They seemed to be looking down at something. They looked like locals because they weren't dressed like the usual out-of-town beachgoers in fun vacation clothes. Their drab appearance blended in with the damp, depressing landscape. Although worried about looking like an out-of-towner, Ha Young could not quell her curiosity. She inched closer, clutching her chest with one hand as her heart tightened. This was a common tick of hers whenever she became nervous.

She finally saw what everyone was looking at. In the middle of the circle was a person lying down. She knew right away that the person was dead. The head and the upper body were covered with a flimsy sheet of newspaper so she couldn't see the face. No living person would be treated that way. White sneakers were on the feet of the corpse. Seeing them, she trembled all over once and pushed her way through the crowd. Then she kneeled at the feet of the corpse and grasped a sneakered foot in each hand. People began whispering, but she didn't care. The feet were damp and heavy. They were only slightly damp, but to her, they felt sopping wet. The fear that weaved through her body like a network of blood vessels converged and charged toward the white sneakers at full speed. She couldn't stop it. Tumbling forward, she hugged the sneakers she was clutching in each hand to her chest. She gave in to a surge of tears. As she wept out loud, her own wretched wailing intensified her fear and woe. Even while bawling, she could still make out the murmur of the crowd.

Who's that? Someone Choon-Shik knows? She doesn't look like a local so how does she know him, I wonder? Even if she knows him, was she that close to him? Who knows, maybe they had a long distance thing for each other. No way, with an older woman like her? We'll soon find out when his family shows up. Anyhow, what do we do about his poor mother? That jerk. I knew that he was lame but never imagined him to be this callous. How could he shove pills down his throat knowing that she has no one else in the world? He could have spared his life if he didn't take so many. Why did he have to be so stupid? I guess he felt hopeless with nothing working out for him. Still, it's not like he was forty or fifty. At twenty, how much life experience could he have had to be that hopeless? What a shame.

Ha Young's wailing was closer to a spasm than crying, so it toned down like an unwinding spring. With the realization that the death she was lamenting had resulted from a suicidal overdose and not from drowning, she lifted her head and grinned sheepishly. Her hair was disheveled and grains of sand were stuck to the edges of her mouth, but no tear smudges remained. Her dry, flushed face shocked the onlookers.

What, was she mad? Well, that explains it.

Each concentric ring opened up as Ha Young made her way out of the crowd. She was soon forgotten when the hysterical mother arrived at the scene, propped on her feet by several people. If it weren't for the mother, some of the onlookers may have followed her, curious, or hopeful, to see if she would do more crazy things. Was it because of the overcast sky? The villagers' faces were especially grim, unbefitting of people who live by a vast ocean.

Ha Young did not look back, but she didn't hurry either, leaving the scene behind as if nothing had happened. Loud sirens caused her to look back, and she saw that an ambulance and a police car had arrived simultaneously. That's when she hastened her steps, cutting across the beach onto a paved road in front of the sushi shops. She felt no panic up until then, but the moment her feet stepped off the plush sand and touched down on hard pavement, she felt a rush of relief. But it lasted for only a brief moment. She had to hide herself somewhere, anywhere.

Ha Young slid open the door of a sushi shop in front of her. A bedroom door all the way in the back opened, and a buxom woman bursting out of her shirt came out yawning and welcomed her in. It was apparently outside opening hours, but the place was not closed. A fishy smell that was different from the smell of the ocean pervading the air outside the shop raided her empty insides. Against her will, her stomach clamored for food, grumbling menacingly. The mingled smell of stale fish, wasabi, soy sauce, bean paste, and chili pepper sauce became overwhelming, making her salivate uncontrollably. She wasn't sure if what she felt was a hunger pang or nausea. It just felt like something she should suppress.

"Do you want to eat something?"

The woman sounded indifferent, like someone who didn't care to serve customers at that moment. Through the open bedroom door in the back, Ha Young could see the back of a man's head and a television screen. Comedians jostling each other, emaciated African children surrounded by pestering flies, two lithe Caucasian bodies intertwined in a lovemaking scene—channels were quickly flipped through until the screen rested on the weekly singing contest emceed by the television host Song Hae. The background mural of the outdoor stage was, incidentally, a beach painted in bright blue like a common landscape painting.

"Maybe just something to drink for now," Ha Young mumbled timidly.

"Well, that's good. It's too early for lunch, and we don't do breakfast."

"Yes, that's fine with me."

She must mean that they don't serve breakfast, not that they don't eat breakfast. Ha Young let out a wry chuckle, and the woman became friendlier.

"Would you like to go upstairs? We have the best view. The beach on one side and a lake on the other."

Ha Young followed the woman upstairs, taking hesitant steps on the filthy carpet. Upstairs was spacious and empty. She liked the space, not because of the view but because she could be alone. In front of her was a refrigerated case filled with beverages. The woman saw Ha Young staring at the beverage case, not the view. She said kindly, "You don't have to drink anything. It'll be lunchtime soon anyway. I can get you a cup of coffee if you'd like. On the house."

"Nope. I'll take a bottle of soju."

What she had wanted to subdue with all her might was neither hunger nor nausea but a pressing need for soju. Soju on an empty stomach was just the thing to revive the tree that seemed to have fallen inside of her.

"Soju? By yourself?" the woman asked, surprised.

"Why? I can't drink by myself?" she countered defiantly, spurred by a sense of urgency.

"No, no. That's fine. Anything to eat with your drink?"

"Just soju for now. I'll order food later."

The woman was about to say something, but she changed her mind and went back downstairs. Soon she returned with a bottle of soju, seaweed salad, and a couple of side dishes made from unidentifiable bits of salted seafood. She laid the food down on the table slowly but somewhat impolitely, and left the table after removing the soju bottle cap with a bottle opener. With great effort, Ha Young waited for her to leave. Despite the haste she was in, Ha Young refrained from drinking straight from the bottle. The first shot of the clear liquid touched her tongue, and then turned rose-colored upon hitting the back of the throat. Pushing forward to create a new path where none existed before, the cool liquid passed over her throat, traveled down her esophagus and settled in her stomach. Sensing every inch of this burning passage, Ha Young shuddered from the electric jolt and the ensuing bliss. With the second shot of soju, branches burgeoned from the main route. The third shot induced even more splitting into tertiary branches. If someone were to ask, she'd be able to replicate in detail the circulatory path of the liquid, including every minute capillary tube. It was like a tree inside her, now fully watered and standing erect. The tree felt turgid, like it was about to spew out fuchsia camellia blooms any moment. That point, when reached, would be the culmination of being alive. She must not be impulsive. She must bide her time in cultivating her tree.

Just when Ha Young's self-control was on the verge of collapsing, the owner returned with a large group of customers. Fussing over the second-story view, they stampeded over to the window overlooking the beach and then to the side of the room with the lake view. Tourists, no doubt. Ha Young felt dizzy, like someone on a boat rocking from side to side due to a great shift in weight. Sure enough, she spilled the next glass of soju she was pouring as if she were actually on a boat. To make matters worse, the group settled down at a table adjacent to hers. One seat short, a man came over to Ha Young's table to take a chair. His eyes roamed over her table, questioning and condemning. By then, the beautiful tree in bloom was already gone. Ha Young started to get up when the owner rushed over to take her order.

"I'll take my meal downstairs."

"Good idea. I'm sure you've had enough of the view."

The woman did not return with the bottle she had seized upstairs. Instead, she laid on the table a paltry array of side dishes, clear clam broth, fish stew, and stale steamed rice. Ha Young didn't remember ordering these. But a sudden and intense hunger overwhelmed her and she ate ravenously. The man in the bedroom had stepped out and was now haggling over the price of fish to be filleted for sushi with the man from upstairs who had eyed Ha Young. While waiting for the woman to reappear, Ha Young watched the fish—either a flatfish or a sole, she could not tell—scooped up from the tank by a metal hook and thrashing around on the cement floor. Inside the tank it had been sluggish, barely alive, but now it was putting up one hell of a fight for its life. The woman bounced down the steps, and Ha Young quickly caught her attention and asked for the bill.

"How was the food?" she asked brusquely, handing over the change. Ha Young quickly left without answering. No one had forced her to stay inside, but she felt a great rush of relief once outside. The corpse with white sneakers and the onlookers were nowhere to be seen. At first Ha Young only darted her eyes in that direction, but to confirm their disappearance she swung her head around and looked searchingly. The people, the ambulance, and the police car were all gone. There was no trace whatsoever of the commotion that the accident had caused. She thought she could at least find tire tracks on the sand, so Ha Young started to head toward that direction but stopped. Did the incident that she had witnessed actually happen? Doubt and accusation made her afraid to go on.

While she was walking away from the beach, a dreary wind accompanied her. It was the kind of wind that could easily have erased the prints on the sand. Having walked for some time, she came upon another area quite different from the row of sushi restaurants. Almost every structure was plastered with signs, most of which were for *chodang* tofu. Original tofu, old-fashioned tofu, all-natural tofu, grandma's tofu . . . each sign boasting of being the very best of the best.

These days *chodang* tofu can easily be found in Seoul, but Ha Young had already experienced the real thing from Gangneung, where seawater is traditionally used as a coagulant instead of salt. It had been a cold and snowy day the first time she'd tried it, and she remembered how the steaming, soft tofu warmed her up inside. She didn't remember the taste being so extraordinary. She was now delighted to come upon this place not because of the tofu but because it was the actual Chodang village.

She was with her husband on her previous visit. It was their first long distance trip after his car accident. They stayed overnight in downtown Gangneung and asked around for directions to Chodang village. They weren't searching for the famous tofu huts but the village itself. One of the huts in the village is said to be the birthplace of Heo Nanseolheon, the renowned poetess from the mid-Joseon Dynasty, and the daughter of Heo Yeob, whose own pen name was Chodang. This unconfirmed piece of information was acquired by Ha Young haphazardly and wasn't included as part of their original travel plan. It was only on the day before, while they were sightseeing at Ojukheon Shrine, that Ha Young mentioned visiting Heo's birthplace. She might not have wanted to go if the Ojukheon shrine wasn't so well preserved. Its flawless perfection actually left her feeling unfulfilled.

Her husband suggested that they make the trip the next day and have sushi by the seaside. Up until that point, they only knew that Chodang village was Heo's birthplace and had never heard of it being known for tofu. When they woke up in Gangneung the next morning, it was snowing heavily. The snow resembled giant, plush cotton bolls, the likes of which they had never seen in Seoul. They drove while listening to a snowstorm watch being issued on the radio. The vertigo they experienced navigating through the storm was as dizzying as being sucked into a sweet but tragic movie scene. On that day, too, they knew they had found the village because of the tofu signs. The village was eerily silent. The snow was still falling heavily, so no attempt had been made to clear the fronts of the houses.

"I'll go and ask." Her husband stopped the car in front of one of the tofu huts. It's always easier to approach a business than a residence. Ha Young squinted and watched her husband's manly figure braving the elements outside, knee deep in snow. The blistering snow made it difficult to see just a few feet away. No one must have come to the door right away, for she heard her husband banging on the door yelling, "Is anyone in there?"

After a long while a head poked out.

"May I ask you something? I've heard that Heo Nanseolheon's birthplace is near here. Can you tell me where it is?"

"I don't know anyone by that name."

"She's a poet and Heo Gyun's sister. You must know Heo Gyun? The guy who wrote *Tale of Hong Gildong*?"

"Dunno anything about that. There isn't a single family with the last name Heo in this village."

Baffled, her husband turned around to face her and shrugged his shoulders with his arms wide open in an exaggerated manner. He had lived abroad for about half a year, and didn't look half bad pulling off this Western gesture. Their conversation was so amusing that Ha Young indulged in frivolous laughter inside the car.

"Ask them if they serve food. I'm hungry," she said, still giggling.

That's how they came to eat soft saltwater tofu and rice at one of the *chodang* huts. There were no other customers, so they were able to kill time in a cozy nook with under-floor heating. It was the perfect place for loafing while waiting for the snow to let up. Later on, the owner joined them for a chat, but neither Ha Young nor her husband asked again about Heo's birthplace. Chodang. Heo Yeob. Weren't they already in a Heo residence of some sort? She wondered if the owners of the tofu place also thought so.

It had stopped snowing but radio broadcasters continued to cover the storm. They reported that more than two feet of snow had accumulated that morning and that snow removal at the Daekwan Pass was going at a snail's pace. Repeated reminders of the necessary gear that every car should have and the precautions that must be followed were made. With more than two feet of snow, it was fortunate that the roads were not closed. Ha Young did not show any kind of anxiety over the perils frantically announced over the radio waves. It wasn't like her to panic. What Ha Young feared was the kind of misfortune that happened without warning. She knew that true calamity always strikes unannounced. Uneventful times, monotony day after day, were what troubled her the most.

Although Ha Young remained unperturbed, her husband still minded her and drove extra cautiously. Somehow he managed to go over the Daekwan Pass before it got dark. Ironically, it was after they had gone over the pass that Ha Young was shaken up. On the other side of the pass, the heavy, wet snow that clung to and split asunder live pine branches had disappeared without a trace. Just like the day before, the bare winter landscape spread out abundantly before them.

Since then, she'd had another similar experience going over the pass. A friend living in Gangneung was getting married in the middle of winter, so Ha Young and a group of her friends rented a van to attend the wedding. Among her close-knit group of high school buddies, this was the last friend to be married, and everyone was excited. There were two other unmarried friends with doctorate degrees in the group, but they had sworn themselves into singlehood and were determined to live out their lives in that fashion. Everyone had come willingly, but the absent bride made her an easy scapegoat for their irritation with the bitter cold.

Maybe if she was twenty-nine. But what's the difference between thirty-six and -seven? It will soon be March with spring in all its glory. What's the big hurry that she has to don a veil in the dead of winter?

You really don't know what the hurry is at her age? It's criminal of you to be so judgmental just because you've settled down and got it good now.

That must have been around the eleventh or the twelfth month of the lunar calendar. It was brutally cold, so much so that the thick frost on the window refused to thaw out even at high noon. Scratching off the frost cleared the view only briefly, because the window froze up instantly again. But after the bus reached the peak of the Daekwan Pass and started downhill, the thick, stubborn frost melted and flowed down like streams of sweat. In no time, the view of the ocean loomed ahead, and everyone cheered.

The instant transformation of the weather from one extreme to another over the treacherous and winding Daekwan Pass represented something of a hope or the will to change for Ha Young. She had no appreciation for the kind of transformation that was gradual; she wanted complete, groundbreaking change.

But she had no idea how to make this kind of change happen.

While mulling over this and that, Ha Young stumbled upon an unusual house that immediately stood out. She had not intended to seek out Heo Nanseolheon's birthplace. With no tofu sign in sight, the Chodang village that the house stood in the middle of looked like any other rural village with thatched-roof cottages. The house looked big enough to have accommodated a noble family back in the day, but now it was quite decrepit. The collapsed central ridge of the roof was covered with a navy plastic tarp. The cheap plastic covering seemed out of place against the aged patina of the mossy roof tiles, but at least it didn't look overly tacky. The village possessed a dignity that could not be undermined by a piece of plastic.

Inside the house was a notice board on the wall explaining the significance of the house and the reasons for its designation as a historical landmark. The years that Chodang Heo Yeob resided there and the belief that Heo Nanseolheon was born there were engraved on a cheap, gold-plated plaque. Dogs, not people, were the first clue that the house was occupied. Both inside and outside the front door, sleeping dogs lounged and awake ones gazed at passersby. They were big in size but not too scary. In fact, even when Ha Young tripped over one clumsily, it neither welcomed nor resisted the human contact. Well, someone must be feeding them, she thought, as they seemed to be living in idyllic comfort.

As soon as she entered the front courtyard, she could see everyday household items laid out on the open wooden deck. Bowls, buckets, a floor mat, spice jars, and a lone shoe—all of these were flamboyant plastic or vinyl pieces. The faucet area in the yard was sloppily patched up with thick cement. Embarrassed by these cheap furnishings threatening the vestiges of the home's former grandeur, Ha Young scuttled back, took a wrong turn, and ended up at the back of the house.

She went around the back of the main building and came upon another courtyard. It was the guest quarters. The courtyard was square and was separated from the outside by a stylish brick wall. Although it was a yard, it was the coziest space in the whole house. This area was also infinitely better maintained than the main building. The green carpet of moss-covered clay ground looked more elegant than any manicured lawn, and the garden nook in one corner was overflowing with zinnias in full bloom. These crimson blossoms, poignant in their forlorn beauty, could easily surpass any tended garden at an upscale hotel. Intertwining strands of the main stem climbed up and branched out, asserting their freedom and determination; it was unlikely that they would succumb to shame after the blooms withered. Ha Young had no idea how old the tree was, but she wanted to believe that Nanseolheon had sat by it and daydreamed. The tree, every inch of its growth steeped in suffering and beauty, had such an aura of eternity.

Ha Young sat sideways on the edge of the wooden deck. She slid her hand slowly over the wooden flooring and the columns made from whole tree trunks. Soft parts of the wood had worn out and the tougher fibers have hardened even more, yielding a unique texture to touch. The virgin wood that had never been coated felt like a living and breathing thing. Ha Young reclined and stretched out. Red peppers had been laid out to dry under the sun near her feet, a surer sign than the dogs of human occupancy. Ha Young let go of her innermost cares and allowed her eyelids to glide over her eyes. Through her thin summer clothing on her back, she could still feel the textured pattern of the wooden floor. As sleep came, she felt herself sinking into the floor by the sheer pull of four hundred years.

When she opened her eyes, the day was bright and the sky azure above the zinnia blossoms. Ha Young had never seen such a sky before in her life. Crimson blossoms weighing down forked branches, moss growing in the yard, and the brick wall with a few missing tiles—like an infant just out from a mother's womb, Ha Young marveled at these sights. The world seemed so clear, unfamiliar, and pure. She was serene to the core. She didn't remember the last time she indulged in such worry-free sleep.

An elderly woman with silver hair was at her feet flipping over the red peppers. Ha Young got up hesitantly and smiled timidly.

"Those are pretty peppers."

"This batch is from the first crop. Didya get enough sleep?"

"Yes. How come you didn't wake me up?"

"What for?"

"This is the Heo family residence, isn't it?"

"That's what they say."

"I've always wanted to visit. Last time, I was near here but couldn't find it. A neighbor said that there were no Heos living in the area."

"They must be right. Treason can wipe out whole clans. No doubt that's how the Heo family line ended, don't ya think?" she addressed Ha Young innocently.

"Can, can I ask . . . who, who are you?"

Ha Young stared at the woman's puckered, toothless mouth and asked with a quivering voice. Surprised by Ha Young's sudden change in tone, the woman mumbled something inaudible instead of replying. Ha Young turned pale as warm blood drained from her face. Peace had not lasted long. Nothing had changed. Ha Young ran out without saying goodbye. Although she didn't go around the yard, she was already outside. The lingering dogs were still unresponsive when shoved out of the way. Not heading in any direction, she quickened her pace like someone being followed. What she was running from was the fear that she somehow always managed to get involved in unhappy events. Truly, it had been a long time since she had enjoyed this kind of perfect rest. But why in the courtyard of an annihilated family?

How long is the life span of a pine tree? She guessed the age of the thick, dense trees blocking the sky to be about four hundred years. The smell of pine was powerful and refreshing. She had calmed down a little but was not completely rid of her fear. The thought that she could never fully escape made her stop running. Nothing grew in the dirt under the permanent shade of the pine branches. Ha Young slumped to the ground and leaned against a tree.

Ha Young turns forty this year. She became a college student at twenty. She was so lucky to get into a school of her choice in Seoul the first time she applied. Her parents and her brothers were all very proud of her. Theirs was a farming family that owned land and an orchard in a rural area. The land that they owned neighbored a developing industrial area, so selling small portions of the land afforded them more than enough money to pay for the children's education in Seoul. The parents would have been happy with any school located in Seoul, but first their son and then Ha Young had made it into top schools, bringing even greater honor to their family. The parents were simple rural folk, but when it came to self-glorification through the successes of their children, they were just as driven as the other parents from the city. As the only daughter sandwiched in between an older and a younger brother, Ha Young, especially, was the apple of their eye. Her father habitually threatened, after having a drink or two, that he'd shoot any fellow who dared to break his daughter's heart. Ha Young, of course, never worried about such a thing. As a confident, well-loved, and well-adjusted young lady, she never entertained the thought that the object of her affection would not reciprocate.

Is there any other time in life more free of worry and full of romantic dreams than one's first summer as a college student? It was an especially beautiful time for Ha Young. She already had her ideal man picked out: Sejoon, a college buddy of her older brother. Sejoon was a true Seoulite, so he liked to visit their home in the country during summer vacations. He was almost like family to them. To distinguish him from her own brother, Ha Young called him Sejoon-*oppa*, but as a smitten high school girl, she used to indulge her infatuation by calling him Sejoon-*ssi* in private, as if he were one of her peers. She was daddy's little girl, but she wanted to be a grown-up in the eyes of Sejoon. The first thought she had when she got into college was that she was now his equal. The girls from her esteemed school had their pick of guys from other colleges who were eager to date them. But during the first semester, Ha Young avoided Sejoon like the plague. Her plan was to shed her little girl image during the few months of her self-imposed separation. This was all in preparation for the following summer. In order to mature, in order to feign indifference, she went on every available date; but only Sejoon ruled her heart.

Sejoon came to stay at their house that summer, but he behaved like a family member and was treated just like family. Days rolled by and Ha Young was beginning to get anxious, as nothing short of a miracle would change their uneventful time together. One day, they had each gone on walks alone, and they ran into each other in the fields. This was their first time together alone. They walked along a stream on a path lined with poplar trees. It's always chilly by a body of water but the air around that place was especially eerie and frigid, like cold water that's thrown on your bare back. They came upon the mouth of the stream where the water emptied into a basin. In addition to the water flowing down from above, it was said to have a natural spring at the bottom from which ice cold water gushed out.

She sat down next to him leaving a little distance between them. Ha Young had never studied a man's face so close up before. From the side, his head bulged out both in the front and in the back. It was the cutest thing she had ever seen. She became curious. If she were to wrap one arm around his head, would she be able make a full circle? His forehead was handsome, as was his nose. She wanted to come up from behind and blindfold him with her hands. It would be fun to feel his eyes move under her fingers, like the rapid eye movement that occurs during a dream. The area around his nose and chin was a bit scruffy, which made him look refreshingly different. His lips looked so firm and sensitive! It was his handsome lips that made his scruffiness beautiful. Without moving, Ha Young outlined with a fingertip the contour of his lips. Surely most people perceived only the firmness, not the subtle sensitivity, of his lips. That's what she wanted to believe. Her fingers trembled with the urge to get closer, to touch him. A vague instinct for lust tickled her yet undeveloped sensibilities. Urged by something irrepressible, her gasping breath headed straight toward his lips. The scruffy part of his lip area felt scratchy, and the kiss was fiery.

"What are you staring at?"

He must have felt her gaze on him, for he spoke sheepishly, rubbing his face with one hand in a downward motion. Startled that she'd been caught fantasizing about him, Ha Young asked him an offbeat question.

"*Oppa*, do you know how to swim?"

"What a thing to ask. 'Course I do."

"Do you know how deep this pool is here? They say that there's a ghost of someone who drowned here. That's why no one comes out alive. None of the village people swim here, you know."

"That's stupid. What, you believe in ghosts?"

"Everyone else does. They're all scared so that means they believe, right?"

"Believing in something that doesn't exist is just plain foolish.

"What if it exists? What would you do then?"

"What would I do? Fight it, of course. And win."

"Then go ahead. Do it, in front of me. I dare you."

How juvenile this whole charade was. This was not her intention. Her intention this summer was to have mature and intelligent conversations with him like enlightened college students. The embarrassment of her first immodest thought probably forced her to play dumb. Something unforeseen happened just then. Sejoon suddenly got up from where he was and dove into the water without even taking his shoes off. His perfect diving form followed by his white sneakers flashed before her eyes. But nothing reappeared. Seconds, minutes ticked by without any movement in the water. Afterward, she had no recollection of how help arrived or how long it took to arrive. Her memory ended after that point in time. It picked up again with Sejoon lying on the ground, his sneakers still on his feet. Shaking off the people trying to calm her down, Ha Young pummeled down on his chest, pounded his abdomen, and sucked his lips. She had never performed CPR or watched anyone do it, but she was trying to resuscitate him. His lips were as cold as ice. No matter how hard she pulled at them, blood did not return to his frozen, blue lips. Others pulled her away, but she managed to get free several times to repeat the act. Even if she had missed the critical time period for resuscitating him, she wanted to believe that the miracle of a loving kiss had no time constraint. After all, the prince charming in fairy tales pulled off this kind of stunt all the time. No one was able to stop her because she was in a state of hysteria. Even nowadays, Ha Young occasionally feels the chill she inhaled from him that day. The chill had frozen into a glacier inside her, dispersing ice crystals throughout her veins.

It took more than just the midsummer heat threatening to putrefy the body to make Ha Young stop; Sejoon's family arrived and the body was handed over to them. They caused quite a commotion, erupting in grief and anger. The main gist of their screaming was that their family lineage had now come to an end with Sejoon's death, that she was the one responsible for this tragedy. This was the most excruciating thing for Ha Young to hear. The bitch who terminated their family line—how that accusation horrified her. She trembled like an aspen leaf in the blistering wind.

But that was nothing compared to what happened afterward. A few days after the funeral, Sejoon's mother reappeared with his two older sisters. They all seemed to have made a remarkable recovery in just a few days and eyed Ha Young with unctuousness and predatory tenacity. Their sympathetic gaze was much harder to endure than the screaming accusations and open hostility. Out of the blue, his mother grabbed her hand and begged her to bear them a son.

You're with child, aren't you? I know you are. It's okay. It's nothing to be ashamed of. Just help us carry on our family line. We don't want anything else from you. And if you want, we'll keep this a secret just between you and us. But you'd better not have any other intentions with your present condition. Just so you know, we'll never forgive you if that happens.

As though possessed, she hissed words to this effect in her ear. The sisters were less forward, but apparently they were the ones who had started all this trouble by instilling the impossible hope in her heart. They had whispered improbable what-ifs to their mother who had taken to a sick bed in her despair. They said they had no idea that their wishful thinking would have such a powerful effect on their mother, for she jumped out of bed instantly. Time will take care of everything so be patient, they said, implying that they, too, were banking on the same possibility on the off chance that they were right. The three of them were determined to claim what was rightfully theirs, Ha Young's body merely a means to an end. In order to dispel their gross misunderstanding, to assert her rights, and to guard her body as her own, Ha Young had to suffer through unspeakable humiliation and harassment. Her father, who had so often joked about shooting anyone who harmed his daughter, said nothing and drowned himself in drink.

For Ha Young, kissing a corpse was the first and only contact she had ever had with a man. She couldn't say this out loud. Whether or not anyone would believe her was of no importance. The fact that her first kiss had been with a corpse was a secret she could not bear.

Once convinced that their hope had been futile, Sejoon's family lashed out one last time. *You killed my son, you ended our family line . . . Let's see how well you turn out. We'll be watching you, we'll be watching. You murderous bitch . . . You bitch . . .* Only after wreaking havoc all over town, bashing her to their hearts' content, did they leave her alone.

Before the year was over, Ha Young's family had left their hometown and moved to an apartment in a satellite city. Her father, who had always been of the opinion that apartments were unsuitable dwellings for humans, acknowledged that they were just the thing for living anonymously. The move was perhaps his sad concession for not having fought off her foes. Ha Young took a year off from her studies and did nothing, spending her days moping around in a daze. Finally, with her brother's earnest plea to resume her life, she slowly prepared to return to school. One night, she stepped out onto the veranda to get some air. Everyone else had already gone to bed. From the veranda, she could see the river that wrapped around the city like a belt, and over and above that, the national highway running alongside the river. The day's bumper-to-bumper traffic had eased and cars sped by sporadically. Why was she standing there? On sleepless nights, she usually read while listening to music. Was she waiting, or beckoning, for something to happen?

In front of her, two cars on opposite lanes of the highway ran straight into each other without swerving. She was too far away to see which driver had been at fault. She rubbed her eyes in disbelief and by the time she opened them again, both cars were ablaze. With barely any traffic at that time, there were no cars in front of either car for the drivers to pass. Unless one of the drivers was insane or had a death wish, the thing that happened couldn't have happened. It was so unreal that Ha Young thought she was hallucinating. *What's happening to me?* Concerned more for herself than for the burning cars, she stumbled back into bed, with the incident already leaving her mind like a distant memory of fireworks. She somehow managed to doze off and when she awoke again, the incident seemed even further removed from reality. The next morning's newspaper, however, gave a full account of the previous night's head-on collision. There were no survivors from either car. It suddenly dawned on Ha Young that that day marked the anniversary of Sejoon's death. This realization shook her to the very core. She began to doubt that the accident would have happened if she hadn't been looking in the direction of the highway.

It was probably from that day on that she began to comprehend that she possessed an uncanny power to harm others against her will or knowledge.

Had she ever felt this power before? She must have. How could she forget Sejoon's mother's blame and accusations? What she'd witnessed by chance simply provided an opportunity for her to throw her hands up in the air and accept what she had tried so hard to ignore. Not that bad things always occurred on the anniversary of Sejoon's death. It was a matter of how she put two and two together. Unless she made an intentional connection, the anniversary of Sejoon's death and the car accident were two unrelated events. An infinite number of good things, bad things, and neither good nor bad things happen in this world day after day. The rhythm of life will continue to make the world go round as long as the world continues to exist. The problem was the feeling she had, the feeling that she was always connected to grief and sorrow. This feeling might have even compelled her to seek out unhappy events to attach herself to. This world was too, too small, and allowed all kinds of associations. One could always find a link, however remote, among relatives, school friends, and hometown acquaintances. Even a bottom feeder and a top dog were connected in some way, if one searched hard enough.

After they moved into the city, Ha Young's family never again spoke about what happened in their hometown. This unspoken taboo prevailed because rehashing that affair would be like rubbing salt into Ha Young's old wound. Her mother mentioned their hometown just once, some time after Ha Young graduated from college. She broached the subject gingerly, as if carefully lifting off layer after layer of bandages on a wound that may or may not have healed.

"I went back there once. For no reason, really. But how much it's changed! There's not a single soul we know who lives there anymore. Oh, and that pool. It's now paved. In fact, they've covered up the whole stream. After we left I heard that factories moved in and polluted the stream. So maybe they sealed it off." After a long silence, she eyed Ha Young cautiously and added, "Well, I wonder whatever happened to the ghost." Thinking that her mother was searching for the ghost inside of her, Ha Young shuddered.

Her father's one wish was to see his daughter happily married, but he passed away before fulfilling this wish. Cancer. When he was hospitalized, her mother never left his bedside. She looked so drained that Ha Young offered to watch him one night. But on that very night his condition took a sharp turn for the worse and he died. She couldn't take her father's death at face value. She couldn't shake off the belief that her presence that night had triggered his death.

She married her current husband in her thirties. She had no

thought of marriage up to that point, but she finally agreed to go on a series of arranged dates. This was purely due to her mother's incessant oh-what-do-I-do-with-my-unmarried-daughter nagging, and Ha Young interpreted her maternal concern as blame for the downfall in the family's prosperity. So she thought it best to get out of their hair.

She hastily married the first suitable guy. He wasn't the handsomest man, but he was kind and affectionate. They had a son and a daughter, their wealth grew, and other good things followed, with an occasional flu suffered by their children being their only hardship. Her mother was so happy for her good fortune that she credited her deceased father for looking after her from heaven. Ha Young didn't appreciate this thought. Why should she be so grateful for things that so many other people enjoyed in life, or think that she didn't deserve them?

Despite such bravado, Ha Young was the one who didn't feel worthy. She lived in vague fear of eventual doom, wondering why nothing had happened thus far. All that waiting—and agonizing—made her wish that she could preempt her ill fate. Her way of preempting fate often took the form of suddenly and arbitrarily running away from home. *I can't live like this anymore! This life is suffocating me!* She engaged in this kind of outburst every once in a while. Her husband was more than understanding about her periodic fits, referring to them as her spring or fall mini-vacations.

This time, it's different. It has to be. Ha Young told herself firmly, staggering out of the wooded area with pine trees. Turning forty this year. As if folding a square piece of origami paper in half with the edges perfectly lined up, she mentally folded her life in half. At age twenty, her life was turned upside down, and she had since lived another twenty years. What may line up perfectly is not origami paper but the recurrence of tragedy. *I must take the initiative. I have to prevent this curse from happening, because I love my family.* The sudden flow of love sent a lump to her throat. She hurried back to the hotel.

Would her mother be home at this time? Her mother-in-law? It's too early for her husband to be home from work. She wants to hear her children's voices, too. It doesn't matter who picks up the phone. She has to let her family know that this trip is different from the other trips. It might be easier to get her point across to either her mother or her mother-in-law rather than her husband. Unable to wait until nightfall, Ha Young dials the number of her home. After two rings, she hears a recorded message: "We can't come to the phone right now. Please leave a message and we'll return your call." A gentle, polite voice—a voice that she's never heard before in her life.

"Hello, who's this? Who's calling? Hello?"

Panicking, Ha Young drops the phone and steps back. Her fingers and toes become numb and she loses all sensation as everything becomes a blur. She is acutely aware, however, of the ice-cold blood shooting through her veins. With the vividness of the blue blood vessels detailed in a poster of the human body, she feels the chill spread.

Long Boring Movie

When I started talking to my older brother about Father, he suddenly started yawning and fidgeting in his seat. I took that to mean that he wanted me to get to the point, so I didn't go into details about Father's recent affairs.

"I'm thinking about having him live closer to us. Incidentally, there's an apartment that just opened up in the building next to us. The owners are going abroad for a few years and don't have any other place to store their furniture. So except for the master bedroom and the living room, they want to leave the apartment furnished. The place is priced really well."

Although I didn't do anything wrong, I still sounded apologetic. I studied his face for any signs of resentment or annoyance.

"Why, has the green belt ban been lifted from Father's neighborhood? Or maybe your hubby is on the verge of bankruptcy?"

He faced me squarely, sitting upright. He was always weary and easily annoyed, but suddenly turned mischievous and antagonistic. I realized the implications of what he was saying and instantly regretted being so timid. But I really didn't want to become defensive or pick a fight with him. Elder Brother was always like this. Without harboring any ill will, he was always sarcastic, and my naïveté made me an easy target for his bullying.

"It doesn't matter to me one bit whether or not the development ban has been lifted. Besides, the heir apparent to their place is alive and well, right here in front of me. And leave Jung Seobang out of this. He's not rolling in dough, but his business is doing well thanks to his hard work. Do you really think I'm in this for the money? I don't get to visit Father often because he's so far away. But when I do, I see how wretched his life is. That's why I want him to live closer. Isn't there a Western saying . . . about how the perfect distance to keep loved ones is somewhere close enough for the soup to stay warm . . . Father will be turning eighty soon. Who's to say that we won't discover his cold body only days after his death?"

"I know, I know. I get your lofty intentions. But what does that make me? Trust me, it's not easy to be constantly compared to a saint like you. You embarrassed me enough with Mother. Do you really have to do this again?"

"What do you mean, you were embarrassed? We took her immediately to the funeral home the moment she passed away, like we promised. What, was there a sign that said she died at her daughter's house and not at her first-born son's?"

I couldn't help but raise my voice in anger, and he immediately backed off. He whined feebly.

"Well, you know how it is with me. A guilty conscience needs no accuser. And the hardest thing for me is facing Jung Seobang. He must think I'm such a loser since my wife has to work for us to make ends meet."

"Elder Brother, would I have brought Mother home if Jung Seobang was that kind of person?"

My brother never liked the fact that Mother came to live with us. She had undergone surgery for stomach cancer, but when they opened her up again, they found that the cancer had spread to all of her major organs. I was hesitant to bring home a terminally ill patient, but I felt that I had no choice. With both my brother and my sister-in-law working full-time, it was useless to expect much from them. Although he couldn't bring Mother home himself,

Elder Brother was opposed to my decision. He was afraid of how he might appear to other people and wanted to split the cost of hiring a caregiver instead.

Elder Brother was a high school ethics teacher and his wife was an elementary school teacher. To everyone else, they both had stable careers that allowed them to provide sufficiently for their two children. Elder Brother thought differently. It wasn't that he griped about his situation. It was more the irritated pessimism he showed toward life that made him appear needy. He gave up his aspirations of obtaining a Master's degree or studying abroad because of our prodigal father, and that permanently damaged his opinion of himself and his career.

If Mother's condition during the last six months of her life were something that a caregiver could handle, I'm sure Elder Brother would have gotten his way. As is often the case with patients suffering from the last stages of cancer, Mother was very lucid, if not overly so. But she had no control of her bowel movements. I don't know what happened, but after the surgery, she could not constrict her sphincter muscle; it was like a rubber band that had lost its elasticity. Being the neatness freak that she was, Mother became completely helpless. At first, we thought this was just temporary. She wanted to think that too. Hoping that her incapacitated condition was due to lack of physical strength, she tried to eat whatever food came her way. During that time, a caregiver was looking after Mother full-time, and I visited two or three times a week with home cooked food. The caregiver, who was very experienced, openly disapproved of me. She said that in all her years of working she had never seen a patient recover from this stage of cancer, and that overeating did not do Mother any good. She wanted me to stop bringing her food. Needless to say, Mother must have gone hungry whenever I wasn't around. Once I knew that, I could no longer keep Mother in that woman's care. Even if I ended up becoming a more abusive caregiver.

What I wanted to take on was not Mother, but her rectum. I couldn't just stand by and watch a stranger clean it and care for it, cursing and shuddering in disgust the whole time. Filial piety was not what motivated me; it was my honest and indignant reaction to my mother being wronged. Why did it have to be a loose rectum? Why, of all people, my mother? For her, this was cruel and unusual punishment. Knowing the kind of person my mother was, I had no choice but to guard the last vestiges of her dignity.

My mother was nearing sixty when I thought that she would finally have a decent chance to live her life. She was freed from caring for her parents-in-law, and Father had moved in after splitting up with his last mistress. They lived in a dilapidated old home, but the yard was big and well maintained—a perfect place of respite for Mother and her friends in the summertime. Idle old folks waiting around for the green belt ban to lift were the only ones left in that declining neighborhood. After Father moved in, Elder Brother and his wife shunned all contact with our parents beyond what was absolutely necessary and obligatory. I thought at least I should visit my parents as often as I could, but once a month was all I could manage. One day on such a visit, my mother's friends were gathered there to chitchat while sharing a watermelon and some chive pancakes. When I arrived, my mother had me serve them, to show me off, no doubt. So I got busy, stirring in more sesame leaves and hot pepper paste to the chive pancake mix and cutting up the fruit and the cake that I had brought into fancy slices to put on the table underneath the zelkova tree. The subject matter of their idle chat revolved around aging and dying.

—I dunno why I keep seein' my mother in my dreams when I never saw her b'fore. I gotta see my Gi-taek get into college 'fore I die.

—Oh, please, I don't wanna hear it. Gi-taek sure's a good

grandson. He must've failed three times 'cuz he don't want you to die.

—You's just braggin' 'cuz your grandson made it the first time. Now, don't be too harsh on Gi-taek's granny. That Gi-taek's no ordinary boy. Her eldest daughter-in-law kept havin' girls, one after another, but he came along jus' when we all thought she was done for sure havin' more babies. Oh, you'd feel that way too, if it were you.

—Yep. We ain't got any business gossiping about other people's precious kids. But don't you remember how that granny went 'round all over town whinin' and cryin' about how she'd die a happy woman only if she had a grandson? It got so bad that on the day the boy was born, neighborhood folks were whisperin' low about a funeral. Yeah right. A funeral. After he was born, she then had to see him with a backpack on strollin' off to school; after grade school she was always harping on 'bout him enterin' middle school; and now it's 'til the boy gets into college? Don't you know that you was born with a long life? It ain't no wonder your Gi-taek keeps failing.

—Hush, you old hag. Stop badmouthin' me.

—I'm just sayin'. We all here have had a pretty good run in life. But if we were to die now, I mean right now, who'd be so heartbroken to see us go? All's I'm saying is that we shouldn't mooch off a few more days in the name of our precious grandchildren, that's all I'm sayin'.

—Hear, hear. Until now, I've been helpful, you see, even if it's just cleaning off a scallion. Never, ever did I leave a single sock or a pair of long johns for them to launder. No siree. But I see my daughter-in-law actin' so righteous and all 'cuz she thinks she's so dutiful in takin' care o' me. Imagine when I get weak or sick? What kind of treatment y'all think I'd get?

—All's I want is to be able to go wherever I damn well please, like this here today. Maybe to the next town when I'm bored outta my mind or to my daughter's when I'm not feelin' so chipper. No mo', no less. I don't wanna live when I'm too weak to do none of that stuff.

—Ain't that wishin' for too much? I pray that I live only 'til I can't use the toilet by myself. I pray to my ancestors, I pray to Buddha, I pray when I pass by a church, and I pray 'fore I go to sleep. Well, I don't care which ghost or God listens. But I hope someone's listenin' up there.

—Never mind the toilet. I'm mo' worried 'bout goin' cuckoo or senile. That'd be my worst nightmare.

—Not me. As long as you're not peeing in your pants, who cares if you're a little crazy?

—Y'all don't know what you're talkin' 'bout. It ain't separate, you see. You go senile, that's why you pee and poop in your pants. As long as you don't lose your marbles, who's to stop you from crawlin' to the toilet?

—Oh, no. You don't got it right. The worst thing in old age is when your body does one thing, and the mind does another. Y'all know how sharp I am. Everyone knows that I never forget an anniversary, a birthday, or any other red-letter day for my family, even distant relatives. Well, apparently, my daughter-in-law don't think that's such a good thing. Anyhow, can you believe that someone so clever as me goes 'round wetting my underpants? Not just in my sleep, you see, but in broad daylight. When nature calls, I can't hold it in fo' the life o' me.

—You, too? Heck, me too.

—That's nothin'. Once in Seoul, I was searchin' high and low for a bathroom 'fore I spilled everythin' in my pants. Just came pourin' out. O' course I was embarrassed, but what was worse was tryin' to hide it from my daughter-in-law. If only I had a husband. I could've at least whined to him about how I's was overworked all my life and needed to take some o' that herbal medicine.

—Well, it seems to me now that Min-young's granny's got

it the best out of all of us. Ain't she the only one who's not a miserable widow? See? The only blessin' that counts are the ones you got in old age.

"Min-young's granny" was a reference to my mother. Until then, I was enthusiastically hopping around, serving, and waiting on them. They, who had exhausted all possibilities in life except for griping about aging, made me secretly revel in my life as someone in her forties. I hummed and flitted around like a dancer with my pleated skirt undulating in the gentle breeze. I was intoxicated with my own youthful zest for life, as if I were a mere twenty-something-year-old. As feelings of pity mixed with disdain grew toward these old folks who had nothing better to do than complain about their bodily functions, I relished my own age and place in life, where imagination and conversation still centered on sensuality and romanticism.

It happened just then.

—I only want to live 'til I can't hold in my farts.

For the very first time, my mother joined in the conversation. Everyone burst out laughing and clapping. I suppose there is no other word in our language that can deliver laughter to young and old, men and women across the board. Even its sound is a surefire form of humor. The fart of a young woman with a baby on her back. The fart of a new daughter-in-law carrying in a table for the family meal. The fart on a blind date from an ambiguous culprit. These situations never fail to tickle people's funny bones and generate much laughter.

Mother's abrupt statement, however, stopped me dead in my tracks, jolting me like the sound of a fast-moving car coming to a screeching halt. It wasn't funny; it was more like a slap in the face. My mother is not the kind of person who would say something crude like this to make people laugh. I didn't need to see her face, which I'm sure was serious, even resolute, to know that she wasn't being playful. It's true that her ability to control bodily functions was getting weaker with age, but I'm sure Mother was worried about more than just that. As a daughter who knows her better than anyone else in the world, I sensed that her fear encompassed all that threatened her sense of dignity and humanity. And what I felt for her was more than just a passing sentiment; it was heartbreaking compassion.

All of our relatives and neighbors knew how Mother was meticulous, shameless, and unwavering in her perseverance. The silent aura of dignity surrounding her was a source of pride for me when I was a little girl. But during my post-pubescent years, when I wanted to believe I was more mature than I actually was, I began to see differently. People who were insecure were despicable to me back then. On the outside, Mother appeared to be a very proud person. But I began to think that she lacked a spine, not to mention pride. Pride should be something qualitatively different from a mere metal skewer poked through a squid filet to keep it from curling up when grilled.

The way I remember things, Father completely snubbed Mother. It was different from verbal abuse or petty squabbles common between spouses. "A cow regarding a chicken" is probably the best description. Their relationship had always been insipid, from the very beginning when they first met in an arranged meeting as prospective marriage partners. This meeting took place during the latter part of the Japanese occupation, and it was a formal occasion with the parents of both parties present. Mother was too scared and shy to even raise her head to take a good look at the young man's face. Although not homely, Mother had never once been praised for her beauty, not even during those years of blossoming youth. In addition to being insecure about her looks, she only had an elementary school education, so nothing was more daunting to her than an arranged meeting. When the groom's side sent word that they heartily approved of her, her parents were more grateful than anything else. Mother was too timid to demand to see the groom once more and conceded to her parents' wishes. Father was a stylish young man who chased after young ladies in trendy, sailor-inspired school uniforms. The only thing Mother had going for her was that she was pleasantly plump in an endearing sort of way, but Father, with his high standards, could hardly have found her all that appealing. His parents, however, were fed up with his womanizing and deemed her to be exactly the dependable, down-to-earth kind of woman he needed. In those days, the filial thing for any decent person to do was to give in to the wishes of his parents unless they were asking him to marry someone with a crooked nose or pockmarks. Defying his parents was especially inconceivable to Father, who, as the eldest son, had been conditioned from a young age to obey them and to care for them in their old age.

Mother found out on her wedding night that she had become his parents' daughter-in-law rather than his wife. Father had solemnly informed her that her duty was to treat his parents with devotion and his siblings with affection. What must have gone through her mind then? She must have bit her lips, remembering that even when lying at death's door, a woman must use as a pillow the threshold of her in-laws' house. One coping mechanism for a woman whose husband regards her the way a cow regards a chicken is to make his parents happy, especially by bearing them a son to carry on the family name. Mother did that. Furthermore, she flat-out refused to compete with his ever-changing concubines and in doing so secured her position like a righteous and dignified queen beside a powerful emperor.

Father, too, was punctilious in treating her as his rightful wife. He worked for the public electric power company, and had a secure and respectable job with additional benefits. He started working there when it was still run by the Japanese government during the colonial period, and he remained after the liberation when the Korean government regained control. Near his workplace, he maintained a secondary residence that he shared with his mistress. He never failed, however, to deliver his paycheck to Mother in its entirety. Mother was immensely proud to receive that paycheck and claimed full rights to it, not caring how her husband managed to support a mistress. That period of financial stability did not last. When President Park Chung-hee's regime came into power, there was a wide sweep of programs implemented to purge social and moral iniquities. As a part of that effort, men holding down government jobs and living with mistresses were pressured to resign. Other men who'd had numerous affairs managed to dodge the bullet, but not Father. The fact that he lived with a mistress was a matter of common knowledge in the company, and as long as the program was in effect, there had to be scapegoats. Father was the first lamb to be sacrificed.

"How could this have happened?" My grandparents bemoaned Father's fate. That incident caused them to curse Park Chung-hee until they died. Mother never saw another paycheck from Father again, but she neither blamed him in frustration nor rejoiced in vengeance. Fortunately, all of his younger siblings were married off and the demands on their purse strings had let up. Areas near Seoul were beginning to be developed, and selling off bits of their land proved to be surprisingly lucrative. With the help of her father-in-law, Mother opened a rice-flour mill, which fared quite well. The only times they had to resort to selling land after that were due to the ups and downs of Father's business ventures.

It must have been during one of the auspicious times for his business. On the day of his mother's sixtieth birthday, Father walked in with a young, willowy mistress and had her formally bow to his parents. Mother didn't bat an eye and carried out her duties as a daughter-in-law that day as if nothing had happened. I was a young schoolgirl then and couldn't decide whether to ignore the other woman just as Mother had or to grab her by the hair and lash out. Which would help Mother? I didn't know, so I brooded silently in the corner. One consolation was that my father, who had always been handsome and dapper, was losing his youthful charm, with the years leaving little trace of wisdom or character on his face. Mother, on the other hand, was aging quite gracefully. I felt smug that Father had gotten what he deserved, but a part of my heart ached. They say that you are solely responsible for your face after age forty. Even if I could turn into Queen Yang, I could never live like Mother. Hers was a life of absolute restraint, and she did not allow a single wisp of anger or pain to escape.

What could I have known back then? It was only when I was about to get married myself that I got clued into the determination, or even desperation, that Mother's pride was made of.

"I'm sure you have nothing to worry about because you two met and fell in love on your own, but I want to tell you just in case. Beware if your new husband tells you on your wedding night that you must honor his parents or that women come and go but parents are for keeps. If he says that kind of nonsense, you can leave him right then and there. Really, I won't blame you if you do. Don't think that he's the only one loved and nurtured by his parents. You, too, are loved just the same."

I must be the only daughter in this country who received this kind of pre-wedding pep talk. That was the first time that Mother had ever expressed her resentment, albeit indirectly, for the humiliation she endured. She had never before allowed herself to indulge in the fallible and human act of complaining.

Mother, who wanted to live only until she could not hold in her farts, was afflicted in old age with the inability to constrict her sphincter. The cruel, unfathomable irony of this infuriated me. This ordeal, from the beginning to the end—becoming ill, undergoing surgery, and losing control of her sphincter—occurred after Father returned penniless to a home that no longer had any assets left.

Since I was the one who accompanied Mother on her hospital visits, I was the first to know about her cancer. The first thing she said to me after being diagnosed was not to tell Father. Although he returned home because he had nowhere else to go, his cow-gazing-at-a-chicken indifference toward Mother remained the same as when he had money and mistresses. Nothing had changed. I felt sorry for my mother, but a part of me found her laughable. What was it that she wanted to hide from him, exactly? The news of her terminal illness would be as shocking to him as hearing about someone's sick maid. Maybe Mother was imitating one of those loving couples on television or the movies where one person spares the other the pain of the truth. Or maybe the last shred of her pride was telling her to avoid Father's unchanging apathy toward his dying wife. That kind of a preemptive strike was the only way that she could ever defy him.

Although no one told him, it should have been obvious to Father from our hushed whispers and grim expressions that major surgery would be involved. Either in real or feigned ignorance, he continued to receive her care, up until the day that she went in for surgery. He ate the breakfast that she had made with the last ounce of her energy and then sent her off without offering a single word of comfort. On that day and the following days she spent at the hospital, we told him, "Mother said not to bother visiting her." He obliged. When she came home from the hospital, he was even more aloof, treating her like a wife returning after she'd run off to her own family after a marital fight. We didn't tell him the truth about Mother's condition without her begging us to keep it a secret because we knew that Father would not have cared. Mother wasn't the only one affected by Father's cold-heartedness. It was heartbreaking for us children, too.

Our father saw that his wife, who had tended to his needs until the day she went to the hospital, returned home unable to control her bowel movements. Instead of realizing the gravity of her illness, he cursed the hospital and accused the doctors of turning a perfectly healthy person into a cripple. They can't get away with this, he fumed. His fury without any real concern for Mother made him seem like a thug keen on extorting money from doctors. It disgusted me even more when I already felt so distant from him. He also mocked us children, blaming us for making her go under the knife when a few packets of traditional herbal medicine would have done the trick. We placated him by saying that Mother's condition was a temporary one brought on by post-surgery trauma. It may have been my mother's dying wish to spare Father from the truth. But like a slave girl protecting a sick friend in front of an inclement master, I seethed with deep resentment.

When I took Mother to my house, Father remained unmoved, scoffing at both of us. He didn't even worry about how he'd manage without her. It was the ultimate insult, and showed his complete disregard for her.

While I floundered in her excrement in the days that followed, Mother nagged me about preparing food to take to Father. Of course, I didn't have the time to do such a thing, but just the thought of making him food with my own two hands was offensive to me. I needed to go to my parents' house to pick up a few articles of clothing for Mother, so I visited him with store-bought food from the market. Father had deteriorated a lot in just a few days, looking grungy and uncared for. "When is that darn rectum going to heal?" He grumbled about her troubled body part, instead of inquiring about her welfare. I grudgingly set the table for him and went to search my mother's wardrobe. I needed an endless supply of undergarments. Tucked in carefully between the layers of clothing, I found scented soaps of all kinds. When our grandmother passed away, we found folded bills stashed inside every *beoson*, but for Mother, it was scented soaps. I also found loosely capped miniature bottles of perfume samples that came free with cosmetic purchases. Mother must have been afraid of smelling like an old woman. It was a fitting act of self-preservation for someone so terrified of the physical and emotional degradation that comes with old age.

That same woman was at her daughter's house wallowing in her own filth. Who was playing such a cruel joke on her and what right did they have? My mother, of all people. I felt angry, angry at the capricious, unruly laws of human life. And my anger found a more tangible, nearby target in my father. He deserved it. He, who had never once complimented his wife on her cooking, was looking distastefully at the store-bought food laid out in front of him and whining about how her rectum was inconveniencing him so much.

I screamed at him that Mother was in the final stages of cancer, with less than five months left to live. Then I left the house without waiting for his reaction. Now that I had said everything out in the open, I felt empty. I wasn't sure why I felt so empty, but the fact that I wanted to crouch down on the street and cry was an empty feeling in itself. I went home and told Mother simply that Father had found out. She didn't scold me for telling him, but she didn't ask about his reaction either.

That night, Father called. At first I didn't recognize the hoarse voice demanding to talk to Mother. This was the first time that he had wanted to talk to Mother directly. He was coughing up phlegm and was making strange noises to suppress hiccups. I handed the cordless phone to Mother and continued to listen in, eavesdropping deliberately.

"Yes, it's me," said Mother in a voice slightly shaken by surprise. Only suppressed hiccupping could be heard on the other side.

"It's me. I'm doing okay. I'm much better now." Uncomfortable with the silence, Mother continued to talk on her own. Then much later, Father spoke.

"I love you. Honey, I love you. I do."

His weepy voice made me realize that he hadn't been suppressing hiccups but tears. I pressed my palm down on the receiver and rolled on the floor with laughter. When I looked in on Mother a few moments later, she had hung up and was clutching her abdomen in laughter as well. In the days that followed, she kept bursting out laughing thinking about the phone call. Mother failed to live out the five more months predicted by the doctors, but her last days were happy ones thanks to the first confession of love she got at seventy-plus years of age. She was up to her neck in her own filth but had not lost her laughter. Since his confession, Father had expressed his love not just verbally, but had also visited her every day. He had even wanted to clean up after her, but that was one thing she would not permit. Maybe she didn't want to disillusion him because she wanted to be loved until the day she died. Father did remain devoted to the end. He took the greatest care in selecting her resting place, and he embarrassed us at the funeral by weeping large tears and making those suppressed hiccup sounds. Compared to Father, we children showed less sorrow, and seemed more relieved than grieved. At least I was exhausted from taking care of her. Elder Brother was the chief mourner, but he had the expression of someone who had just finished watching an endlessly long, boring movie. He must have been bored to tears as he waited to be freed from the self-blame of not having been a very good son.

"Well, in any case, thanks. I, too, was thinking that we can't leave Father there forever."

"It's settled then. He's still in good health and it'll be easier to visit him or have him visit us. I'm not saying that I want to be responsible for him one hundred percent. I just want him nearby."

"You realize that it still makes me look bad."

"Why do you think it makes you look bad?"

"How would you know what it's like to be the eldest son?"

"Fine. I'm just a sparrow and you're a phoenix."

"Time is a scary thing. What's happened to all his dreams and abilities that he now has to depend on his children to take care of him? I bet he feels sorry for himself."

"Do you think that Father can't remarry because he's broke?"

"Well, he's not turning away women because of his devotion to Mom. Our father? Don't make me laugh."

"You're so clueless. Do you know that he's gotten quite a few propositions from matchmakers? I already looked into a couple of them."

"He probably goes around pretending to be loaded when he's living off his children like a parasite. I really thought that he'd make something of himself before he got too old."

"Why are you being so harsh? Well, at least he still has his house."

"Can you even call that an asset?"

"You asked me a minute ago if the ban on the green belt has been lifted. Every year there are rumors that it might have in that neighborhood. There's huge potential, and that's what counts. Lots of women, many of them much younger, are interested in him, I'll have you know."

"I can't have that. When Mother was alive, I was in no position to meddle in his love life. But it's different now. With her gone, he could even decide to include his new woman in the family register. Would you be okay with that?"

"Elder Brother, there's no need to get all worked up. Father has already made his position clear. He wouldn't even let me bring up the subject of a second marriage. Do you know why? He said he wanted to leave his firstborn son at least the house. When I said that I wanted him to live near me, he told me in no uncertain terms that since I was already doing well for myself I was not to covet the house. To tell you the truth, I was a bit insulted when he said that. Of course I don't have an ulterior motive. But he doubted me first, instead of taking my good intentions at face value."

"Honestly, who else has a daughter like you? I'm a little insulted, too, for your sake."

I knew I couldn't convince Elder Brother that I wasn't as filial a daughter or as nice a person as he thought, so I just let him think what he wanted. It was too complicated to explain even to myself.

I figured that Elder Brother had more or less given me the go ahead, so I contacted Father to settle a few loose ends before his move. He said that we could meet anytime because he came into Seoul every day. The place he frequented in Seoul was an underground plaza with an entrance to the Lotte World theme park. The plaza was also connected to a subway station, so he could easily commute to and from home with only one transfer. He told me to stop by anytime because he was there almost every day. I laughed because he sounded like he owned the whole plaza. My parents' house always seemed so far away because I spent so much time stuck in traffic driving there and back. With the urbanization of my parents' neighborhood and the development of a new subway route, it was now only a hop and a skip away from Seoul. I inevitably thought of their ten-thousand-square-foot property. It was conceivable that Father, who was now closer to eighty than seventy, could still end up a rich man during his lifetime.

With no one maintaining the house after Mother had passed away, it was starting to show signs of neglect. Mother had always tended the garden diligently, not because she liked trees or flowers but because she didn't want the house to appear unkempt. She was like that. She had spent her whole life keeping up appearances.

The Lotte World underground plaza was a glitzy, wide-open

space. With only a few days left until Christmas, the place was bustling with end-of-the-year crowds. In front of a supermarket entrance a temporary booth selling trendy lingerie was set up to lure young women inside. Right next to it, in front of the fountain, an unknown singing group—young kids still wet behind the ears— was performing to raise money for needy families. There were many built-in seating areas in the plaza but not nearly enough to accommodate the masses there that day. Some people were even sitting on the entrance steps to the supermarket, blocking foot traffic. Among those seated, some were obviously waiting for others in their party to arrive while others had met theirs and were busy chatting. Still others were just sitting around, staring into space. Weaving in and out of all these people sitting was a rapid current of people in a hurry, taking short, irritable steps. Father was not difficult to spot amidst this sea of people. That's because the elderly had their own hangout in the middle of the plaza. They were sitting in a large circle, most of them men, with only a few women present.

Father was easy to spot because he was singing in front of the group. It was my first time hearing his singing voice—sappy and unctuous, yet self-assured like that of a man in his prime. Although he didn't have a microphone, his voice seemed to overpower, or at least interfere with, the young vocal group singing, "One More Thing I Still Need to Do in This Life." Perhaps that was an exaggerated perception due to my embarrassment that we were related. Father was singing the words from a decades-old pop song, "How I've Traveled Thousands of Miles to Jinju," with his eyelids gliding down in a sentimental display. That wasn't all. He'd changed the lyrics from "wrapping my arms around a tree trunk" to "wrapping my arms around another man's woman." He did this while actually putting his arm around the waist of an elderly woman sitting next to him. He was smoother than a serpent slithering over a fence.

It probably wasn't a coincidence that a woman, decidedly a minority in that group, was sitting next to him. She didn't seem at all upset to have Father's arm around her, for she quickly snuffed out the cigarette between her lips and began harmonizing with him. If he were a stranger, I could have laughed in amusement. But as his daughter, I probably should have blushed in embarrassment instead. I did neither, sinking deep into my own thoughts. I had the sudden realization that this wasn't the first time I'd seen him like this. The image of my father that I dug up from the depths of my memory seemed vaguely familiar and connected.

It was also by chance that I recalled a particular memory of my father. On a few occasions when I was a schoolgirl, I had to run errands at the home my father shared with his mistress. He never flirted or joked with her in front of me, nonetheless I was shocked by how different he seemed. At home, he was always stiff and uneasy, but there he seemed carefree and relaxed. The father I saw in the middle of the Lotte World plaza was definitely comfortable in his own skin, just as when he was living with his mistress. Was my father's promiscuity an escape from the binding duties of being an eldest son and husband? In that relaxed state, Father had seemed vulgar to me when I was young, but now, I wasn't so sure. Perhaps even debauchery, mastered over a lifetime, can become a tasteful art form. My presumption that Mother had aged gracefully while Father hadn't may have been off the mark in the end.

No one can see a day into the future and a person's life can't be judged until the coffin has been nailed shut. Who knows how Father will live out his days? I'm not sure if I'll ever regret this decision, which may very well lead to the responsibility of caring for him on his deathbed. Mother, who lived her life with sealed lips that held in her sighs, suffered a humiliating end with her loose sphincter. Was I hoping that Father, who had made a mess of his life and neglected his family, could also reverse his fate and die gracefully? No, it wasn't that. Then was I trying to repay him for making Mother happy in her last days? No, it wasn't that either. I wouldn't say that I sided with my mother to that extent. What may be closer to the truth is that I wanted to experience the perplexing, logic-defying nature of being a caregiver again.

When Mother passed away, Elder Brother took on the responsibilities of chief mourner with the lethargy of someone watching a long, boring movie. No one wants to watch a long, boring movie a second time. But when the movie is profound and abstruse, one might watch it again hoping to understand it better.

I approached Father with a smile on my face, and only then did he loosen his arm from the woman's waist. She snapped up another cigarette and wedged it between her lips. Father winked at me and clicked a lighter for her before getting to his feet.

Lonesome You

Every single graduation ceremony she'd attended had been cold. Bitter cold was the one thing that all her and her children's graduations had in common. But the coldest graduation ever was the one she experienced from the comfort and warmth of the school's official residence. Temperatures in the countryside always felt at least five or six degrees colder than in the city. Without any consideration for rural children, whose clothing was often shabbier than city children's, the elementary school principal went on and on with his speech for more than thirty minutes. It was the same message every year. Even his passionless, bellowing voice was a constant. What were the children thinking about as they wriggled their frozen toes? Her anger was so great that her thoughts turned murderous. Covering her ears or shaking her head delivered no relief from the torturous oration. Just when the children's frozen toes had turned numb and her fury had melted into quiet resignation, the speech ended. It was simply despicable that there was only a thin wall between where she lived and where her husband worked. The school principal was her husband.

This mid-year graduation was her first. She vaguely recalled that these events were called cosmos graduations, but today's oppressive late-summer humidity had choked out the last whiff of breeze that could have encouraged those willowy flowers to bloom. Pavarotti, which was a spacious café, was well air-conditioned inside. Like a blanched tomato, her senses were confused by the sudden chill thinly coating her overheated body. All of the wait staff were wearing body-hugging black uniforms. The contours of their bodies suggested a pure, lanky innocence that alluded more to adolescence than adulthood. Was this what people referred to as unisex these days? There was no way to recognize the gender of these young people. All of them had smooth, white faces without makeup and straight hair that was cut short or tied neatly into ponytails. Unlike their tight pants, baggy tops hung loosely over their flat-chested torsos. She felt an urge to furtively slide her hand over their androgynous thighs or hips, which she guessed would feel hard and frigid like a popsicle. If she were to touch a boy, it would be an act of sexual harassment. She shuddered at the burgeoning animalism inside her, pushing its way out through the encrusted chill.

How long had it been since she'd had such a queer feeling? This may be the first time in her life. She knew, and had been told, that people of a certain age should not frequent cafés in college towns. But this place was not at all shady or improper, and the music was low enough so that you could actually hear the person talking next to you. The cello music they were playing gently swaddled the interior space in subtle waves of pastel tones. The café was a clean, comfortable place with a wholesome atmosphere. The only thing that stood out, if there was anything at all, was the modern black uniform. Even before her husband arrived, she fretted that he would stick out like a sore thumb. To her, the sophistication of this place was that impeccable.

It was Chae Jung, their daughter, who chose Pavarotti as a meeting place for the two of them. Even at the time of Chae Jung's graduation, she and her husband were separated. She was supposed to meet her husband, who was coming into the city that day, in front of a bronze statue. The university was home to several statues. Instead of checking to see if he had found the right one, he plopped down by the first one he saw, making it impossible for his family to meet up with him. Moreover, that was the day that they were to meet the parents of Chae Jung's long-time boyfriend for the first time. Even in retrospect, the anxiety and embarrassment he had caused her made her blood boil. Because she had tried to overcompensate for her sense of inferiority to their future in-laws by stressing their family values, the events of that day were even more humiliating. But when she finally did find him after the ceremony was over and more than half of the people had already left, she wished that she hadn't. Instead of a proper winter coat suitable for that cold day, he was wearing a quilted jacket worn out from bad laundering on top of a faded pair of cotton pants that were too short and stopped above the ankles. Even if he weren't meeting his future in-laws, he was a sorry sight to behold. Chae Jung must have felt the same because she said in a tearful whisper, "I can't believe him! He must hate us both to come dressed like such a bum." Chae Jung had a bad habit of attributing everything she disliked to bums and hobos, but she didn't mind it just then. If the in-laws weren't there, surely harsher words would have come out of her own mouth.

Her daughter's graduation remained forever burned into her brain because of the way her husband was dressed. For Chae Jung, the most memorable fact must have been that her father got lost. That was the first thing she worried about for her little brother's graduation. She visited his school first and handpicked the café as a place where her parents could easily find each other without drawing too much attention to themselves. As it turned out, all that trouble may have been for nothing because mid-year graduations seem to be less crowded.

Did Chae Jung not want her parents to show up separately? This thought suddenly crossed her mind. Yes, it was possible that Chae Jung, who was now a mature, married woman with children, would have thought through such matters of propriety. But she was no longer interested in impressing her future in-laws.

Marrying off a son felt different somehow. It was so liberating to feel that she had no reason to feel insecure or indebted. For heaven's sake, the kids were married already. Let the parents think whatever they wanted of her family. This kind of audacity felt just like having a firm grip on the hilt of a sword. Although she approved of her son's girlfriend waiting faithfully for him while he served in the military, she wouldn't say that she prayed for them to be together. She wanted it known implicitly that her preference for a younger bride overrode the girl's loyalty; such was the twisted mind of a mother-in-law. Her son was currently living with his wife's family, but even that was nothing to be ashamed of. They have been married for less than a month now, and they are scheduled to leave soon to study abroad. If anything, the girl should be grateful for not having to live with overbearing in-laws, as was the tradition.

A boy—or maybe a girl—in a black T-shirt brought her a glass of ice water and then briefly hesitated. She reckoned that he or she was waiting for her to order. She was curious to hear the pitch of his or her voice, but deciding not to rush the customer, the waiter or waitress left with a generous smile unusual for someone so young. She had about an hour before the ceremony. Chae Jung had urged her not to be late because she was sure that her father would be on time. She thought that Chae Jung's opinion of her father's punctuality had less to do with love and respect than the belief that her father was a simpleton who did not know how to be fashionably late for anything.

Instead of waiting intently, she was staring blankly out the window when he arrived. He had on a suit and a rusty brown tie that was on too tight. She was about to stand up and wave, calling out, "Over here," when his booming voice rang out through the entire café.

"Is this Café Pastarotti?"

All eyes landed on him. Most of the patrons were young teens probably still in high school. Whispering, "Who's Pastarotti?" they giggled in their seats. Instead of shouting or waving her arm, she ran over to him and dragged him to their table. He seemed relieved to have found his wife.

"So I did find the right place. Did you wait long?

Once they were sitting across from each other, they had nothing more to say. There was plenty of time left until the graduation ceremony. He took out a raggedy handkerchief and wiped the beads of sweat oozing from the smooth, bronzed top of his head. His nickname during his tenure as a principal was "Brass Potty". He always perspired so much. But he hadn't always been bald. In his youth, the coarse bristles of his black hair made him look a bit untamed. When he violently shook his head, shouting, "Ahh, I'm so hot," a shower of sweat drops splashed in all directions. Did she love him then? She knitted her brows as she unearthed an old memory. Things that disappear over time—like love or hemp-like strands of hair, should leave at least a shadow of their former splendor, shouldn't they? That, however, seemed highly unlikely.

We mustn't fight, she thought. It would be cruel when neither of us has any means of self-defense. While she was thinking this out of the blue, he finished wiping up his sweat and began to order.

"Over here, get us two cups of hot coffee. I had it in my mind to order more expensive ice coffees, but how can I when it's so darn cold in here, huh?"

She jumped out of her skin when his crude voice blasted throughout the room. She thought she heard more giggles from the teens who had mocked him before.

"C'mon, come and take my order. Don't have all day here."

"They'll come. Just be patient, will you?"

"Why sit in here all day? Let's just pay for taking up seats here and leave."

"We have lots of time. Isn't it nice here? It's cool inside and we get to watch all these young people."

"In a country that can't produce a single drop of oil, I can't believe so many of our resources are wasted on these kids who have nothing better to do than hang out all day."

Whenever he opened his mouth, he couldn't help but sound like an ethics textbook from the Koryo Dynasty. This is no good, she thought. If someone could read her mind and asked exactly what was no good, she wouldn't be able to explain. That's how muddled and irrational she was at that moment. Coffee arrived. "I've come to like my coffee black now. It's not bad," he said, guzzling it down as if he were drinking spicy beef soup.

"So, when are they leaving? The kids," he continued.

"In a few days, I'm sure. They have to be there before the semester starts in America."

"Why didn't you keep them until they go? The new daughter-in-law, I mean. The son's family should show her how things are done."

"Son my ass," she snapped irritably, unable to suppress her sudden frustration.

"What'd I say? Did I say something wrong?"

She was about to retort, "When do you ever say anything wrong?" but she let out a wry chuckle instead. Until the late 1970s, her husband was an ordinary grade school teacher. Even after he became the vice-principal and later the principal, he used to reminisce about those years teaching as the best days of his life. But how good could it have been as a teacher in a rural elementary school? Maybe he considered his heyday to be the time when at least there was room for upward mobility, when he could strive to become the vice-principal or the principal. This was during the Yushin Reformation when the spirit of the *Saemaeul* or New Community Movement throttled the last fresh breath out of children. It was suffocating for her to think about those times. His class was wallpapered with copies of the Charter of National

Education and he was famous for making every student, including the ones with learning disabilities, glibly recite it by heart. Their rote memorization wasn't merely perfunctory. When the town held a regional competition to test students' in-depth knowledge of the charter, his class snagged the first prize. He later became the vice-principal and then the principal during the Chun Doo-hwan and Roh Tae-woo regimes. As political power changed hands, so did the gigantic photograph of the President hanging from the highest place in his office. He didn't hang the picture because he ran a public elementary school; he would have done the same whether he was a principal or an important member of the President's cabinet. What she had a problem with was his blind subordination. Like a servant handed off to another master, he gave no thought to the character or the values of the person he served. The fact that that person was his master was the only thing that mattered to him. When a new photograph was hung, his manner of speech and behavior aped the person in the picture. His tirades during the morning assembly were undoubtedly replete with quotes from the incumbent chief of state. If he were an ambitious opportunist keen on getting ahead in life, she would have tolerated such behavior. If he were a fawning peon of a public employee who complained of his wretched servile life in the privacy of their home, she would have comforted him. How could she have not? She would have thought it noble of him to carry out his patriarchal obligation to support his family no matter how low he had to stoop in life.

But he was someone who needed no such comforting. Is there any human being more maddening than someone who doesn't need to be comforted? His willingness to serve the system was neither forced nor self-willed. Rather, it stemmed from his innate nature, from the essence of his vacuous personality. She really didn't want to think about any of this. But today was the last day of their separation that was justifiable in the eyes of society.

When her daughter got admitted to a college in Seoul, she left her husband behind and took the kids to the city. At her high school, Chae Jung was the first student ever to get into a reputable school in Seoul, and she was honored with a huge congratulatory banner bearing her name above the front gates. It goes without saying that they, as parents, were incredibly proud. The glory was hard earned after years of relentless, hands-on parenting. True, it had been exhausting for her, but the experience had also boosted her confidence in raising high-achieving children. She could have burst with joy when her daughter earned the right to finally march out of that small town and swim in bigger waters. Chae Hoon, who had just entered high school at that time, was a few years younger than his sister. Fortunately, her determination to send him to an even better school and her husband's refusal to let their young daughter live alone coincided. Thus began their separation, which was perfectly natural and justifiable to others and to themselves. The first place they rented in the city was a basement unit where they could hear every sound made by the upstairs tenants. Listening to the urinating or loud chewing noises coming from upstairs was a happy reality check for her that she had, indeed, escaped the principal's residence. Distant now were the memories of the same old tedious lectures given at the morning assembly and the squirming children dying for the agonizing tirade to end. Such were her memories of those days, as insufferable and dreadful as torture.

Taking care of the kids was only an excuse; she realized after leaving that what she really wanted, what she had been wanting for a long time, was to not be the principal's wife. After the separation, almost all of her husband's monthly salary was deposited into her bank account. How he could manage with the remainder was a mystery to her. But her life in Seoul entailed many expenses that could hardly be covered by the amount he sent, so she took the money without any questions or reservations. Not long afterward, she started working to afford private tutoring sessions for Chae Hoon. She was helping out a friend who owned a discount cosmetics store in a mall adjacent to an apartment complex, and she ended up buying the business from her friend. In addition to cosmetics from domestic brands, she increased the inventory to include knickknacks imported from overseas. She proved to be an able businesswoman, and luck was on her side. Perhaps it was the kids who brought her luck. When their extracurricular activities required the most money, her income peaked accordingly. As the kids grew older and those expenses dwindled to almost nothing, a major department store opened nearby and wiped out small businesses. Before she started working, the three of them needed every penny her husband sent so they couldn't refuse any of it out of concern for his situation; when she was bringing home a paycheck, the amount he sent seemed so trivial that she didn't bother to worry about how he was faring. Her husband, who was always loyal to the powers that be, was for some reason forced into a very early retirement.

The news of his retirement arrived along with his announcement that he would move to an even more remote area. They happened to own an old house and some surrounding land in an area that was outrageously close to the Demilitarized Zone. He decided to live there, and thus she didn't have to worry about his joining her in the city. Thinking about her newly retired husband made her chuckle, knowing how much he would miss lecturing into a loud microphone every morning. In the ensuing months, his pension money continued to be deposited into her account. Apparently, the kids visited him occasionally. His rural lifestyle did not impress them much, for they had told him to "hang in there for just a bit longer." They often told her the same thing, apologetic that their parents were living apart for their sake. Or, perhaps there was another motive. It may have been in their interest to prevent their parents from separating permanently so that they wouldn't have to worry about them or be responsible for them. Keeping their parents together was their best bet to gain independence from them.

Not once did she visit her husband in the countryside. She wanted to show the kids how indifferent she was toward him. If he did such a good job of looking after himself there without any help from her, then maybe he, too, wanted to make this separation work. It was like a battle of wills between them. She didn't ask for his participation in this battle, but she might as well have. It was what she wanted from him anyway, so why should she care how he lived? Like an old hut rotting away and collapsing into a pile of dust, their relationship suffered a silent demise—silent enough to go unnoticed by the children living under the same roof.

"Is that the only suit you have? You should have worn something else today," she said, looking at the deep creases in the fold of his pants, which were made of linen. His shirt collar also had a faded but visible spot, perhaps a *kimchi* stain.

"What's wrong with this suit? You said so yourself that it was first rate."

"Even if it's first rate, you got it as a wedding gift from our daughter-in-law, didn't you? It was fine to wear at the wedding, but you put it on every time we see the in-laws. What would they think?"

"Not all the time. I haven't worn it since the wedding. In this summer heat, you couldn't pay me to put on a suit and tie."

"I mean all the time for the in-laws. We haven't seen them since the wedding. You should have put a little more care into your outfit."

"More care than this? Chae Jung, she's been callin' and buggin' me the past few days to dress in a suit. And this is the only summer suit I've got, so what could I have done?"

"All right, all right. Let's just drop it."

It was no use belaboring the point.

"What's more important than the suit is appearin' like a normal couple to the in-laws, in my opinion," he said quietly before getting up from his seat to pay the bill. She saw something close to compassion flit across his eyes and was taken aback. He pitied her when it should have been the other way around. Hah, the irony. She looked at her watch. It was time to get to the graduation ceremony.

The ceremony was being held inside an auditorium, not outdoors, probably because mid-semester graduations had fewer attendees. There were more than ten in the in-laws' group standing by the door—the parents, their son, their other daughter, her husband, and a few others. Chae Jung was not there because she had gone inside to save seats. Thanks to her, the two sets of parents got the best seats in the house side by side, and the other family members were able to sit together as a group next to them. The two women sat next to each other with their husbands on either side, and throughout the ceremony Chae Hoon's mother-in-law kept whispering in her ear. Having lived with her new son-in-law for almost a month, she sure had a lot to say, most of it about how the two kids got along so well. Curiously, there was much bragging cleverly disguised as humility and amusement carefully masked as hardship.

"Now I know what they mean when they say that daughters are useless once you marry them off. We did assume as much with our older daughter, but the youngest, well, my husband dotes on her so much. And I guess I did my share of spoiling her rotten, not ever letting her wash the dishes. Now that she's married, she's the first one in the kitchen fussing over her husband's meals. You know what else? Every morning her father drinks freshly squeezed vegetable juice, and she demanded to know why her husband doesn't get any. Nowadays, she comes down before I'm up, squeezes the juice, and takes it upstairs. If she's making juice anyway, she should make enough for her father too, but she makes just one glass. I think it's so rude of her, but do you know what my husband says? 'Look how our little girl's all grown up and looking after her new husband.' He's so pleased with his youngest son-in-law and is amused by everything he says. Granted, our Soo Jung married well, but Jung Seobang sure did quite well for himself, wouldn't you say?"

"Certainly."

Coerced into agreement and resenting it, she simmered with anger at this woman who was intentionally messing with her. So, it seemed that the in-laws were delighted with the newlyweds, carrying on as one would over a pretty flower or a cute baby and filling their home with much laughter and joy. And in contrast, she thought not of her own dreary living conditions but her husband's home in the country that she had yet to see. The vision of an isolated house inhabited by an aging man—and all the desolation and squalor that it entailed—played in her mind like a tacky old movie.

"Still, they say a son-in-law must always be treated well like a guest. It can't be easy for you. They could have come and lived with us . . ." Having said this out of courtesy, she trailed off. It made her angry that she had no choice but to trail off. Whether or not he understood the subtle psychological warfare going on between the two women, her husband stuck his neck out, his eyes fixed on the graduation ceremony.

"No, no. Jung Seobang is so easy-going and pleasant to have around. The kids have been best friends since their freshman year, so he's been coming around to our house for several years now, hasn't he? Before I knew he was going to be my son-in-law, I treated him like he was one of my own. He ate at our table like family, and we've gotten very close over the years. Now that he's one of us, well, that just makes him even more endearing to me. But I'm nothing compared to my husband. A few days ago was the *jesa* ceremony for my deceased father-in-law, you know.

Our oldest lives in the States, and he hasn't attended in a long time. Now our other son is obviously the next in line, but my husband made Jung Seobang offer the rice wine first, insisting that the new addition to the family be properly introduced to the ancestors. He's like that—doesn't mind bending the *jesa* rules a bit. Well, our ceremonies tend to be informal anyhow. We use portraits instead of calligraphy posters, and as for the food, we don't usually prepare what's proper but what the ancestors used to like eating when they were alive. I tell you, what my husband lacks in formality, he makes up for in interesting ways. He talks to the ancestors as if they were still living, chatting about our daily lives or pleading with them to go easy on us when we're faced with problems. This time, he was so funny talking about his new son-in-law that there was more laughter than somber respect at our *jesa*."

Reliving her happy memory, her in-law giggled. What did she mean, "one of us"? No matter how much this world has changed, Soo Jung, by anyone's standard, has become one of *us* instead of our Chae Hoon becoming one of *them*, she thought. When it came to bending formal traditions, the in-laws were nothing compared to them. She couldn't remember the last time she attended a *jesa* on her husband's side of the family. He wasn't the eldest and his older brother's house was deep in the mountains in a distant rural area. Except for when she was a newlywed, she never went with her husband. At times when he thought he'd be too tired to teach the next day, he only sent money and didn't go either. After he became the principal and was no longer burdened with a teaching schedule, he continued to be lax about attending *jesas*. He must have taken Chae Hoon with him only a handful of times. His justification was that *jesas* were meaningful only for those ancestors one had seen and remembered.

Given their attitudes, Chae Hoon probably grew up giving little importance to *jesas*. Still. To think that he had bowed to his wife's family's ancestors before having her bow to his own. She felt bitter. Stupid, stupid Chae Hoon. What an idiot. The more she thought about the matter, the more outraged she became. Perhaps she was taking the resentment she felt toward her smooth-talking in-law and blowing it out of proportion, turning it into betrayal from her son. She wanted to kick her seat out from under her and storm out of the ceremony. Instead, she grabbed her husband's hand. She needed someone to walk her out, hand in hand. Hardly noticing that she was holding his hand, he was still entranced by what was happening onstage. He was like a nervous student waiting for his name to be called to receive an award. She gently withdrew her hand.

She knew what the stage meant to him. He liked stages. On a stage, his voice took on an authoritative tone, and virtuous words that no one could refute flowed out of his mouth. However small the gathering, the stage symbolizes power and authority. And as a person of power standing on the platform, he could not tolerate even one inattentive person. What he demanded from the audience was not mere attention: it was respect. He had been so committed to his responsibilities as an authority figure onstage. Who could stop him now from fulfilling his duties as an attentive audience member offstage?

The reason he was less authoritative with his family wasn't because he was a loving family man. There was no need for him to assert his authority because he assumed that it came naturally with being the man of the house, as long as he fulfilled his role as the breadwinner. For him, that meant living on as little as possible and handing over most of his paycheck to his family. His effort in this matter bordered on obsession. This was true during their years of separation, which he accepted without any question, as well as after his retirement. What was his life like these days, she wondered. She looked at the hand she had grabbed a moment earlier—coarse and dirty under the nails. Like stepping on a foreign object and stumbling, she was startled by a new emotion stirring inside her that she hadn't felt when she had first grabbed his hand.

Doctorates and Master's were given out and it was time for Bachelor's degrees. She wanted to see her son receive a degree with her own eyes. Chae Jung was in charge of taking pictures, and several of their family members were also equipped with cameras. Throngs of picture-takers, who obviously outnumbered the graduates, blocked her view of the stage. Her in-law began talking again. Amidst the noisy movement in the hall, the whispered breath on her earlobe gave the talk an air of intimacy.

"Don't try so hard to see. We should be fine as long as the pictures turn out well. What remains of important events, except the pictures? By the way, didn't the wedding pictures come out well? We sent you all the copies from the photographer as well as the ones our family took."

"Yes, we received them, thank you. We also took pictures but you were so kind to send so many more. You shouldn't have."

"Oh, when our kids were growing up, we always took tons of pictures at every milestone. It's a hobby, and we take such pleasure in documenting their life histories. We never missed an award ceremony, so of course we went all out for a once-in-a-lifetime event like this wedding. Pictures always tell the whole story, and I'm always reminded that things should be done properly even if it's just for show. When I was organizing the wedding pictures, I just felt horrible about not sending them on a honeymoon."

"Not sending them? They were the ones who insisted they didn't want to go. Wasn't that the case?"

No longer willing to take any more abuse lying down, she faced her in-law squarely. The wedding had taken place at the peak of the vacation season. And with only a month left until their departure for America, the kids had so much to do in preparation: applying for visas, sending ahead some of their bags, and renewing their driver's licenses to name a few. They didn't want all these loose ends hanging over their heads during their honeymoon, so they decided to postpone it and stop by Hawaii on their way to the mainland. The decision was made by the couple and the parents were only notified. Why was this an issue now?

"Of course, of course. But as parents, oh, we just felt . . . so bad. This is the last wedding for both families, so we wanted to give them everything possible. That brings me to my point. We made a reservation for them for a three-night stay on Jeju Island after the graduation ceremony. They don't know this yet. It's a surprise. They're done with all the graduation requirements and finally have some free time, so I'm sure they'll be happy. Too bad that they have to hop on another plane so soon after the trip, but what's the point of wasting a few days here in Seoul with nothing to do anyway? No doubt, they'll spend that time being dragged around by their friends for one last drink. Don't you think?"

"I suppose so," she answered bitterly, her patience dangerously close to being pushed over the edge. For whatever reason, her in-law then pulled out a white envelope from her handbag and gave her a glimpse of its contents: round-trip plane tickets and a voucher for the Hyatt Hotel. Her in-law gently placed the envelope on her lap and whispered, "You give this to them later."

"Why?" she asked with shock, redness spreading to her ears.

"Oh, does it really matter who gives it to them? It doesn't come with our names printed on it. The kids will be happy to receive it from you. We'll just send them off with some spending money. It'll be more natural this way."

What were the true intentions of this woman, who was so friendly on the outside but full of hidden agendas? She floundered in shame, feeling that she had fallen into her in-law's trap. Her bewildered hands somehow managed to firmly push the envelope from her lap. But before she could do anything else, her in-law slipped the envelope into her purse and tucked it into a side pocket with a quick and graceful movement. Her face burned with either anger or shame. She could not tell which. The ceremony suddenly ended at this inopportune moment and the audience became a confused mob heading for the exit. Trying not to lose her balance as she was swept along by the crowd, she somehow made it outside. The sweltering afternoon heat made the air thick like congealing taffy. The word 'awful' kept escaping from her lips. The monolithic mob slowly dissolved into an amorphous mass of scattering people. She wasn't sure if she could find her husband, Chae Jung, or the in-laws. Not a single patch of shade offered her solace where she was cast off by the milling crowd, so she stood there like a torture victim resigned to her fate.

Her husband was the first to find her. Pointing to the group standing under a large zelkova tree, he called out, asking why she was standing there by herself. Upon seeing him, she remembered the envelope, a white triangle sticking out of her black handbag like a starched pocket square on a waiter's uniform. She quickly pushed it deep into her bag and then followed her husband to the tree. Everyone was gathered there. Except for Chae Jung and her husband, no one paid her any attention, as they were too busy taking turns posing for pictures with the graduating couple. Buried in flowers and presents, Chae Hoon was smiling from ear to ear like a fool. At the ceremony, she had seen her in-laws holding a huge present wrapped in flashy wrapping paper, and she had scorned their showiness because they could have easily given it to the children at home. But apparently everyone on their side came prepared with gifts. Did she need to feel ashamed for being empty-handed? No matter how hard she tried to stand tall and proud, the course of events that afternoon shoved shame down her throat. Could it be ridicule or pity for what was contained inside the white envelope?

Chae Hoon was still busy taking group pictures and exchanging greetings. Upstaged by their group of avid picture-takers, Chae

Jung, the self-appointed cameraperson on the groom's side, was standing off to the side quietly observing the scene.

It was like this at Chae Jung's graduation also. The parents of both families met for the first time, but the in-laws completely dominated the whole affair. They surrounded Chae Jung, taking pictures and fussing over her, sometimes acting with dignity and sometimes with playfulness. She and her husband were ignored like a bowl of cold rice. She didn't get too upset, though. She thought that was the standard treatment for the girl's family, and with a younger son to marry off in the future, she even hoped to learn a thing or two about being in the dominant role. That is to say, things weren't so unjust when you had a chance to reverse the roles. She also didn't mind the envious stares directed at Chae Jung for meeting a boyfriend while in school and being doted on by her prospective in-laws at the graduation ceremony. *But look at us now. Who can I blame when my own son is a fawning fool?* Like a powerful matriarch whose anger had been roused, she glared at her son.

Chae Hoon must have felt his mother's stare. She quickly caught his roaming eyes and drew him toward her like a magnet. He was her dear son, but at the moment, he looked like a fool with a sheepish grin on his face. To make amends for having neglected her, he took off his graduation cap and placed it on her head. Immediately recognizing her chance to shine, Chae Jung shoved a camera in front of them. But she resisted his gesture, breaking free from the cap. *What do you take your mother for?* Before she could get the words out, her husband's voice rang out.

"What's da matter? If you're happy, just say so. I dunno why you're acting so jealous. On a day like this. Hoon, I guess your mom here doesn't want to. But I sure do. Lemme try it on. Whatdaya call this cap, a mortarboard?"

Spurned by his mother and standing there feeling embarrassed, Chae Hoon jumped at his father's rescue attempt, putting the cap

on his father's head and affectionately wrapping his arm around
his father's. In addition to Chae Jung, everyone with a camera
on the in-law's side zeroed in on the proud father and his filial
son. Her husband instantly became the center of attention. Like
a provincial farmer from the 1970s who had sold off his cattle
and land to send his son to college, he posed naïvely for picture
after picture. *Look how happy the father is. Jung Seobang better get
his advanced degree from America soon and bring his father even
greater honor.* Well wishes blossomed and the atmosphere became
celebratory again. Time ticked on, arrogantly unhurried.

*It's so beautiful by the lake and at the outdoor theater near the
democratic students' memorial tower. What are we doing here
taking all these pictures with the same backdrop?* Someone called
out and put a stop to all the picture-taking activities. No one
objected, and the group began migrating en masse toward the
more popular gathering spots. The two families naturally broke
into smaller cliques consisting of their own kin, and Chae Hoon
took turns walking alongside his mother and his mother-in-law,
strategically adjusting his pace as he did so. Acting as a bridge
between the two families, he kept them from separating as the
space around them became more and more packed with people.
Whenever he returned to her to take her arm after intimately
whispering to his mother-in-law, she resisted him with a scowl.
She had no idea where he had learned to juggle two allegiances
at once. Students were performing with traditional instruments
at the open-air theater, and throngs of people were gathered by
the tower. It would make an ideal spot to slip away unnoticed.
The mother-in-law must have thought that the envelope had
switched hands by now. There had been more than enough time
and opportunity.

She had not forgotten the envelope tucked inside the pocket
of her purse. How could she, when it was like a splinter stuck to
her undershirt, scratching away at her flesh? When Chae Hoon

disappeared among the crowd of in-laws, she tugged hard at her husband's sleeve. An impulsive idea coincided with an opportunity. How could she think of such a thing? Her own audacity shocked her, making her heart pound and knees knock. Once she was sure she had successfully escaped with the money like a thief in the night, she swelled up with pleasure like a balloon about to burst. Perhaps it wasn't pleasure, but spite, a malicious spirit that delighted in mischief. She felt it sprawling out, growing beyond her control. How thrilling it was to have the power to do harm! She bit down on her molars to suppress a smile.

Her husband kept asking where they were going as he was being dragged away, but she didn't answer him. Assuming that she was searching for a restroom, he followed her without a fight. When she saw the front gates, she calmed her frayed nerves and turned to him.

"I wanted us to make a quick and quiet exit. The in-laws are sending Chae Hoon and his wife to Jeju Island today as a graduation gift and for their honeymoon. If we stay, they'll have too many people to say goodbye to when they have so little time to pack for their trip. And after they leave, I'm sure it'll be very awkward with the in-laws as to whether or not we should have dinner together. I see no reason to. We're not even that close."

"Really? The in-laws think of everything, don't they? Even so, it wasn't right to leave without sayin' a word. What if they look for us thinking that we're lost?"

"Don't worry. I've dropped enough hints to Chae Hoon so I'm sure he knows what we're up to. He'll come up with a suitable excuse for us."

"Shouldn't we have given the kids some spending money? Well, I'm sure I don't have to tell *you* how to take care of these things ..."

His words were laced with sarcasm. Granted that he had neither cooperated, nor approved what she'd done, she resented

it nonetheless. She herself couldn't comprehend why she poured
so much heart and soul into something that put a damper on—or
at best postponed for a day—the kids' happiness. Self-scorn and
rejection made for a strange kind of loneliness, a kind she had
never experienced before. There was still time to undo what she
had done, but she intended to push forward stubbornly. The thrill
that had exhilarated her whole being was gone without a trace;
what remained was spite, the determination to rain on someone
else's parade.

"Let's have dinner together, you and me."

His invitation was more businesslike than affectionate.

"When the sun's still shining like this?"

The sun was hazy but the heat was relentless. This was
unbelievable heat, considering that the first day of fall had come
and gone by a few measures of the lunar calendar.

"But now that we're here, isn't it better to get dinner out of the
way? Eating by myself is so depressing . . ."

How was it that this man was so candid? His tackiness,
shabbiness, ineptness—all these things hung from him like
sagging baggage, an obvious sign of someone who ate alone on a
regular basis. She didn't want to look him in the face.

"How about if I accompany you to Barani today? Why are you
so surprised? It's not like I want to go somewhere I shouldn't."

Barani was the name of the neighborhood where he lived.
She'd learned the name from Chae Jung, who thought it was a
pretty name. She, on the other hand, didn't like the name at all. It
made her think of a bunch of old folks sitting outside and waiting
with their necks sticking out, on the off chance that someone
might visit them.

Her husband's face briefly showed surprise before turning blank
again. Then he informed her that they had to take the subway.
She followed him silently. She felt sorry for herself, for trying
too hard to compensate for her sense of loss. Things had already

gotten off to the wrong start today, but there was no stopping now. The train, running on a newly built line, was clean and well air-conditioned. Her husband explained apologetically that they must transfer to the national railway at Wangshimni, ride it all the way to the terminus, and then change to a bus. She pretended to listen, but nothing registered in her mind. She knew less about Seoul than her husband. Once she set up her business, she never moved once during the years she spent in Seoul because she was afraid of losing her regular customer base. Of course, most of her regular customers were apartment renters who moved often. But the ones who left were replaced quickly enough. What was important to her was that she had a steady influx of regulars, not so much who they were. For the sake of her regular customers, she learned to become a good conversationalist well versed in world affairs. She made the small store feel cozy and welcoming, a place where they could drop by to chat even when they didn't have anything to buy. After the big department store opened, however, her store turned into a waiting room for the department store shuttle bus. At first, the customers came into the store pretending to look around before running out to catch the bus when it pulled up. Then they eventually stopped setting foot inside the store, ignoring it on their way to and from the department store. It was as if her small shop had never existed.

They had to climb several flights of stairs to transfer to the national railway, a much older line. The last stairway that led above ground was narrow and hidden in a remote corner. Above ground, the sun had not set yet. The evening sun hanging from the corner of a skyscraper was still sizzling like burning coal. The national railway station was, unfortunately for them, out in the open without a single patch of shade. It seemed like a place where passengers came not to catch a train but to be punished. The pavement was roasting from the day's worth of heat it had absorbed, but the people standing on it waited with impassive faces, as if they didn't care what happened to them. Her husband's bald head was beginning to develop a dull sheen from sweat. If she were to touch it, it would surely be sticky like tree sap. She shuddered at the thought. The national railway trains apparently did not run as frequently as the subway trains. A schedule posted on a cement pillar indicated that it ran every twenty minutes. In that time, she thought, she would have to endure indignity more than the heat.

Their wait was rewarded inside the train with air that was just as cool as the subway's. But the view outside was completely foreign, and it was hard to believe that such a place even existed in the vicinity of Seoul. It was neither city nor country, with abandoned fields occasionally carved by streams syrupy with rotting pollutants. Curved bridges leading to god knows where were held up by massive cement pillars, their foundations deeply embedded in swampy bogs. Rusting metal and rotting planks stuck out of carelessly piled heaps of garbage, and tough weeds, with their heads cocked and ready to spurt out poison, threatened to overtake rundown houses nearby. Then suddenly, a row of square townhouses loomed close to the railroad, revealing their rooftops with laundry hanging from clotheslines and humble gardens blooming with zinnias and cockscombs. Regrettably, no neighborhood kids showed up, running after the train and waving their fists in the air.

It dawned on her like some great revelation that her husband was very much like the national railway train. Once this idea entered her head, the passengers around her seemed to be of a different race than the subway riders. Her husband was sleeping or pretending to sleep with his eyes closed. What am I doing, she asked herself. Losing her son was as sudden and debilitating as falling into a pit. At an age where one could stumble even on firm ground, she never dreamed that there'd be such a pit hiding in her path. She looked upon her sleeping husband with the disbelief of someone who had grasped nothing but a handful of straw as she fell endlessly into life's bottomless abyss.

The train came to a stop and many people were getting off. Urged on by an irrepressible feeling, she shook her husband. Confused and disoriented, he got off the train with her. He was about to board again, saying that they had one more stop to the terminal, but she pulled him toward the steps.

"We have to go somewhere."

"Where, all of a sudden?"

"The kids are going on their honeymoon today. Why don't we have some fun of our own? What's waiting for us in Barani except the mosquitoes?"

She recalled that Chae Jung always took a load of mosquito repellent with her whenever she visited her father.

"You're the one who wanted to go to Barani," he said in a quiet, admonishing tone. Then he took the lead, walking briskly and entering a barbeque joint. Instead of an air conditioner, a fan oscillating like an airplane propeller was hooked to the ceiling. At the center of every table a large hood hovered just above the hot grill, but the hall was still filled with smoke and the smell of spices. Maybe because it was dinnertime or because the locals favored it, the place was crowded, with almost no empty seats. The food arrived and she wasn't displeased to see her husband grill the meat skillfully. This pathetic man had understood 'having fun' as sharing a slab of barbequed meat. But she hadn't objected due to her sudden hunger pang. The meat was ordered by weight, and it arrived, along with a charcoal pot and some side dishes, but the rest was self-service. Her husband took care of everything, from grilling the meat and cutting it up into bite-size pieces to changing the burnt grill plate. He explained that he occasionally patronized the restaurant when he needed to boost his diet with an affordable, hearty meal.

Having satiated himself until he smelled of the barbecue from head to toe, he stepped out of the restaurant, commenting once again how inexpensive this place was, given the amount they had eaten. She had left ahead of him and paid him no attention. Someone descended from a cab in front of the restaurant, so she grabbed it, motioned to him, and shoved him in. She got in next to him and told the driver to take them to a nearby love hotel with a nice view. She said this without a flinch and with a slight emphasis on the word "love." Then she turned to her husband and asked, "This is your first time going to a place like that, right?"

"Looks like it ain't your first time."

"Actually, it is for me, too," she said firmly, to end the discussion. There was not a shred of doubt that neither of them had been to such a place. Even if one witnessed the other enter such a building, an extramarital affair would not be considered the purpose of the visit. Those were the kind of people they were. It was laughable, but true. Did that make them a good couple? How did they end up like this? A sense of defeat drained all the energy from her tense shoulders. The cab driver took no pains to hide his disdain for the perverted old couple and dragged them all over the city. Fortunately, he then dropped them off in front of a three-story, villa-like building overlooking the Han River.

It was her husband who paid the cab fare and walked up to the front desk.

"Will you be resting for a short while?"

"No, we'll be staying the night."

Blushing at his reply, she turned to the window at the end of the hallway and looked up at the clear sky. The sun had finally gone down.

"Well, you must have more money than I thought," she said caustically, stopping at the stairway where it made a sharp turn. He had received the key and she was following him up the stairs. She knew him to be an unrivaled cheapskate, but he had paid for dinner and the hotel without so much as a whimper. He never had a dime to spare, for reasons she knew only too well. At times she may have been embarrassed by his frugal ways, but she never resented it. They were a couple with no feelings left for each other, not even suspicions of infidelity. Even for such couples, money supposedly remained a touchy subject, and she was surprised and ashamed to discover that this might be true in her case as well.

"You know that it was Chae Hoon's graduation today. I thought we may go out to eat with the in-laws so I've been puttin' aside some money for the occasion."

She didn't know how to react to his quiet and somewhat dejected explanation. The room was dim and cozy, not as racy as she had imagined. Outside the window, beautiful houses, either vacation homes or hotels probably, stood scattered on the hillside across from the Han River. The hotel building had a garden below with a well-manicured lawn that was so close to the river you could almost stand on its edge and soak your feet in the water. She stood for a long time looking out the window and listening to the water running in the shower.

"Ah, that felt good."

When her husband walked out of the bathroom, she almost yelped in surprise before turning her eyes away. The lower half of his body, clad only in underwear, was hideous to see. The little remaining flesh on his thighs sagged like sacks of water, and scrawny calves with sparse hair stuck out below red, knobby knees. Feeling goose bumps spread throughout her body, she shuddered with loathing. It was a feeling different from disgust. The feeling of disgust has a residual veneer of interest to it. What she felt was pure loathing. This kind of emotion was not possible between a married couple who had lived together and made love for many years. They were never a lovey-dovey couple even when they lived together. On hot summer days, her husband did often walk around the house only in his underwear, and she used to reproach him by saying that kind of behavior would make it impossible for them to live with a daughter-in-law. Back then, his habit caused her more worry than aversion. Certainly, she was not charmed by the sight, but she was indifferent to it, as if seeing an old wardrobe, desk or table—something that sat where it should for a long time.

Oddly enough, the surprising emotion caused by the sight of her husband took her mind back to the white envelope. A telephone lay right in front of her eyes. The fact that she must call by the end of the day was a scripted part of her plan, but she still felt butterflies in her stomach. Her son's mother-in-law answered the phone. She skipped the usual greetings and went straight into her act.

"Whatever shall I do? I completely forgot to give the envelope to the kids. My husband was in such a hurry to leave, you see. He said that on a day like this it's best to leave the boy alone so he could spend more quality time with his wife's family. He said that you might be uncomfortable with us hanging around. He's like that, overly accommodating sometimes. It turns out, he had a plan of his own. I'm at his friend's vacation home in Chungpyung right now. He spends a great deal of time alone on the farm, so whenever he comes up to Seoul, he goes out of his way to make the time with me special. He is just too much, sometimes. Oh heavens, look what I'm doing. I called about an urgent matter and I'm digressing. What are the kids doing now? They couldn't have left since I have the tickets with me here . . . Will the plane tickets and the hotel voucher be valid tomorrow? We'll head to Seoul first thing tomorrow morning, so please send Chae Hoon to our store. I still can't believe how we blundered like this. What do we do now that we've ruined their plans?"

"Oh, no. You haven't ruined anything. They left on their trip as planned. The reservation is still good even if they don't have their tickets. Please don't worry about them and enjoy your time there." Her in-law spoke matter-of-factly without any sneering undertones.

Although she had been succinct, there was enough underlying disdain in her own speech to offend. It may be true that you learn to imitate what you scorn. She was the one who had spoken so glibly the whole time.

How could this be? All the effort that went into disrupting, or at least inconveniencing, their warm and fuzzy happiness had amounted to nothing. The thrill of playing an elaborate trick on them had backfired in the form of plain and simple ridicule. A deep sense of failure now furthered her sense of inferiority, making her misery intolerable. Her husband spoke with a concerned voice.

"You did or said something wrong to the in-laws, didn't you? I hope you weren't foolish."

"What did I do that was so foolish? You don't know anything," she snapped angrily, suppressing a sob.

"Oh, I know you're smart. So, so smart. I always thought so, but I gotta admit that you did look a tad foolish next to Chae Hoon's mother-in-law today."

She remained silent, afraid that her sob might break loose if she spoke. Her husband spoke again, this time in a gentler voice.

"You've all been saying that Chae Hoon's major doesn't lend itself to a job these days without a degree from overseas. That's why I didn't object, but frankly, I'm worried about their expenses. All I'm good at is not spending money, and I feel terrible about how long you'll have to continue to work."

"Oh, don't you worry about me. Why do you think that we need to help the kids with their expenses? We've done more than necessary up to this point."

"What did we do for them exactly?"

"When the kids got married, I told Soo Jung not to worry about wedding gifts or new furnishings. Do you have any idea how much all that is worth? Her parents immediately understood what I meant and said that they'd leave some cash aside in dollars. After they burn through that lump sum, I'm sure Soo Jung will get a job or something. She's the one who coaxed Chae Hoon into studying abroad. Don't you think that she's prepared to do that much at least?"

"Even so, we gotta do our part. Let's scrimp and save and do what we can to send them some money every month."

"Do our part? Hah! I can't spend any less than what I'm spending now. The business is dying, so I'm planning to close the store soon. So don't expect me to bring in any income. If you really want, you can 'scrimp and save' and send that money or go on a trip to America. Doesn't matter to me."

"I'm trying to spend as little as humanly possible. You know that, don't you?"

The sad resonance of his words made her spring to her feet.

"Get some rest. I'm going out to get some air."

She left as quickly as her feet would carry her, leaving her husband lying on the bed. Because she wanted to escape but had to prevent herself from doing so, she left without her purse. The second floor hallway was as quiet as an empty house. The emergency exit at the end of the hallway opened easily, and outside was a small space where one could slip out for a smoke. She went down a spiral staircase leading to the garden on the ground floor, and there was a small pond and a bench under the shade of a tree facing the river. No one was taking advantage of these amenities, for the place was deserted.

Looking up at the three-story building, she saw that some of the windows were lit and some were dark. The light coming from the windows was not bright but muted. The emptiness she felt after having wasted her whole day grew inside of her, growing into a vast emptiness, the sense of having wasted her whole life. She felt infinitely small and worthless. Did she know that she would end up feeling this way, and was that why she had scuttled around all these years trying to fill the void? She had desperately tried to grab on to something, anything, even a handful of straw. Opening her fingers, she now realized that what she had seized in her final, desperate attempt was her husband's boney shin. This revelation was also the manifestation of a deep despair that made her think that she couldn't possibly go on living with him.

She did not drag him to this place with the expectation of sex. She considered herself beyond the age of desire, but even when she and her husband were younger, they were hardly a couple with overactive libidos. They had sex routinely until their separation, and with neither being the first to suggest it, they settled naturally into mutual abstinence. Thus, they lived as two perfect strangers without any physical contact. If there was even an ounce of physical intimacy left between them, she might not have been so repulsed by his legs. If there was some connection between the lack of physical intimacy and her loathing, perhaps she shouldn't have taken that aspect of their relationship so lightly. What she yearned for today was definitely not lust. If a friendly act like scratching each other's backs could have filled the void, wouldn't it be nobler and lovelier than lust? Now that she realized the impossibility of this prospect, she began to regret the time their bodies had spent completely apart. She had no idea that it would be such an irreversible mistake.

She gazed at the flowing river for a long time, long enough for her husband to have fallen asleep, before returning to the room. It was cooler in the room than by the water, and her husband was snoring in his sleep in his worn-out underwear with the blanket kicked off to the side. Before she could feel repulsed by his appearance, she felt concerned that he might catch a cold. She reached for the light, flower-print blanket, and while doing so, she couldn't help but see his legs up close. They were covered with mosquito bites, some swollen red at the peak of inflammation and some healing down to brownish patches. There were so many. How could those tiny creatures be so cruel as to suck the blood from those scrawny legs? What was his life like, that he'd allow himself to be mutilated like this? From the dirt under his nails, she could see the impoverished and exhausting life he had eked out. His monthly income was more than enough for him to live comfortably in retirement, if he wished. A hot lump of compassion rose to her throat as she looked at her husband who so willingly shackled himself to his patriarchal responsibilities. She gently stroked the mosquito bites on his shin as one would caress a piece of antique furniture beat up and grimy from years of wear.

That Girl's House

During a writers' conference last summer, I participated in a poetry recital that was a fundraising event to help North Koreans. I assumed that the event was for poets only, but I was told that veterans from various fields, including me, were being asked to recite their favorite poems. I was taken aback by being referred to as a "veteran," but I guess no one is brazen enough to weasel out of helping our fellow countrymen in the North. I agreed to do it—not so much out of obligation, actually, but because I had a poem I wanted to share. At that time, I was obsessed with Kim Yong-taek's poem "That Girl's House." Kim Yong-taek is one of my favorite poets, but I wouldn't say that he is *the* favorite. Likewise, I don't know if "That Girl's House" is even his best work.

Reading this poem in *The Green Review* came as a complete shock to me because I was sure that the poem was about the story of Gop-dan and Man-deuk, who were from my hometown. Jang Man-deuk, who is now well into his seventies, still had a penchant for literature, as he did in his youth. He told me that up until recently, he still got woozy with excitement every year during the spring literature contest. Naturally, I assumed that he got more than woozy and submitted his own writing. I assumed this because I know all about that kind of dizzy excitement and how you can't suppress it. If it were some unknown poet's name instead of the famous Kim Yong-taek's in the byline, I would not have doubted for a moment that it was Jang Man-deuk's pen name. I read the poem over and over. Vague images formed by the words gradually became vivid, like photographs being developed in a chemical bath. Forgotten memories from my past unveiled themselves one by one, even those of hidden, apprehensive beauty, and I sipped away at a bottle of wine as overwhelming nostalgia and grief sank in.

Gop-dan was the youngest and the only daughter of a family with four big, strong sons. Her hardworking farmer of a father and his dependable sons were always the first ones to thatch their roof in the fall. Although this was hardly a big job for five brawny men, Man-deuk would be up on the roof before them prancing around in excitement. In our small village, Man-deuk was the only middle school student and thus exempt from menial labor, but he was always a willing volunteer to help Gop-dan's family, who hardly needed it. One of Gop-dan's brothers was Man-deuk's friend. But all the townsfolk knew that Man-deuk was motivated not by his friend but by that girl, Gop-dan. Yes, when the elderly townsfolk saw Man-deuk on the roof strutting his stuff as smoke rose from the kitchen while a hot lunch was being prepared, they shook their heads, saying, "When you adore your bride, you bow down even to the pole in front of her house." As evidenced by such claims, the expectation of marriage between the two kids was a publicly acknowledged matter.

The relationship between the two of them was the object of envy among those of us who were younger. Our hearts fluttered when we gossiped about their romance. I suppose it wasn't impossible for two young people to be in love without the formal approval of their parents in a conservative rural village in the 1940s. Sometimes there was talk of couples carrying on secret romances or even illicit love affairs. Such gossip was scandalous enough to make the parents hang their heads in shame and plague the accused with a lingering stigma.

People referred to Gop-dan and Man-deuk's relationship as a "courtship" instead of a "flirtation" or a "love affair." And I'm sure they did this to differentiate their relationship from those other scandalous associations. Such differentiation by the villagers was a form of affection and yearning. Although men studied at the schoolhouse and women became barely literate by looking over the shoulders of male students, modern education was a distant dream for the villagers who lived at least eight kilometers away from the nearest town. But this dream was something that they wanted to afford to their children, if possible. I think they thought of romance in a similar way. They harbored an irresistible curiosity toward the newfangled ways of life enjoyed by educated city folks. Thus, Gop-dan and Man-deuk's relationship had the seal of approval not only from the younger generation but also from the officious older folks who criticized every little thing. Even before the two ever had any feelings for each other, it was the elderly who delighted in imagining, with their eyes half closed, the two of them together. Both Man-deuk and Gop-dan's families were independent farmers who owned just enough land to yield them sufficient annual harvests. They also knew how to be generous to others who were less fortunate. Man-deuk only had older sisters and Gop-dan older brothers, so the two were the cherished favorites in their respective families. They say children valued in their own homes receive special attention and treatment from others as well. This was certainly true for the two of them.

Unlike other coarse rural children, Gop-dan had fair skin and long eyelashes. I had no fitting description for her long lashes until I read Kim Yong-taek's poem. As he stated so eloquently, they were long enough for big snowflakes to rest upon. When that snow melted into dew and her moist lashes cast a shadow on her dark pupils, her tender expression was beautiful enough to make a statue fall in love. Man-deuk was so clever that he knew ten things after learning just one. And he, too, was as handsome as the jewel in a crown. The two of them were a rare sight to behold in these rural parts. If Man-deuk was a dragon born from a swamp, then Gop-dan was a lotus blossoming in a bog. I don't know who said it first, but everyone unanimously agreed that the two made a handsome couple, that they were a match made in heaven. The two families were of equal standing in the neighborhood. Both sets of parents were simple and honest folks; they approved of their child's prospective partner, albeit chosen by others, and looked with affection upon their children's transformation into attractive, well-adjusted adults. Amidst the monotony of our simple lives, Gop-dan and Man-deuk were the pride and joy of our village. But anyone experienced in matchmaking knows this: One may feel compelled to bring together a couple seemingly so perfect, but more often than not, the individuals involved feel absolutely nothing for each other. For better or for worse, falling in love is beyond the scope of human intentions; it falls under the jurisdiction of the gods. When humans try to meddle in the gods' affairs, they can play all kinds of tricks on well-meaning matchmakers and unsuspecting couples.

Man-deuk and Gop-dan, however, did not betray the villagers' hopes. This was apparent from Gop-dan's undue shyness toward Man-deuk. People gossiped endlessly about the time Gop-dan broke her water bucket. With just twenty households constituting the upper and the lower sections of our village, we only had one well amongst us. Transporting water was a chore reserved for women, and no self-respecting housewife used her hands to hold up the water bucket carried on her head. You didn't earn your stripes as a seasoned homemaker until you could walk confidently with both hands free, even turning your head left or right. Girls looked upon their mothers with awe while feeling the pressure that one day they must perform the same feat. Little girls were eager to try carrying a water bucket on top of their heads, and they practiced with a smaller-sized bucket called a *banguri*. Used more for play, many *banguris* were broken in the hands of their owners. In our village, it was a common practice to call a girl a *banguri*, meaning a little squirt.

Gop-dan was a cherished daughter and had two older sisters-in-law, so she did not have to fetch water. But she still owned a *banguri* because she was at an age when she had to try everything that her friends did. She was very much a beginner who could not take a single step without holding the *banguri* on her head with both hands. She was walking in this manner one day when she saw Man-deuk approaching. He was running toward her to help her, but shrieking "oh my goodness," she let go of her hands to lift up the shoulder straps of her dress. Of course, the *banguri* slipped off her head and shattered into pieces. She must have been fourteen or fifteen, with her bosom coming in like apricot seeds. In those days, it was customary for women to wear dresses held up by straps tightened just above the bosom. Above the dress, they wore a very short, cropped top with sleeves. With arms raised up, bare armpits showed and breasts jutted out. In our village, there was no shame among young women in revealing a little skin in this manner. It was not an unusual sight to see a child on a mother's back reach to the front, grab her breast, and nurse. Immodesty associated with female breasts is often culturally taught. In our town, a mother's bare breast was about as exciting as a rice bowl whereas baring a belly button was considered indecent exposure. Considering this, it was no small matter for a young girl like Gop-dan—it might be different for maidens of marriageable age—to conceal her bosom at the expense of breaking her *banguri*.

Man-deuk was the first in our village to go to a middle school in a nearby town. When he did, Gop-dan also nagged her father to enroll her in a branch elementary school two and a half miles away. This happened some time after the *banguri* incident. Gop-dan's school was called the Simplicity School, and it had no age limit and focused on vocational skills. There were even young fathers among the male students. It was the same for the middle school. After graduating from elementary school, Man-deuk had stayed home for a few years to help his family with the farming. His oldest sister, who was married and lived in the city, insisted on modern education for her younger siblings, so Man-deuk enrolled in middle school a few years behind other students.

The simplicity school was located on the way to town in a village called Ginaegol, the largest village in our surrounding area with fifty-plus households. Two hills and a creek had to be crossed to reach the school. Naturally, Man-deuk and Gop-dan walked to and from school together. There was nothing unusual in how they appeared to others. Gop-dan always walked far behind Man-deuk, who took long, arm-swinging strides in front of her and then waited. Back then, it was considered proper even in married couples for the wife to walk a few steps behind the husband instead of walking next to him. Man-deuk had twice as far to walk than Gop-dan, and at times when he became impatient with her dawdling steps, he took off by himself.

Although the area had plentiful sources of water, with small streams branching out everywhere like fishing nets, the brook running below the bridge in Ginaegol was especially beautiful. The water was not deep but the gulch was, with its steep walls speckled with myriad wild flowers that continually bloomed and withered from early spring to fall. Except for the shadow of wild flowers, the surface of the water was crystal clear; tiny waves rose and broke playfully. Schools of fish swam below and white pebbles and grainy sand lined the bottom. The brook had a mud bridge. Two big logs were laid across the gulch, with braided ropes and tough vines forming the rungs between the two logs. A mound of mud had been patted down below the logs to form a walkway as cozy and romantic as a path running through a forest. But when it rained a lot or the soil thawed in the spring, the bridge became a booby trap with a slippery surface and hidden holes. For the most part, people crossing the bridge were inconvenienced only temporarily because someone always made repairs right away. The short but unpredictable intervals before the repairs had been made and the long monsoon seasons were the problem. Girls especially were scared to cross the bridge that might be full of hollow pits. The deepest part of the water was only waist-deep, and it was actually safer to go down into the gulch, take off one's shoes, and wade across the water. The boys had the manly job of walking ahead with long sticks in hand and cautioning the girls away from the deep, treacherous parts. Man-deuk did not allow Gop-dan to cross the brook behind other boys, lifting her dress up to her navel and getting her long underpants wet. On the way to school and even on the way back, he somehow managed to meet her in time to help her cross the muddy, hole-ridden bridge. Oh, how Gop-dan fussed and yelped in distress and how Man-deuk indulged and patted her in reassurance! The bridge was hardly long, but rumors of how they constantly ended up in each other's arms while crossing abounded. The rumors were not vicious. The elderly, otherwise behind the times in so many ways, considered the two young kids adorable, not indecent. Man-deuk and Gop-dan would surely marry someday, and their flirtations were regarded as natural and beautiful as a pair of birds rubbing their beaks together. So the villagers called the mud bridge a love bridge, and that, too, was meant without malice.

Man-deuk probably opened his eyes to literature as a middle school upper classman. He used to carry around a copy of the poetry book *The Dance of Agony* under his armpit instead of in his book bag. He looked very hip and intellectual walking around like that. Most of the young men in the village, even those who had never set foot inside a government school, were literate in Chinese characters because the village school functioned almost as a mandatory educational institution for young boys. Most of them could read the title *The Dance of Agony*, but fully grasping its meaning was another matter. All they knew was that the letters were in traditional characters, but each character exuded an exotic and highly colorful feel. Wherever it came from, the phrase "high color" was very popular among the young people in our village during that time. Anything that seemed exotic or modern was referred to as "high color."

Man-deuk was the one who popularized the reading of Choonwon's works in our village. Choonwon's works, such as *The Earth*, *The Tragic Tale of King Danjong*, and *No Emotion*, circulated among young people and were read until the pages became tattered. As the pages frayed, the eyes of impressionable adolescents reading them twinkled like the stars. Soon, however, the Choonwon fans in our village became disappointed and confused by the rumors that he had led the movement for changing everyone's surnames into Japanese and gave speeches driving young men into battlefields. This rumor was started by none other than Man-deuk himself. It was not an exaggeration to say that he had the emotional pulse of his peers under his thumb, and he could tighten or loosen his hold as he pleased. The realities of village life were getting harsher every day at the end of the Second World War. But the young people suffered more from deprivation of the mind than actual poverty and were therefore quite vulnerable to manipulation. The books popularized by Man-deuk naturally brought together like-minded youth to discuss literature and to rant about the current state of social affairs. Of course, Man-deuk was the central figure in these gatherings. Although he was a few years older than the other middle school students, he was still just a teenager. The gatherings served more to boost his ego than to help young activists protest against oppression. During the meetings Man-deuk sometimes recited poetry, including his own, in a somber tone. Gop-dan was partial to one recitation that always moved her to tears. It was the last part of one of Imhwa's poems.

When he came to the part, "Oh! Wider than the sky above," Man-deuk's voice would be overcome with emotion. Gop-dan said listening to him made her fearful that she would lose him to the big, wide world one day.

Gop-dan sometimes showed me the letters she received from Man-deuk. "I don't want them to go to waste . . ." she'd add shyly, because I hadn't asked to see them. Since love letters are usually meant for one pair of eyes only, it actually made no sense to say that they'd go to waste. Her showing me the letters meant that they didn't contain anything racy enough for someone else to read. It also meant that she wanted to show off parts of his writing that had impressed her. One thing I remember from one of the letters was that he had compared the bladder cherries growing under her fence to "dwarf guardsmen holding up red lanterns." Most of the houses in our village grew forsythia as hedge plants in the backyard. Underneath the forsythia grew wild bladder cherry plants. In spring and summer, they remained forgotten like inconspicuous weeds hiding under the bright canary-yellow forsythia blooms. One noticed them only after most of the thickets became withered and tawny. Then the ripened bladder cherries stood out prettier than the autumn foliage with their petite lanterns looking as cute as buttons. That was also the time when the flaming orange of the persimmon fruit upstaged the yellowing leaves, and the peppers in the fields changed color from plain green to ruby. Still, bladder cherries were mere weeds with no use other than to serve as playthings for bored girls to chew in their mouths and pop. As with all the other houses in the village, our house had bladder cherries growing in abundance under the fence. So among all the ever so ordinary, widespread bladder cherries, only Gop-dan's were worthy of becoming dwarf guardsmen with lanterns. Could it be that Man-deuk wrote from experience? Yearning for his love, he may have once tried to burrow a hole under her fence only to be stopped by the dwarf guardsmen holding up red lanterns. How else could Gop-dan's bladder cherries become so special among so many ordinary ones?

In addition to bladder cherries, apricot trees grew profusely in our village, so much so that our village name in Chinese characters means the apricot village. Every home had one. In spring, along with the forsythia blooms, apricot blossoms transformed the whole neighborhood into a floral paradise. But the delectable-looking fruit were actually wild apricots with a very sour taste. Although some people saved the seeds to use in herbal remedies, no one, not even the children, ate the fruit. So they fell to the ground, rotting in heaps. Our village was a beautiful place. When the apricot trees came into full bloom, milk vetches and violets covered the fields and knolls. Milk vetch blossoms spread evenly in wide rolls of plush carpet while violets scattered in random clusters. By the time the rotting apricots had seeped into the ground to nourish the soil, wild roses going down with one last fight would fill secluded pathways with beauty that was as breathless and intense as the gleaming moonlight.

While reading "That Girl's House", I recalled that the apricot trees in Gop-dan's house were, indeed, special among the many growing in our village. Just as her rooftop had the shiniest golden sheen among the countless thatch roof houses. Just as her bladder cherries stood out from all the rest. Gop-dan's house was the first house in the upper section of the Apricot Village. The creek water flowing down from the hills wrapped around her house and fed into a fertile strip of rice paddy owned by Man-deuk's parents. The apricot tree in Gop-dan's yard was a big one, strong enough for her father to tie a swing for her and her friends. To Man-deuk, the shower of pearly white petals that fell from that tree and floated downstream must have seemed like love letters carrying bits of her love.

In the spring of 1945, did any apricot trees, bladder cherries, violets, and milk vetches bloom? They must have, but somehow it just felt to me like they didn't. I wondered if Gop-dan and Man-deuk's love came to an end before the flowers bloomed. As one of the older students at a four-year middle school, Man-deuk was drafted into the military immediately after graduation. He only had a few days before he had to report for duty, and the two families wanted to marry the kids in that time. It was not uncommon for young men to be hurried into marriage before entering military service so that they could at least start a family and carry on the family line. Man-deuk was, in fact, the only son in the family. Although the *saju* letters for fortunetelling had not been exchanged, the whole village knew that he and Gop-dan were as good as betrothed. But Man-deuk adamantly refused to get married. That was his way of loving her. He didn't care what anyone else thought, but he dragged her around trying to convince her of his way of loving. The chill of early spring had kept the last of the snow from thawing, but he must have talked to her under the muted moonlight until roosters crowed at the crack of dawn. Whether or not Gop-dan accepted his viewpoint is anyone's guess. Even if he hadn't dragged her around but had taken her to a place like a rice-cake mill to spend the night instead, her parents and the villagers would have trusted him not to have laid an improper finger on her bosom. It was like that in those times. It may have been the innocence or stupidity of the times, but such were the convictions we held firmly in our hearts.

A Japanese flag and another flag signaling the residence of a soldier summoned to war flapped ominously in the wind by the front door of Man-deuk's house. Drinking parties went on for days at the house but the authorities turned a blind eye to the bootlegged liquor. Ten days passed by in the blink of an eye and Man-deuk left. Convincing Gop-dan to wait for him until the day he returned alive and well should have been the easy part. She certainly had no intention of marrying anyone else and her parents were not the kind of people to force that on her. It would have taken time and effort, however, to explain why he wasn't going to marry her before leaving. As her name suggests, Gop-dan had a heart as soft as ripples of luxurious silk, but she was no pushover when it came to being dissuaded from the judgments she deemed to be correct. No one said anything out of respect for Man-deuk, because the villagers considered him like their own son-in-law, but they knew he was going off to a place where his life was on the line. They thought it was very noble of him to spare Gop-dan the pain of widowhood in case something happened to him. Man-deuk and Gop-dan were the golden couple; they were like the village mascots whose happiness the villagers wanted to guard as if some misfortune would befall them if the two became unhappy. And Man-deuk never offended the good will of those simple-hearted folks, his behavior in all matters good and honest in their eyes.

After Man-deuk left, other young men became conscript soldiers or workers one by one, so the only men left in the village were those past their prime or the elderly. In Gop-dan's family, except for the eldest brother caring for her parents and the third brother working at a factory in the city, the other two brothers were drafted into service. Thus, her house full of strong, young sons became practically an empty nest. The authorities took not only manpower but also food, leaving the once-bountiful village with worries of food shortages. Strict food quotas forced parsimony on the generous people who used to make enough fried pancakes to fill a wicker tray, which they would share with their neighbors. Hard times did not end there, and news worse than an epidemic began circulating. People had long known about comfort women because the town hall had put up public notices about how young women could be paid to work in Japan or the South Seas. Supposedly, they could earn enough money abroad to send home regularly. Not a single family, however, opted to send their daughter away, and no one dreamed that young girls would be forced into such a work force. Soon, rumor had it that town hall administrators and patrol officers had been allotted quotas and had resorted to blackmailing families and abducting young girls. While people dithered in disbelief, a horrible incident occurred. Since it happened in the same district, one couldn't just brush if off as a rumor. Authorities were searching for caches of food in the outskirts of town. One scared couple assumed that they had come to take their daughter away and hid her in a haystack inside a barn. What they didn't know was that the quota enforcement officers routinely stuck their sharp-edged poles into possible places where grain had been hidden. The impaling of the haystack and the parents' screaming, "Please, don't!" were said to have occurred simultaneously. In one version of the story, the girl's flesh tore off with the pole and remained stuck to its tip; in another it was not flesh but her ruptured intestine. One story had her die at the scene but in another she was carried off in a cart to a hospital where it was not known whether she lived or bled to death. It was a ghastly incident with a huge ripple effect. Terror gripped the entire district, and families with young daughters lived in perpetual fear.

Gop-dan's older brother, who worked at a munitions factory, came home one day with a middle-aged man who had gaiters over his calves and cleats nailed to the soles of his shoes. He was a surveying engineer at an important construction site in Sinuiju, a city in northern Pyeong-An province. Gop-dan's parents had recruited him as her husband after hearing the rumors of the horrific incident. The man had been married once before. His first wife had been driven away after ten years for not bearing him any children. Instead of looking at Gop-dan's pretty face, he kept staring at her slim hips, wondering out loud if she'd have trouble giving birth. Tilting his head in doubt, he didn't seem to be all that impressed with her. But Gop-dan's parents had no other eligible bachelors to choose from. And the aged groom-to-be was a capable man doing important work for the war effort and thus automatically exempt from military service. So without a second thought, Gop-dan's parents gave away their precious daughter to be his second wife.

There was no telling how Gop-dan felt in consenting to the marriage. They say the sight of blood can drive a normal person mad. The same can be said of bloodstained rumors. Gop-dan's parents weren't the only ones who'd lost their rationality. The whole village had. Village elders who delighted in Gop-dan and Man-deuk's puppy love were now of the opinion that the best they could do for her was to not offer her to the Japanese. Gop-dan's mother, especially, was a soft-hearted, delicate woman who couldn't even twist off a chicken neck to make a meal. The gory rumor must have shaken her to the core. I'm sure Gop-dan would rather have died than betray Man-deuk by marrying someone else. But she, too, was softhearted and incapable of ending her own life. All she could do was become numb and lifeless, like someone drained of all human emotion. The marriage ceremony took place at Gop-dan's house. As she took her leave with her new husband three days afterward, her face was expressionless and eerie, like a corpse wearing makeup.

Thus, she left home for far away Sinuiju, and before she could make the first trip back to see her family, Korea was liberated from Japanese rule. She left home at age nineteen and never returned to her home with the yellow thatch roof. Our village fell just below the 38th parallel and the passage to Sinuiju way up in the North became blocked indefinitely. Man-deuk returned home alive. In the spring of the following year, he married Soon

Ae, a girl from the same village. She was a pleasant girl with a cute, round face, but she was certainly no match for Gop-dan. On his wedding day, Man-deuk was hung upside down according to the tradition of breaking in the groom. The young men from the neighborhood, many hardened by military service, pounded the soles of his bare feet so hard that Man-deuk wept out loud. He, too, had become tough as nails on the battlefield, so was it really his friends' playful smacking that made him weep? He probably wanted to cry his heart out. At least that's what the villagers thought because they still wanted to interpret Man-deuk's every move in relation to Gop-dan. The celebrated romance between the two could not be forgotten quickly, and it must not have been easy for Soon Ae to be the new bride under those circumstances. Before the villagers could see how Man-deuk and Soon Ae got on as a married couple, they moved to Seoul. Man-deuk was the only son in his family, but his older sister had found him a job and brought him into the city.

After the Korean War, the Military Demarcation Line that replaced the 38th parallel placed the Apricot Village in North Korean territory. I hadn't kept in touch with Man-deuk and Soon Ae but my occasional visits to my hometown had supplied me with the news of their well-being. That was no longer possible after the war. Once in a while I thought of them and figured that if they hadn't died in the war they'd be living somewhere under the same Korean sky. These occasional remembrances soon gave way to a permanent amnesia. Life in Seoul was like that, where even among relatives, wedding invitations or news of death were received with a greater sense of obligation than kinship. People with no immediate relation were bound to be forgotten before long.

It has been less than ten years since I saw Man-deuk again in Seoul. My uncle, who is now deceased, had wanted me to accompany him to a hometown reunion. As is often the case with gatherings among displaced residents, the elderly made up the bulk of the attendees. The meeting was held annually, but for people like my uncle who were there for the first time, it took a long time for them and the other villagers to recognize one another. To make this effort easier the organizers divided the seating area into neighborhood districts, and from there the attendees themselves broke into smaller villages. The Apricot Village consisted only of my uncle, me, and an unfamiliar older couple. My uncle was nearing eighty at the time and passed away the following year. Unable to set foot on his hometown soil, he had at least wanted to be near its people. His children treated this desire lightly, assuming that ridiculous demands came with old age. That's how I came to accompany him to the gathering. The gentleman from the Apricot Village didn't seem to recognize my uncle either. I bowed to him politely to show respect for an elder from our hometown but didn't pay much attention to who he said he was. If he hadn't approached me later with a business card, I may never have recognized him. The name on the card was Jang Man-deuk, a rep from some electronics company. Something stopped me and I took a closer look. Only then did the younger version of himself that had been buried in my latent memory surface. He and I were never that close. Girls my age knew that he was Gop-dan's and so the proper thing for us to do was not to pay him any attention. I'm sure it was the same for Man-deuk. He was such a celebrity in our village, and celebrities can't be expected to recognize their fans. His face was still young and his body lean for his age. I told him that he looked just the same after all these years and then laughed in embarrassment. I was contradicting myself because I hadn't actually recognized him.

It was even harder to recognize Soon Ae. Back then, I was snobby about going to school and never socialized with older girls who stayed home to learn sewing and other domestic skills.

I couldn't say with confidence that the woman standing next to Man-deuk was actually her. She came up to me first, saying that I hadn't changed a bit, so I assumed that it was her. Man-deuk and Soon Ae looked like a happy and affectionate couple. It seemed a shame to just go our separate ways so we exchanged phone numbers before parting. Surprisingly, Soon Ae called me often, so we sometimes met for lunch or went shopping together. When we had gotten closer she confessed to me that her husband had never gotten over Gop-dan.

"Young friend, everyone tells me that I have it so good in life, but I'm like the apricot fruit from our village that looks delicious but tastes sour. I have no one but you to confide in. Who else would understand what I'm talking about? My husband makes a good living, never cheats on me, and is good with the kids. Others see him bending over backwards to please me. But no one knows the kind of mistress I have to put up with. Gop-dan is stuck on him like a leech, but I can't humiliate her in front of people or grab her by the hair and fight. It's absolutely maddening. I'm so glad that I ran into you because who else would understand my situation? Do you know that he still writes her love letters? He can't be, you say? That's what I thought at first. Oh, he justifies it by saying that he's writing poems, but I took a peek once when he wasn't looking. "Apricot blossoms alight on your shoulders," or "apricot blooms come alive every year, but my beloved will never again return." That kind of gibberish is not poetry but a love letter, am I right? And do you know what else? You should have seen him when we traveled to China last year. I was a fool to go along with him in the first place. After we went to see Baekdu Mountain, we got on a Yalu River tour boat at a place called Dandong something or other. At one time during the tour, we got close to North Korean land. The boat got so close, and seeing North Korean children playing on the shore made me emotional. In fact, all of the South Koreans onboard had solemn expressions on their faces while the Chinese continued to enjoy the ride unaffected. That much I can understand. But my husband, he lowered his head over the side of the boat and wept out loud. A silver-haired guy weeping and shaking all over. Moved to tears by the tragic division of our country, do you think? The land that we could see from there was Sinuiju. To be so near, so close to Gop-dan must have killed him. I wanted to push him overboard. Swim toward that wench, I wanted to tell him. There's more. There was a time when he wanted to immigrate to the States. He claimed that he wanted to raise the kids overseas when neither he nor I could speak a word of English. He had a good job here and we were doing just great, so what do you think his true intention was? I'm no dummy. I knew that you could go to North Korea with American citizenship. I told him to go by himself and to have a good life with that wench. He looked at me like I was a mental patient, but he ended up not going. He'd never give up the kids. I'm sure he couldn't have endured this miserable life if it weren't for them."

That was the gist of her story. True, she would have made no sense to anyone who didn't know the history behind Man-deuk and Gop-dan's days of youth and romance. But it was also true that her resentment was based on a repertoire of just a few incidents. She didn't have much evidence beyond those few incidents, and I was getting tired of listening to them over and over. Just when I was beginning to sympathize more with Man-deuk than her, I received the news of her death. She had been taking medication for several years due to high blood pressure, and one day she suddenly collapsed. Without regaining consciousness, she died within three days. At the wake, I was stunned to see a funeral portrait of her in her late twenties. I suppose the trend nowadays is to use younger photographs at funerals because no one wants to stare at a wrinkly face. But with the seventy-year-old Man-deuk shedding tears before us, a portrait of his much younger wife seemed inappropriate. Her children must have sensed the guests' disapproval because they took pains to explain that she had requested that an old photograph not be used for the funeral. After her death, it turned out that she had left behind a portrait for this purpose. Before I knew it, I was mentally comparing the younger Soon Ae to Gop-dan. No comparison. Gop-dan possessed unusual beauty that increased with imagination over time, and the woman in the portrait had a youthful but blatantly plain face. I felt genuine pity for Soon Ae. She must have spent her whole life battling a formidable rival in love—one that never aged or erred.

I never had the occasion to see Man-deuk on my own after his wife's death. Two or three years after she passed away, I ran into him at a support group event for comfort women. I was surprised to find him there, and perhaps because I had been influenced by his late wife, I couldn't help but think that his presence there had something to do with Gop-dan. I looked for him after the event and ran after him like someone in hot pursuit of a criminal. He was walking away from the conference site with slumped shoulders and I called out to him. Omitting the usual pleasantries, I asked him abruptly if he'd remarried. He said no and added that he had no such intention in the future either.

"Why? Is it because you can't ever forget Gop-dan? What made you come here? Are you still deeply bitter about what happened with comfort women? Because of one woman after all these years? That's really something. You think that if it weren't for the Japanese, you and Gop-dan could have lived happily ever after, don't you?"

Instead of addressing my outburst, he walked ahead and led me to a coffee shop. At that age, he still had an air of invigorating charm, but I looked at him askance as if I had inherited Soon Ae's resentment. He spoke in a soft, low voice.

"My wife only imagined that I never got over Gop-dan. I can't even remember her face, to tell you the truth. If my wife hadn't persisted in reminding me all the time, I would have forgotten her name too. If I did miss Gop-dan, it was because of the vague, nostalgic longing for our youth that we all have. Is it so wrong to indulge occasionally in memories of our beautiful hometown? That's also why I cried on the tour boat. I couldn't believe that the land looming right before my eyes was really North Korea. From another country it seemed so close when it had seemed so far away from our own country. That's what moved me to tears, not the fact that we were near Sinuiju. Why did I come here today . . . Let's see. I'm not sure if I can explain it even to myself. Recently, I read an article in a Japanese magazine showing how the Japanese were trying to make light of the comfort women issue. Is there any evidence that the women were forced to perform such a service? Isn't Korea trying to exaggerate the number of recruits? That kind of thing. They showed no remorse or responsibility, and I couldn't stand it. Although Gop-dan's face is a vague image in my head, there is something that I feel unmistakably in my heart—the despair she must have felt in being married off like that. In honoring the sacrifices of the comfort women, I wanted to include those who have evaded conscription but suffered in other ways. Those who experienced it directly and those who were affected indirectly were all victims of imperialism. What price did some women pay to be exempt from such a fate? If someone jumps off a ten-story building to avoid an armed burglar, does that absolve the burglar of his crime? We can't forget, it's not humanly possible to forget, the atrocities against man and God that wiped out love and laughter from all corners of our land. Can you understand how I feel, how I want the sorrow of the escapees to be remembered along with the sufferings of the actual victims?" Huge teardrops hung from the corners of Jan Man-deuk's eyes.

Thorn Inside Petals

In the morning I received word that my sister had died. This was less than two months after she had been sent back to the States. In my befuddled state, I asked where the funeral home was. That was a ridiculous question and it made my niece-in-law laugh. That's when I realized that my sister hadn't died here, but in America. Still, to laugh like that. Perhaps because her voice came through the phone line, she sounded upbeat and not as if she were mourning.

"Would you go if you knew where it was being held?" she asked.

"There's no reason not to. She's my one and only sister."

Saying this out loud brought forth suppressed tears. It was a daunting realization that I was the only one left out of five siblings.

"Auntie, America isn't Busan or Daegu."

"So where are you now?" I asked.

"Banpo, where else? Have you forgotten where we live?"

"So I guess America is too far away even for the eldest daughter-in-law."

"My husband just left. Thank goodness it's the off-season, otherwise he couldn't have gotten a ticket on such short notice. What's in America that so many people go there all the time?"

"Are you saying that you couldn't go because you couldn't get a ticket?"

"Auntie, our youngest is a high school senior. How can the mother of a senior go anywhere?"

Her voice was firm and righteous, almost incredulous that I could ask such a thing, and I was momentarily taken aback as if someone had yanked me from behind. Indeed, I am quite aware that in our society, you can get away with bending quite a few rules caring for a high school student, especially a senior. My niece-in-law wanted to hang up so she could contact other relatives.

"But what do I do now? Do I just sit here and do nothing? How can I do that? How?" I whined, but she had already hung up. Realizing that I was talking into a dead phone line, anger flared up instead of sorrow. How could they have shipped off my sister like that, on what proved to be her very last trip? I knew that I could have done more for her as well, but my niece-in-law's treatment of my sister on her first real visit with them was inexcusable.

My sister immigrated to the United States in the 1960s, so more than thirty years have passed. During that time, she never once set foot in her home country. Even when her eldest son, who was educated and married there, found a job in Korea and returned permanently, she did not come. She could have come afterward to visit them, but she did not budge as if she was rooted to American soil. Understandably, she had no compelling reason to visit. Much to her credit, her other children had grown up to be successful adults there. And her eldest son went back to the States so frequently that he didn't give her much chance to miss him. He was in high school when his family moved overseas. As a bilingual perfectly comfortable in both languages, he landed a cushy job in Korea that allowed him to spend three or four months out of the year abroad. My niece-in-law's grumblings that air travel was ruining her husband's health always sounded more like bragging to someone like me, whose children have no ties to the international community. In my family, I am the one who has traveled the most overseas, thanks to my sister. She was the oldest of the five siblings and I the youngest, and the three brothers in the middle all died just before or after their sixtieth birthdays. The remaining two of us naturally became closer despite the distance. We called each other often and the few times she mailed me an airline ticket, I went to stay with her for a month or two. Of course this kind of thing only happened within the past decade, after she became financially better off.

Her return visit after thirty years' absence was fraught with trouble from the very beginning. My nephew's eldest son—the brother of the aforementioned high school senior—was my sister's first grandchild. He was born in the States and moved here during his childhood when his parents relocated. The purpose of my sister's trip to Korea this spring was to attend his wedding. That was her very first and last visit. I had gone to the airport with the other family members, and when she stepped out, we were all stunned. Multicolored quilted coat, sunglasses pushed up above tightly curled permed hair, and sandaled feet with cherry nail polish poking through. This look was more than just outdated for a grandmother who was over seventy years old; it was tacky. Her luggage was just as inconsistent. An enormous duffle bag that was badly stained and held together at the seams by duck tape came out alongside an expensive new Louis Vuitton suitcase that still had the tags on it. That stylish suitcase embellished with understated gold trimmings did much to alleviate our disappointment over her appearance, and instilled hope in our hearts. After all, she was coming home after thirty years to attend her first grandson's wedding, wasn't she? I'm sure my sister didn't have to nag her well-off children to send along gifts for their nephew. The new bag differed qualitatively from the immigration duffle, a sure sign that it was laden with gifts. It might as well have borne a label that said as much. My sister's concerned expression when the luggage was being loaded into the car confirmed our assumptions.

At home, my sister unpacked the duffle bag, but she behaved so strangely with the new bag that no one dared to ask her about it. She got upset with the less-than-careful children, as if they had kicked around a sacred ancestral tablet. Then she shoved the bag into a dark corner, saying that it didn't have much inside. In our eyes, something was not quite right about her. She was acting like an underground dealer handling stolen property. Furthermore, the hopelessly pathetic gifts that she proudly dug out of the duffle bag made us even more curious about the new suitcase. There were more than twenty bags of instant coffee and even more tubes of cheap, made-in-Taiwan lipsticks. The common Lancôme pressed powder compacts were among her more expensive gifts, but there were only a few. The rest of the duffle contained her clothes, which were so gaudy and cheap that I was embarrassed for her. Oblivious to what was going on, my sister was busy trying to allocate the bags of coffee to everyone she could remember, including her in-law's second cousin. My eyes met my niece-in-law's.

"My sister's so out of it, eh?"

In a pitiful attempt to lighten the mood, I joked in my imperfect regional dialect. Thirty years ago, people couldn't get enough of anything made in America and a bag of instant coffee was a welcome gift. I guess my sister was unaware that most people these days preferred ground coffee over instant coffee. The change in my niece-in-law's face, from uninterested boredom to a blatant smirk, did not go unnoticed. *Stay quiet and wait a little longer*, I reassured her with my eyes. I was again banking on the new bag. After digging and digging through the bottomless duffle, my sister now resorted to counting off on her fingers to match up the number of gifts with the number of recipients. My niece-in-law excused herself to go to the kitchen to make preparations for a meal. I wondered if she was going to cook up a fifty-dollar corbina fish. Once or twice a year I had the occasion to visit my nephew's family, and they treated me every time with warmth and respect, even when my sister wasn't around. Once, they gave me one whole baked corbina, which they said was the real thing from the town of Younggwang.

As I suspected, the meal was a feast fit for a holiday. Laid on the table were stewed short ribs, stir-fried glass noodles, fried fish fillets, and several kinds of *kimchi*. I knew that my sister could eat all these things to her heart's content in the States, so I pushed the plate of corbina in front of her.

"Elder Sister, have some of this. This is the real thing from Younggwang and costs more than fifty dollars each."

"What? For a small fish like this? That's sinful ... In America ..."

She pushed the plate away, hardly believing her own ears.

"Elder Sister, what they have in America must be a different species altogether. How can you even compare it to Younggwang corbina?"

But she was resolute in her opinion that the fish from America was the real thing and that the ones found in Korea were mass-imported from China. She spoke doggedly about the cheaper cost of living over there compared to here, citing, like a penny-pinching housewife, the exact prices of radish, cabbage, garlic, and other staples. Although this kind of talk was not wholly unusual for someone who had just returned from abroad, my niece-in-law responded with cold, exaggerated apathy. A silent but fierce feud was growing between the two, and I felt obligated to step in as the only person who could. At the risk of making a fool of myself, I tried to change the subject.

"Elder Sister, how come you haven't opened your Louis Vuitton bag? You're waiting for me to leave, aren't you? Don't be mean like that. You have wedding gifts for the new bride in it, am I right? Each of your children must have sent something. Things like that, you should boast about. It makes them look good. Well, you should know that I'm not going anywhere until you show me everything."

"Auntie, were you planning to leave today? Jang-Woo's wedding is only a few days away. Stay here until then. I'm sure you two have a lot of catching up to do. And we'll soon be sending the wedding box to the bride's family, so we need you to properly oversee that, as family elders should." My niece-in-law's face immediately softened into a smile. She was a simpleminded woman. Depending on how you dealt with her, she was easy to please and she rarely harbored hard feelings. She was about to become a mother-in-law herself, getting on in years like us, so she knew how to treat her elders. She and I both had a certain feeling beyond simple curiosity about the new bag. We wanted to get it out in the open. Suddenly, my sister stood up muttering, "Jeez." We didn't have a chance to tell her that she didn't have to get up in the middle of her meal. She returned to the table in a flash, carrying a thick envelope.

"I was going to show this to everyone anyway. Your younger brother and sisters sent sizeable sums. They wanted to buy the newlyweds one gift each, but I suggested that they give cash instead. Money's the best gift, right? They weren't sure how much to give, so I decided on the amount: a thousand dollars each. I'm sure they thought it was daylight robbery. It wasn't easy for them because they're so Americanized now. Americans are so frugal, you know. Most wouldn't shell out that much even for their own children. But they're good kids, you see. They put up the money without a single complaint."

My sister had three more children living in the States, so that would add up to three thousand dollars. From what I knew about her children, they wouldn't have spent more than a thousand dollars each on actual gifts. I knew from my visits to the States that all of my sister's children lived in big, fancy houses. They said, however, that their homes and even their college educations were financed by loans. I guess living beyond your means like a hollow rice cracker is the same, whether here or there. Jang-Woo was a nephew in name only, for they'd never had a chance to really get to know him. For my sister to get them to cough up that much money must have been nothing short of extortion. She had every right to be triumphant.

I think my niece-in-law agreed. Oh no, they over-extended themselves, she fretted, but she was obviously pleased. But then, what was in the bag? Curiosity, diverted by the envelope, resurfaced. The more my sister tried to banish the bag to a dark corner of the room, the more it seemed like we had a dubious guest in our midst. I hated feeling uneasy like that. I could tell my niece-in-law felt the same way, and I felt awful for her.

After the envelope made its grand entrance, everyone seemed to have lost their appetites. Only my sister ate slowly and obstinately to the bitter end, fiddling with the side dish plates as if unsatisfied with the food in front of her. I glanced nervously around the table, apologetic on behalf of my sister, who was still holding onto her spoon. I don't know why I felt so apologetic but this irrational feeling compelled me to say more.

"Elder Sister, stop eating now. You've had enough, so let's unpack your other luggage. I'm dying of curiosity."

"I unpacked everything, didn't you see? I even dragged out the envelope from the pouch all the way at the bottom of the bag and made the big announcement. What more do you want to see?" she asked accusingly, putting her utensil down slowly.

"You didn't unpack your new suitcase."

"There's nothing in it, really."

"But it can't be empty."

"No, no, I don't mean that. I don't have anything more from America, you see." Her words trailed off, and she sounded coy again, like a dealer of stolen goods.

"Oh, c'mon. You think we're still crazy for American goods here? Who cares if it's from America or from China? We just want to know what you're guarding with so much care."

"If you really want to see, then all right."

She got up from the table and headed straight to her room. I was beginning to get upset, as if I'd unwittingly conspired in a nasty scheme. This was not my intention. What was purely playful curiosity had somehow turned serious. Inwardly, I began blaming my nephew and niece for the unpleasant atmosphere, for holding back their love for a mother who had returned after three decades. I was only caught up in what they were doing. No one asked me to explain, but I felt the need to justify myself.

The spare room had been used to store odds and ends and was cleaned up hastily for my sister. The built-in storage cabinet was cluttered when she opened it. Shoved deep inside, leaning at an angle, was the Louis Vuitton suitcase. She took it out and laid it out in the middle of the room. Encircled by family members, she opened it slowly and painstakingly, fumbling with the clasps. When the bag finally opened, the contents sprang forth. Something resembling the cool breeze of a bamboo forest stirred up and hit our noses. We stepped back, stifling cries of surprise. Beige clothing made of hemp. Before we could mentally assess the surprising contents of the bag, my sister picked up each item, naming it by its traditional title: embroidered silk outerwear, top middle layer, a body blanket, a mattress, a face covering, hand wraps . . . these were traditional dress pieces for the dead.

"Mother, please stop. Please."

My nephew was the first to protest. His wife ran out of the room, covering her face with her hands, and the other family members followed to comfort her. Before I could assess the situation and understand why my niece-in-law needed comforting, I got busy stuffing everything back into the suitcase. First hiding the offending objects from view seemed like a smart thing to do.

"I told them in no uncertain terms that I wanted the whole set," she said shrewdly. She wore a determined expression that was quite out of character. The whole set implied that every piece of formal clothing according to tradition was included. But so what if it was a complete set? And why now, just before her first grandson's wedding? Not worried by all the trouble she had caused, my sister yawned loudly and said that she wanted to go to bed early. After perking up my ears to what was going on outside, I rolled out the plush futon my niece-in-law had prepared for her. Whether or not she knew that she had just become the undisputed black sheep of the family, my sister closed her eyes and fell asleep. My thick-headed sister. I watched her for a moment and left the room. My niece-in-law was practically foaming at the mouth as she fought with someone on the phone. In contrast to her highly agitated voice, the rest of the family sat in ominous silence.

"No? What do you mean, no? If it's not that, then what? Her precious daughters claim they know nothing about this, and now you're telling me that I've got it all wrong? That I've misunderstood? A seventy-something-year-old shows up here with burial clothes, so of course I'm going to think that you sent her here to die. All three of you, you had her go from house to house to work like a maid, and now that your children are grown up and she's getting weaker, you sent her here. What do you take me for, a fool? I know that I'm the eldest daughter-in-law, but if you think that I'll go along with this just because I'm the eldest, you've got another thing coming. Both you and I married into a poor, immigrant family and worked hard to make something of our families. At least you used her, but we left long ago and I never benefited at all from the in-laws. So I have every right to say what I'm saying now. Why do you think we left the States when we had it so good there? My husband had plenty of career opportunities and life would have been easier for me there as a mother and a wife. But I wanted to return to Korea to start over.

Freedom from the in-laws was more important to me, you see. It's not that I don't see where you're coming from. Just when she was becoming a burden, an opportunity presented itself with this trip. I can understand that. If you had just given me a heads up, I wouldn't be this upset. I know that you didn't have the most proper upbringing, but I never thought you were this kind of a person. Even our worst enemy wouldn't have sent along funeral clothes for our family's first wedding. That's what kills me. As for Mother, I can easily ship her back to all of you, but I can't understand why you hate me so much to send these morbid things on the happiest occasion of our lives. Do you think that if you live in the States long enough you can ignore what's right and wrong where the family is concerned? You keep denying everything, and I don't know what you have up your sleeve. But just know that I won't be a sitting duck."

Embarrassed that I was listening, my nephew snatched the phone away from his wife and yelled. "Shut up, woman. Are you out of your mind? Do you know what you're saying in front of the kids?"

"Your mother's sleeping. She must be jetlagged. I planned on spending the night here, but I think I'd better get going." I left their house in a hurry. No one held me back. I was a loved and respected person in my own right, with adorable grandchildren, a devoted son and daughter-in-law, as well as a daughter who was constantly nagging me to live with her. I wouldn't have lost sleep if these fools didn't ask me to stay, but not knowing what was in store for my sister made it difficult for me to leave.

As soon as I got home, I made an international call to the States. Nieces were easier for me to deal with over the phone, so I called my eldest niece who lives in Laguna Beach on the outskirts of Los Angeles. Apparently she had also received a call from my niece-in-law and was aware of what happened. However, she didn't understand what the big deal was.

"My sister-in-law accuses me of sending funeral clothes with Mom, but how could I have known? She left directly from Elder Brother's house in San Francisco. I just sent Mom the gift money and didn't have a chance to see her off in person. Even if I had known, why should I have stopped her? She's free to do what she wants. Maybe she wanted to have the clothes with her just in case something happens to her in Korea. She was probably trying to be helpful to the family in Korea, I bet. Isn't that why people make funeral preparations in advance? She waited and waited for a leap year and almost begged us to get her the clothes. Do you know how expensive the set was? It's a trend among the elderly here to buy their burial clothes during a leap year. Korean-Americans these days are much better off, you know, so they can afford things like this. At first, I didn't want to burden others so I bought her a set myself because it wasn't as expensive as I thought. I got her something similar to what everyone else gets, but Mother was not pleased because she believed that the fabric was imported from China. She insisted on Korean-made linen from Andong. Considering what she means to us, how could we have refused her one wish? So I gave away the set I bought, and we chipped in to buy her the most expensive Andong-made set. Now do you see why she's so attached to it? So why is everyone overreacting? Auntie, you know how hot L.A. is. But sometimes you see older women with fur coats on at the first sign of a chill. At that age, they want to show off what they have. It's cute. It's the same with Mom's burial clothes, so why can't we just take it for what it is?"

After hearing her, I began to doubt that there was any conspiracy behind my sister's bringing her burial clothes. Perhaps my niece-in-law's reaction was based solely on the morbid nature of what it represented, especially in contrast to a celebratory occasion like a wedding. But how could I explain the age-old taboo hovering over us to my niece, who could equate fur coats with burial clothes? Before hanging up, I told my niece that I didn't think her mother should stay here long.

The mayhem over my sister's burial clothes did not end there. Within a few days, I was asked to come over to see the wedding gifts that arrived from the bride's family. Because most of the groom's extended family resided overseas, the wedding gifts were to be given to immediate family members. Still, the bride's family was gracious enough to send gifts for my sister and me. We both received beautiful silk fabric. Mine was enough to make a traditional *hanbok* only and she was given extra fabric for a matching outer garment. I was pleased because the difference in the value of our gifts was an appropriate one. I also liked the fact that hers was an opulent pastel pink, and mine a more subdued gold. Gushing over our new in-laws' good taste, I unfolded the silk fabric and draped it over my sister's shoulder. My sister suddenly broke into a broad smile and got up in front of the full-length mirror. Then she rolled out the silk from her shoulder down to her toes. Elegant pleats stretched out before us, silky ripples that seemed to whisper sweetly and melt away the recent troubles that burdened our hearts. The mirror reflected my sister's blissful expression, but what came out of her mouth was astonishing.

"This would make fine burial clothes, wouldn't it?"

She smiled vaguely, baring her white teeth and quietly asking for our affirmation. Even I was shocked by what she'd said, so it's no wonder that my niece-in-law exploded in anger. I had hoped to join in on the reconciliatory atmosphere made possible by the wedding gifts and finally spend the night there with my sister. But with the turn of events, I quickly abandoned the idea and left in a hurry, like someone being chased. My niece-in-law saw me off with my share of the fabric and an envelope containing money for custom tailoring. Patting her shoulder, I asked her to be patient with my sister, who may not have been completely of sound mind.

"I talked to my nieces and nephew in America, and they have absolutely no intention of dumping their mother on you. Not only are they completely devoted to her, she receives enough pension and medical benefits to live comfortably. I know something about that too—America is a good country for old people. One thing that's certain is that she didn't come here to die, so please don't worry. Be good to her while she's here, though. After the wedding, I'll talk her into not staying here too long."

I consoled her the best I could. Still, she must have been fed up with burial clothes because she never did make a dress for her with the fabric. My sister wore a jade-colored *hanbok* to the wedding. After the wedding, my sister spent another month at her son's without any trouble. Considering what my sister did for me in the States, I should have returned the favor by inviting her to our house for an extended stay and taking her on short trips to the countryside with my daughter. But I was hesitant to do so. I was afraid that my sister, who had upset her own daughter-in-law, could easily do the same with my daughter. During her stay, my niece-in-law became a totally different person, sullen and ill-tempered. It was obvious to everyone that my sister did nothing to endear herself to her daughter-in-law.

Another incident occurred that proved to be the last straw and I had to take it upon myself to ship my sister off like an unwanted piece of luggage. Although it had nothing to do with burial clothes, it was far spookier. After receiving an urgent call from my niece-in-law one day, I rushed over there. I found my sister sitting amid scattered petals of fabric. She must have been snipping away all night to go through all of the pink silk fabric she'd received. The petal snippets were shockingly uniform in size and shape, making her act even more eerie. She looked at me with the same pallid smile she had when she was trying on the fabric the other day. "Elder Sister, what are you doing?" I called out frantically and rushed over to her. When I embraced her, I half expected her to resist me wildly in her madness. Instead, her body was as light as charcoal ash. I stepped back in surprise, as if I had just embraced a gust of wind.

"Am I still the only one to blame," my niece-in-law demanded, glaring at me. I felt nothing but sheer hatred for her at that moment, however I had no choice but to take her side. That meant being the one to send my sister back. That task didn't turn out to be so difficult. Again, I called the niece with whom I felt the most comfortable and said that her mother wanted to return. I told her that she'd be on a plane on such and such a date and time. "Sure, Auntie," she said, and that was it. Because I took care of it, the arrangements were made quickly and without complications. If I had left it up to my niece-in-law, I'm sure more unpleasant words would have been exchanged.

Unlike the day she arrived, my sister showed up at the airport glowing with understated sophistication. She was wearing the jade *hanbok* from the wedding and even embroidered socks and rubber clogs to match. Her hair, which had grown out during her stay, was neatly tied up into a bun. The traditional outfit and the up-do perfectly suited her petite frame and flat shoulders. Her luggage, too, had changed. The battered duffle bag was gone and new, proper suitcases stood in its place next to the Louis Vuitton bag. Two new suitcases meant that there were enough gifts for the relatives back in America. I don't know about sibling love, but my niece-in-law certainly had enough pride to fill those suitcases.

"They say life is good in America, but Korea mustn't be too bad, especially for old folks. Look how in just a few months your mother is oozing with elegance and charm." I beamed, directing intentional praise and flattery to my niece-in-law. It was true that I was grateful to her for putting up with such a difficult mother-in-law all this time and sending her off in style like this. In front of the departure gate, it was nice to see that people were hugging and rubbing cheeks like Westerners. Like them, I embraced my sister. She had plenty of family members seeing her off, but I was the only one among the whole entourage who could embrace her like this. I was the only one who was truly sad to see her go. A pang of sorrow brought tears to my eyes, but my sister did not react at all.

My niece-in-law thought that she had confiscated all of the petal snippets—a whole basketful to be exact—but the night before when she was helping to pack, she found more scattered among the layers of burial clothes in the Louis Vuitton bag. This was her final spiteful remark about her mother-in-law, whispered in my ear as we left the airport.

"So what did you do?" I asked breathlessly.

"What could I have done? I just ignored it."

"Good thing you did," I said, rubbing my chest in relief. Although my nephew offered me a ride, I flatly rejected him and headed toward the bus station. I didn't want to look at my niece-in-law any longer than I had to. Her revulsion and unforgiving attitude to my sister's eccentric behavior were despicable to me.

How could I have known that my sister would die just two months after that? I guess two months could be considered a long time. Sending her off like that and not contacting her once during that whole time. It wasn't that I was uninterested in how she was doing. It was just easier for me to wait for communication from her side. I was afraid of hearing bad news that I could do absolutely nothing about; I also wanted to take the easy way out by interpreting no news as good news.

My eldest niece picked up my sister from the airport, so I suppose she was the one who cared for her until the end. When I had visited the States, my eldest niece was so kind and generous to me, and she was very well off so I could stay at her home in comfort. I was told that she lived in one of the most expensive neighborhoods in America, probably comparable to one of those hilltop houses in Korea with impeccably landscaped gardens. The lower yard of her house was almost an acre in size and led straight to a beach. When you stand at the edge of that vast yard, you can see white waves smashing against the cliff like vicious predators attacking helpless prey. I had once asked my sister if she thought the fierce waves were scary, and she said there was nothing scary about the Pacific Ocean. Why wouldn't it be scary just because it's the Pacific Ocean? I never got to ask. Another day, we took a walk around the neighborhood. My, oh my. Vibrant flowers everywhere in full, luscious bloom—the place was as impressive as any botanical garden. Yellow wild flowers blooming in empty fields or peeking through cliff walls looked like oilseed rape flowers in season, but I was told that they were wild mustard flowers. My sister pointed out each of the houses and the people living in them—famous movie stars, rich lawyers, and retired government officials. Good Lord, how successful were Kyung-Ae and her husband? Amused by my bewilderment, my sister commented that not all of the Koreans in that neighborhood were so privileged. "That house over there with four dogs and two swimming pools belongs to so and so, who is hiding from creditors. That mansion with construction work going on over there belongs to the pachinko kingpin who you read about in the papers a few years ago." She continued to show off her knowledge of the area and its people. In keeping with the posh neighborhood, the road we were on looped around leisurely like the smooth back of a slithery serpent. Cars rarely passed by. My sister seemed so full of vigor that day, but the pilgrimage proved to be a strenuous one for both of us as we moaned with aches and pains at home that night.

We walked around all day but how come we never came across a single neighbor or a passerby on foot? Did the people my sister talked about really live in those houses that she pointed out? I don't know why I suddenly started having these doubts after hearing the news of her death. Just when I was thinking that my nephew must have returned from his mother's funeral, he called me. It was unusual for him to call me directly without going through his wife. He said that this was his first day back at the office and that he naturally thought of me. He wanted to send a car over so that I could meet him for lunch. I didn't say no, figuring that he needed a kind ear more than a lunch companion. From my years of living I know that sisters come to resemble one another more and more with age. I suppose that such a resemblance can alleviate the pain of loss at times like this.

Given the warm welcome I received, my nephew seemed to be a regular at the upscale Japanese restaurant. He was waiting for me in a private room. He greeted me warmly by grasping both of my hands—a show of affection he would never have allowed in front of his wife. Thin slices of high-grade beef infused with the flavors of various vegetables boiled away in a stew pot. Tender morsels melted in my mouth, but my appetite failed me. My nephew didn't eat much either, favoring sips of his rice wine over the broth.

"She died at a home, you know. One of those homes for the elderly who are not all there mentally. I've heard that many of those folks live longer than their peers. I was so angry and frustrated about Mother passing away so suddenly at a place like that, that I gave Kyung-Ae a hard time. Then after the funeral, she told me something. Why is it that she knew this and I didn't? What makes me sadder, Auntie, is that even if I had known everything about Mother, nothing would have changed."

Unlike his usual reserved self, my nephew continued to chat away. Drifting with the rhythm of his voice, I imagined that I was sitting across from my sister instead of my nephew, listening to her story:

I went to America in the 1960s so it was a time when Korea was still very poor. My husband's older brother was the first to immigrate to the States after failing in his business. His wife's sister was married to an American so that's how they ended up there. After only a few years, my husband's brother was back on his feet and doing well. He used to send a hundred dollars for my mother-in-law's birthday. At that time, a hundred dollars went a long way; it was more than enough to throw an extravagant party. My mother-in-law began boasting about her son's success overseas, and my husband grew increasingly tired of his workaday life. What he felt was a sense of failure more than dissatisfaction. He was at an age where your fate was pretty much sealed in Korean society. One's mid-forties was the time when those who would get ahead already had and those who wouldn't had already been passed up. The fact that he graduated from one of the elite schools made him feel worse. His mediocre job paled in comparison to the successful careers of his classmates. He habitually threatened, "I'm going to quit this damn job!" but the sad truth was that no one was begging him to stay. The glory tales from his brother made my husband trivialize his life even more. He saw himself as a victim, pushed aside and marginalized by unseen forces. American society, where justice and principles prevailed, where sweat resulted in just rewards—that was the ocean he was meant to swim in. He wasn't a particularly naïve person who believed everything he heard. But those were the times when frustration with social ills boiled over, and escaping to another country was a fantasy everyone entertained at least once in their lives. Hopping on a plane to leave their old life behind was an immediate step up in status far more enviable than any upward career move.

My husband persisted in nurturing this dream, and our family finally embarked on such a journey. My mother-in-law had recently passed away, freeing us even more from ties to our home country. There were six of us. A big family. My husband's brother was running a restaurant in Los Angeles with his then divorced sister-in-law. As a traditional Korean restaurant catering to the immigrant Korean community, the place reeked of *kimchi*, fish sauce and other smells worse than any dingy food joint in rural Korea. Displaced Korean customers hungry for home cooking and nostalgic for those smells frequented the restaurant, but we, who longed for new experiences in a foreign land, felt nothing but disgust. My husband took it the worst. When his sister-in-law wished to run her own business, his brother offered him her position. Having diligently studied English in hopes of starting a new life in America, my husband would have turned his nose up at any job, no matter how lucrative, where only Korean was spoken all day long. While he was trying relentlessly to get his foot in the door of mainstream white society, he whittled away our moderate savings. Once the relationship between my husband and his brother turned sour, I could no longer work at the restaurant either. I was left jobless, worrying about my children's futures. My brother-in-law's pride and joy came not from his job but from his children attending prestigious schools. Work like a dog and spend like a king, he always used to say. We, on the other hand, may have ended up raising our children like dogs thanks to my husband's inflated ego. One piece of advice I got from those around us was that even if my husband found a decent job, I would have to work also to make ends meet in this society. And those concerned friends referred me to various part-time jobs. But I never lasted long at any place. Unlike my husband, the extent of my English was only a few words I'd learned in high school. To make matters worse, my timid personality prevented me from ever opening my mouth. I dreaded walking into a home to cook and clean for a family I couldn't communicate with. As an immigrant minority, dealing with white people was far more difficult for me than dealing with an overbearing boss. The one-on-one interaction with foreigners these jobs required proved to be too stressful for a shy person like me.

The first real full-time job I had was at a frozen food company. My job involved sorting out frozen shrimps according to size and packaging them. The weekly pay was proportionate to worker output, and among all my colleagues, I earned the least. Of course, that was because I was the slowest worker. But I liked my job. I liked the fact that I earned as much as I worked, and I also liked that I had colleagues. Most of my colleagues were heavyset Mexican women. They were a jovial, friendly bunch, and they were much less intimidating than the whites. Interestingly, I could better understand English spoken by Mexicans than by whites.

One day, I was given an office job. It was simple enough work, recording the incoming and outgoing inventory. But the pay was much better and I was spared from the hard labor that left my hands painfully frozen and chapped. How such an unexpected windfall fell into the lap of the newest and the slowest worker was a mystery to me. I soon found out the reason. A supermarket returned a large quantity of our shrimp they had ordered, claiming that different sized shrimps were mixed together in the packages. On each package, there is a special indicator that shows the worker responsible for putting it together, and a close inspection revealed that I was the only honest worker who had sorted the shrimps correctly. Thus, I had rightfully earned the promotion, but I still could not shake off my feeling of guilt for being promoted. "I'm sorry," were my most frequently uttered words to the company president, the inspectors, my colleagues. I was humble to anyone and everyone, hoping to preempt jealousy and resentment. Albeit exaggerated, my humility was not feigned, as I truly felt bad about what happened. Gradually, people began jeering at me. I don't know who ratted on me about what, but I was soon relegated to a room with a scary machine that ground up fish whole, including the bones. Cleaning that gigantic machine was extremely laborious work, and I heard that a worker had once lost an arm when he operated it incorrectly. Being of faint heart, I quit my job. One lesson I learned from this experience was that I shouldn't automatically assume a subservient mindset. Another thing I gained from that job was a tip given to me by a Mexican colleague about a trustworthy job referral agency that was run by a Japanese person. I was quite fluent in Japanese; my heart swelled with hope that I could improve my situation since I spoke Japanese.

I was not wrong to hope. The director of the agency was a middle-aged Japanese woman. Her speaking to me in the sprightly tone characteristic of the Japanese language was in itself a welcome relief, and what's more, she showed genuine interest in getting to know me. She encouraged me to talk, and talk I did, having yearned to speak freely for so long. She graciously smiled at my comments, agreed with me occasionally, and asked appropriate questions. She gently probed me about my job skills and expectations, making me wish that I had come better prepared with marketable skills. Because of our conversations, I began thinking for the first time about what I wanted to do and what I would be good at. For an unskilled, desperate job-seeker ready to jump at the first offer of a paid position, this privilege gave me a new kind of happiness. I didn't have a college degree, and the high school I went to was known only for producing prospective housewives. I never worked prior to coming to the States. All this I confessed at length to the director. While talking about my past, I reminisced that sewing was my favorite class in school. During those years, most girls never dreamed of advancing beyond high school, and the curriculum reflected their practical need for cooking, sewing, proper etiquette, and other domestic skills. Dressmaking was one such class, and it was immensely popular among the students because the teacher was a modern, fashionable woman, rare for the times. We were also fortunate to have been provided with quality sewing machines. Under her tutelage, we not only practiced stitching but also learned all of the important basic skills such as measuring, cutting patterns, and producing unique outfits from those patterns. What I learned from the class proved to be so useful time after time that the sewing notes were one of the first things I took with me when I got married. Throughout the years, I rarely relied on store-bought dresses for my daughters.

My sharing the stories of my past had more to do with unleashing the suppressed need for conversation than consulting her about a job. We were similar in age and shared a language with which I could express the subtleties of my feelings. I felt a connection from the very beginning. I told her that job hunting aside, I would like to visit her occasionally. Before this, I had never been that bold with anyone. But I think she never lost sight of her professional objectives while conversing with me. She soon matched me up with a dressmaking job. Run by a French woman, the boutique sold custom tailored clothing to a few select clients. The pay was high, and what I earned at the frozen food company was incomparable. Worried that the director had overestimated my skills, I meant to politely decline the job offer. But when I went to see her, she happened to be very busy that day and handed me off to the person who came to take me to the shop. Thus, I was thrust into my new job without further ado.

The boutique was located in a clean, quiet street behind a residential area where many Japanese lived. Perhaps because I was referred to a French boutique by a Japanese woman, the place felt like the embodiment of an unexpected friendship between the two countries. There, everything appeared larger than life, and even the obsessive-compulsive cleanliness impressed me. Although there was no window display visible from the outside, a glass case presented itself upon entering through heavy doors like the ones seen in European cathedrals. Inside the display case, sad but dignified-looking mannequins were posing elegantly in stances of greeting, wearing abundantly pleated dresses made of satin, chiffon, and other costly fabrics. Past this small reception area was the French woman's office, which was brightly lit and efficiently organized. Her face, gaunt and devoid of any wrinkles, did not give away her age. The most striking thing about her was her thickly painted lips that made her look like she was biting down on a mouthful of orange poppy petals. Adjacent to her office was a workroom full of sewing machines operated by Arab men. I never heard the French woman and the Arab tailors converse. She spoke to me in simple English and sometimes in Japanese. Whichever language she chose, she always spoke in a barely audible whisper, so it was easier to intuitively sense what she was saying instead of trying to grasp her every word. In fact, there was very little need for words. Unlike the silence imposed upon me since I'd come to America, I was at peace with this kind of silence; it was more of a dispersed stillness rather than a forced detachment. My job at the boutique was cutting the fabric according to the patterns given to me by the French woman. As I was taught by my high school teacher, I cut the front and back or left and right sides by facing the armholes the opposite way. Although this was a common practice for minimizing yardage for solid fabrics, the French woman thought it was very clever of me. I could tell that she was beginning to like and trust me more and more. Although my husband was still in the doldrums, I took comfort in the fact that I had found meaningful work all by myself, averting any immediate financial crisis and gaining a foothold as immigrants in this country.

We were never short of work at the shop, but I never came into contact with any of the clients. Occasionally, I saw people whom I thought were clients, but they always turned out to be intermediaries. It was unbelievable to me that even in America there was an exclusive upper echelon of society who purchased custom clothing by ordering over the phone or by sending hired help. I conjured up images of these high-class clients based on the foreign horror novels I'd read as a schoolgirl. In one such novel set in the Middle Ages, a powerful and rich lord sequesters a chosen group of aristocrats in a castle to cut themselves off from the world overrun by the bubonic plague. Although inside a tightly sealed environment that a needle, or even time itself, cannot penetrate, they continue to live in fear. To ease their fears, they hold festive galas night after night. On one such night, they are astonished to find a mysterious guest mingling among them. To their horror, the mystery guest was no other than the plague incarnate, and the attendees at the ball die off one by one. The dresses made at our boutique were exactly the kind suitable for pompous aristocrats in such stories.

More than the intricate, flowing dresses that the French woman patterned, I was fond of her other creations—silk slippers embroidered with fake pearls, veils that showed off the exquisite nature of French tulle, and voluptuous corsages cut from fabric scraps by long, shiny shears. I used to silently watch her work with an expression of intense concentration, almost intoxication. Dresses made from black, silver, or purple fabrics were adorned on one side of the chest with corsages. Although made in similar drab colors, a corsage could imbue an impractical, lifeless dress with surprising vitality. Its seductive charm came from the undeniable feeling that it was full of vigor, that it might suddenly detach itself and jump off the dress. Perhaps the French woman was playing jokes on the somber dresses that she completed. I used to watch her put the final touch of mischief on the dresses with an entranced expression on her face and could not help but think that she wore the same expression when painting her lips every morning. The image of her wan face without the orange lipstick horrified me.

Because I felt that I had the easiest job at the boutique, I tried to compensate by staying late and cleaning up the store after everyone else had left. Darn guilt. It always followed me wherever I went. Before long, I was entrusted with a key to open and close the shop. Alone in the French woman's immaculate office and standing in front of a huge mirror holding my beating heart, I tried on the dresses that hadn't been picked up yet by their rightful owners. I couldn't resist the temptation of forbidden pleasure and the thrill of doing something wrong. Like a little girl trying on her mother's clothes, the dresses tailored for Caucasian women hung like a tent on my small frame. But the luscious feel of the fabric and the budding corsage on my bosom teased out the hidden temptress from the depths of my soul. Oh, how I loved that time of the day when all my senses came alive! It was a time set aside for me to savor long forgotten emotions—gentle sweetness, the anxiety of imminent misfortune, and the impatience of restless passion.

The boutique was apparently far more reputable than I had first thought. One day, a TV station crew barged in with all their oversized equipment. I was the only one surprised, for everyone else seemed to be expecting them. Lights glared, cords were plugged in, and the staff moved microphones and cameras while talking in loud voices. They spoke in English, of course. I understood what they were saying, but the ruckus they were creating made me anxious because it threatened the silence I had relished there for so long. One of the crew members was Asian. He had a pleasant, familiar face that made me wonder if he was a Korean. When I initiated conversation in Korean, he shrugged his shoulders with his palms facing up, gesturing that he didn't understand. He returned to work indifferently, but I continued to observe him. When one of the machines he was handling refused to comply, I heard him curse in Japanese. He may not have spoken Korean, but I could speak Japanese. I waited for him to finish what he was doing and approached him again in Japanese. This time, he responded enthusiastically. It was a mistake to ask him if the boutique was famous enough to be aired on television. I found out from him that the station was doing a feature on unusual jobs and that the French woman was renowned for making burial clothes for upscale clients. What I had tried on alone in the store were burial clothes. I quit my job that day. I knew that I couldn't hope to land another cushy job like this one, but I could no longer be a part of that boutique. I never did find another job like that one and suffered through countless menial labor jobs until my husband secured a good job for himself. But I have never once regretted my decision to quit. And I never went back to the referral agency.

I'm reminded of the story of a young woman wasting away after discovering that the man she was sleeping with was a skeleton. I know that the past is irreversible. My job didn't require me to come in direct contact with dead bodies, so arguably I did a dumb thing by quitting a perfectly good job. It was beyond my power, however, to shake off the stigma associated with corpses ingrained in me by years of culture and tradition.

A Ball-playing Woman

From the bus terminal, Aran walked past her home toward the sculpture park. Her home was too small at times like this when she needed to loosen the knot in her chest and calm her nerves. What the villagers called the sculpture park was simply an open patch of grassland. It was said that a certain sculptor developed the surrounding farmland many years ago by setting up a teahouse and bringing in three-dimensional artwork to the open area. There was no longer any trace of the teahouse, but scattered pieces of sculpture still remained. The sculptor was believed to be dead or to have immigrated overseas, and the sculpture pieces stood abandoned in their grotesque or severely damaged form. When Aran visited the park, she often wondered whether the sculptor had rented the land or simply taken over idle space.

Perhaps there is such a thing as destiny even for land. Despite its proximity to the city and convenient access to public transportation, the area failed to appreciate in value. Originally a wasteland, the neighborhood was comprised of residents displaced by development projects. They were brought here and dumped like garbage, with less than four hundred square feet allotted to each family. With such an inauspicious beginning, the area never grew to its full potential, and instead reached its peak with rental apartments and townhouses. Both were low-income housing with a little more than four-hundred square feet of living space. Aran lived in a multiplex, the first home she ever owned, located at the edge of the neighborhood. Although her home was far from the bus terminal, it had a wide open view of the park.

The park didn't have a single bench, and the sculpture ruins scattered here and there served as makeshift seats. A marker indicating the artist's name and an explanation of the work could sometimes be found, but it was rare for it to match the piece actually displayed. Worse, a marker left without an artwork was like a tombstone standing on an empty grave, sad and ridiculous at the same time. Moreover, not a single marker was modest in the explanation it offered.

"This work of art incorporates the use of tin. What is tin? It is what humans have obtained from Mother Earth using fire. The intimate yet tense interrelationship among these three forces— humans, earth, and fire—makes my soul tremble. I don't believe creative impulse can exist without the trembling of the soul."

This was typical. Such arrogance . . . Aran stopped to read the sign next to a heap of metal and mumbled her disapproval. At the end of the metal heap resembling congealed lava, she found a spot as flat as a millstone and sat down. She rolled up her blouse sleeves, revealing milky forearms marred by three cigarette burn marks left by Hun. The burn spots had puffed up at first into cherry-red blisters but quickly shriveled into tawny welts. Still, no one would mistake them as anything other than burn marks. Aran didn't smoke often. Whenever the squalor of life got the better of her, making her vacillate between hope and hopelessness, she reached for a cigarette. The attraction was not the bittersweet flavor of nicotine; it was the captivating image of Miss Kim with a cigarette between her fingers. Miss Kim was a tenant in Aran's home who worked as a bookkeeper for a hotel coffee shop in the surburbs. Money, money, money—that was all that Miss Kim talked about and cared about. And it was no wonder, because she earned little but had plenty to spend on; she had nobody to mooch off, but several family members to support.

Miss Kim never succeeded in quitting smoking even though she lived in constant fear of her manager sniffing her out and firing her on the spot. After hours of abstinence at work, she would come home in the evening to relish a leisurely puff. Aran once asked if the cigarette tasted as good as she made it seem, and Miss Kim answered that she smoked not for the taste but for the respite it provided from her crappy life.

"Whoa, can you really get that from smoking? Can I try it, too?"

Aran bummed many a cigarette this way, but she only succeeded in imitating Miss Kim's gestures, not in tasting any respite. On the day she discovered that Hun had failed the bar exam for the fourth time, Aran felt truly crappy. So she fished out Miss Kim's cigarettes and smoked three in a row, clouding up the tiny common area that served as both a living room and kitchen. That's when Hun walked in and snatched the lit cigarette from her hand. He pressed the burning stick into her forearm, furious with her for moping around when he had failed only four times. Aran was thirty years old. It wasn't *only* four times to her. What Hun sought to crush, besides the impatience of a thirty-year-old, was the body of a thirty-year-old. Like a doting grandparent tending to his beaten and bruised grandchild, he blew on the raw burn spots and began slowly but expertly caressing her. Her body broke down, like an overripe peach releasing its sweetness in full self-abandonment. She continued to cling to him afterward and had to further endure his ridicule that she was a desperate, oversexed old maid. But Hun could not have been more clueless as to what she was desperately clinging to. It wasn't sex; it was the last ray of hope growing ever so faint and the small possibility inching beyond her grasp.

At work, it was a mystery why a pretty girl like Aran was still single. There were no more male coworkers drooling over her because all of them had now become husbands and fathers. Less attractive girls who were overshadowed by Aran had all managed to find their Mr. Right. Some of them left the company after marrying while others continued to show up at work with their pregnant bellies proudly jutting out. Aran knew as clear as day how laughable her beauty was to them. On top of her good-for-nothing beauty, she was poor. And for her to stand her ground, unperturbed, at the same company until age thirty was due to her firm belief that one day she would be the object of everyone's envy and praise. She was determined to marry a successful guy—a guy who had passed the bar with flying colors for instance—in front of her colleagues at this very job. What Aran had clung to was not Hun's tired body; it was the hope that one day, oh, someday, a butterfly would emerge from the cocoon and spread its wings.

Son of a bitch . . . that son of a bitch . . . Aran screamed into the void with an explosiveness that surprised even herself. Rolling down her sleeves, she realized that she would have to switch to the short-sleeve uniform in a few days. Instead of sighing with worry, Aran sniggered. It would be no big deal to quit her job before then. From now on, she didn't have to put up with anything. Not a thing. Telling the son of a bitch that he was a son of a bitch. Walking away from a job that led nowhere for women after years of devotion and hard work. Refusing to share five hundred square feet of living space. Could all this be a mere dream? She wanted to share this surreal freedom with someone so that it wouldn't blow away like a puff of smoke. But not Miss Kim. Miss Kim had enrolled in a ten-million-won savings plan several times, but her incessant need for cash always forced her to cancel before the maturity date. For Miss Kim, ten million won was an amount that she could only dream about having just once in her lifetime. Wouldn't talking about an amount more than thirty times that be cruel to her? It would be nothing short of torture. And when tortured, the human reflex is to fight back in self-defense. Aran had no intention of exposing her good fortune to that kind of ill will. But it was good to have thought of Miss Kim. Try as she might, ten million won was an amount that lay beyond Miss Kim's reach. Thirty-five times that—this calculation gave Aran a realistic understanding of her windfall. Her sense of self swelling up like a balloon, she floated up from the edge of the disfigured sculpture that had been the subject of an absurd pseudo-philosophy. Aran felt like she was walking on air. True, that feeling was elation, but it was also anxiety at the same time.

"Pain of Existence" was the title of a piece now long gone but for a signpost stuck in the ground. So pompous . . . She was about to pass by it with scorn but suddenly stopped as if her feet were glued to the ground. She remembered something about the title. She must have seen it around the same time last year because the park was filled with the most beautiful colors back then also. After failing the bar for the third time, Hun had left on a trip to let off some steam with the money she had given him. She hadn't heard from him after a few days, so she called the Exam Village without any success in locating him. It was a beautiful weekend, so she headed toward the sculpture park to walk off her despair. That was the day she saw the "Pain of Existence" signpost standing here without any accompanying artwork. On that day also, Aran had scoffed at the title, thinking that it was only a cheap play on words compared to the real heartache and headache that she actually felt. From a distance, a ball rolled toward Aran. Behind it, a couple was laughing and clapping their hands. They were young parents of a waddling toddler. The ball that the toddler had kicked was rolling down a gentle slope, but the parents perhaps believed that their child had powered that ball. They were laughing out loud and clapping as the child ran after the rolling ball. The white rubber ball was much larger than a baseball, large enough to be held with both hands. Although an ordinary plaything, a ball like that was becoming an increasing rarity in those days. Aran quietly watched its movement, strangely mesmerized. The starting point of that ball's momentum was not the boy's foot but Aran's childhood. Facing the ball rolling in from her childhood, Aran tensed up with anticipation.

It must have been Children's Day. The neighborhood was filled with laughter as even the shantytown kids had gotten at least one inexpensive gift. Aran had picked out a rubber ball as her gift. Her mother came home late the night before and, feeling bad about not having bought a gift, she took Aran to a nearby stationery store. In addition to school supplies, the store was well stocked with various toys in preparation for Children's Day, but most of it was cheap knickknacks sellable only in a poor neighborhood. Aran picked out a rubber ball that was the cheapest of the cheap toys. Dismayed by her modesty, her mother urged her to pick out another toy like a doll, but Aran shook her head in refusal. She didn't choose the ball out of consideration for her mother's pocketbook. She chose it because that was what she really wanted. She played with the ball for many days until it eventually became deflated, but during that time she proved herself to be quite adroit with it. She could go around the whole block keeping the ball tossed in the air with one hand. In front of the other neighborhood kids, she dribbled the ball while circling her leg over the top. A few of the kids thought they could perform the same stunt, but no one was able to do what she did with such ease. No matter where the ball was thrown, bounced, or rolled, it always returned to Aran. When that white ball finally lost its bounce, Aran got tired of playing with it.

Aran expected the ball that the toddler had kicked to roll directly toward her as if obeying a basic law of physics, like a metal chip being pulled by a magnet. The ball, however, suddenly disappeared from sight. The child stopped running and burst into tears. The parents, their laughter dissipating in the wind, ran toward their crying child. "Don't worry, I'll find it for you." After assuring the kid, Aran combed the grass patch where the ball had vanished. Near the "Pain of Existence" signpost, there were two big holes in the ground, probably made when the sculpture was moved or stolen. She couldn't see inside the hole with her naked eye in bright sunlight, so she reached her hand in. It was so deep that only after putting in her whole arm up to the shoulder could Aran feel the smooth, round firmness. She was in luck because she found the ball in the first hole. "I found it! Hold on just a minute, I'll get it out for you," she said without looking at the kid who had stopped crying in the meantime. While continuing to yell out reassuring words, she tried her hardest to get the ball out. This was easier said than done because the diameters of the hole and the ball were almost the same. She could touch the ball but couldn't scoop it out. With her shoulder blade deep inside the hole and only after digging out the dirt around the ball with her fingernails, Aran just managed to pull the ball out. But the kid had not waited for her. Holding onto each parent and swinging between them, he was already quite a distance away. A gentle breeze caressing the child's soft hair and carrying away the parents' happy chatter tickled Aran's cheeks. Blushing with shame and anger, she shoved the ball abandoned by its owner back into the hole. She felt violated and grimy, like the dirt under her fingernails.

The two holes near the "Pain of Existence" sign were there just as before. Was the white rubber ball still in there? Aran dropped to the ground and stuck her arm in one of the holes. Her fingers touched a plastic bag and damp dirt; in the second hole she felt the ball. No longer firm, the ball came out easily without any digging. The ball was in sad shape, covered with a year's worth of dirt, so Aran took it to an outdoor pump that drew underground water. At first, the neighborhood residents had flocked to the pump thinking that it drew mineral spring water, but they abandoned it after the city officials declared the water undrinkable. Aran turned the spigot and water flowed out.

She washed the ball and once its white sheen was uncovered, she tossed it onto the grass. With love from the sun and the earth, the ball regained its bounce, and Aran began nudging it with the tip of her foot. Rolling and spinning the ball freely on the bright green grass, Aran felt exhilaration spread through the veins of her body all the way down to her toes. It was an unexpected but absolute pleasure. She wasn't handling the ball; she became one with it. From the claustrophobic darkness of binding fate, she stepped out into the open sunlight and basked in it. Connecting with the ball was helping her get used to her unfettered freedom. Her new, dream-like reality definitely needed some getting used to.

It was about a month ago that she read in the newspaper about Chairman Jin Hyukboo's death and about a week ago that she received a phone call from his eldest son, Junggi. Aran's first thought in hearing the news about the deceased was something along the lines of, how fortunate that her mother had passed away first. If she were alive, she would have insisted on Aran joining the Jins to properly mourn his death, no matter how much she might be mistreated. When she was a young child less than ten years of age, Aran was forced by her mother to attend the well-publicized seventieth birthday party for Chairman Jin. The abuse Aran got from his family that day remained a painful memory for many years. It also afforded Aran a convenient and effective way to defy her mother until the day she died. Whenever they got into an argument, Aran cited the details of the humiliation she endured that day as a result of blindly following her wishes. There was one thing, however, that she never mentioned during those fights: how it felt to be hugged by her father. The party was in full swing and Aran had walked straight up to the seat of honor. It was neither courage nor audacity that enabled Aran to do this; it was the powerlessness she felt in acting out the part of her mother's puppet.

"How dare she! Who does she think she is?"

She was soon bombarded by the angry stares of the outraged members of his immediate family. Her lips twitched as she suppressed a sob. Pushing others aside, Chairman Jin rushed to her and declared that she was just a little girl who had done nothing wrong. He embraced her. Aran was just tall enough at that time for her ear to rest on the old man's chest. Listening to his pulse twittering like a small bird, Aran instinctively understood that this elderly gentleman was important in protecting her from all kinds of abuse from other people. Still embracing her in his bosom, Chairman Jin made his way through a crowd of people and handed Aran off to someone, probably a hotel waiter, outside the reception hall. That person took Aran into an elevator, walked her out through the lobby, and put her in a cab. Based on what she pieced together from her mother later, Chairman Jin was her father. As old as the hills, even as a grandfather, he would not have been a very young one.

In all likelihood, her mother was his mistress. But Aran never witnessed her in this role. So the label "mistress" did not conjure up the same image for her as what conventional social wisdom dictated: wicked beauty, habitual indolence and extravagance, insuppressible sexuality, and shameless greed for money. Until she died, Aran's mother worked as a domestic help. Instead of going from job to job, she only worked at a few homes of widowed or single professional women in academia. Her insistence on being selective with clients almost bordered on paranoia, for even when better-paying jobs came along, she invariably turned them down when men, either married or single, were part of the household. Her days as a mistress were evident only in a faded photo album. In it, Chairman Jin and Mother looked more like father and daughter than lovers. It was peculiar that Aran was included in every photograph and that pictures of just the couple were noticeably absent. Obviously, the album was for Aran's benefit.

Chairman Jin holding Aran in his arms and gazing at her sweetly looked just like a grandfather with his first grandchild. This was the family from her childhood although she had no memory of it. The photos must have been taken before his wife found out about their existence. Apparently that period did not last long, because the Aran in the pictures never grew up past preschool age. As is common with faded old photographs, facial expressions and clothing looked outdated and stiff but an underlying nervousness still lived and breathed within the still images. Her mother never revealed exactly how or when his family found out about them, and Aran never asked. She had no doubt that it involved much dirty laundry that neither of them cared to discuss.

Her mother probably demanded that Aran be added to his family registry in return for making a clean break from Chairman Jin. Things must not have gone her way, for Aran often heard her sighing in frustration that they had not kept up their end of the bargain. When it came to that issue though, Aran knew that her mother wouldn't just sit around and sigh. She had no intention of rekindling her relationship with Chairman Jin, but she did everything in her power to remind his family of Aran's existence. Invitations to graduation ceremonies, awards from writing contests or art fairs, and copies of her report card were regularly sent to his home. Aran's attendance at his seventieth birthday party was no doubt part of this endeavor. But it took another ten years for Aran to get her name listed on his family register. She was in high school when Junggi, his eldest son, contacted her. Junggi came to meet her for the very first time to inform her that his father had retired a couple of years ago from overseeing the main operations of the corporation. At that time the distribution of his assets had been finalized in his will, and Aran could now be added to the registry without financial complications. Junggi didn't forget to add that the inclusion came with the stipulation that she sever all ties from the family. She was only a high school student. In retrospect, she was old enough to know what she needed to know, yet she probably didn't know much. None of this mattered to Junggi because the person he wanted to deal with was Aran's mother. Aran served only as the indirect channel of communication.

"I have no idea why your mother so desperately wanted you to be a part of our family. You don't gain a dime from it, really. And it's not like we come from a long line of power . . . Do you know where our money comes from? Our grandfather worked as a foreman among menial laborers."

He sneered with affected sympathy. Aran knew that it was intentional, that he didn't even try to extend her the slightest courtesy as a sibling. Kind of like Nolbu, the evil brother in a famous Korean folktale, he was a mean and devious man who wanted to mar or spit on what he was forced to give away. Ever since that meeting with him, Aran used the same words to scorn her mother whenever she had the chance. Her mother had to endure greater abuse from her daughter after Aran officially became a part of the Jin family. And to her daughter's abuse she always gave the same reply: she was never after their money or power but simply wanted the truth to be known. Proud to the end . . . Aran was sick and tired of her mother's pride and arrogance. She knew that what her mother said outwardly and what she felt inwardly were two different things. Declaring that she now had no more regrets in life, her mother quickly lost her energy for life, became ill, and died before Aran entered college. Did she really have no regrets in life? Didn't she feel disbelief and disappointment at being empty-handed after such a long struggle that eventually did her in? It was easier for Aran to think so. She despised anything too complicated. And what she despised about her mother was her convoluted way of thinking and living, her twisted mind that manifested itself in complete hypocrisy. Three years after her mother's death, Aran heard through the grapevine that Chairman Jin's wife had died also. She felt no emotion regarding her death, as she was so busy working during the day and taking college classes at night. *Her hapless mother . . . If she were alive . . . Who knows, she could have married Chairman Jin and become part of his oh-so-great family . . .* She could have entertained such a thought, but she didn't. Not only was she busy living her life but she didn't ever want to think about his terribly stuck-up, intolerant family.

When the Jin family, who wanted to sever all ties with her, contacted her out of the blue, Aran was puzzled but not daunted. The fact that she had nothing to expect from them gave her the courage to stand up to them. Aran also took comfort in the realization that as coldhearted as they may have been, they were not twisted people. The meeting took place at some apartment, not an office. When she arrived, the atmosphere was somber. Waiting for her were several gentlemen including Junggi, some middle-aged women, and a silver-haired elderly woman. The women were all wearing mourning clothes that suited their grim expressions well. Aran would not have been surprised to learn that they had never cracked a smile in all their lives.

They were probably Chairman Jin's sons, daughters, and their spouses. A month had passed since his death, and the fact that they were still wearing mourning clothes seemed pretentious to Aran. She was wearing a canary yellow two-piece outfit. She looked good in most colors, but she knew that she always commanded a presence in bright yellow.

"Some daughter . . . Didn't even come to the funeral . . ."

The oldest-looking woman with silver hair sized up Aran from head to toe with a sharp eye and mumbled under her breath as she looked far into the distance.

"Don't waste your breath, Sister. Look how she's dressed. She's hopeless."

"You called me here for this? Wasn't it you people who wanted to have nothing to do with me?" Aran ignored the women and addressed Junggi.

"Sisters, may we be alone?"

One word from Junggi was all it took for them to shuffle toward the bedroom, and only the men remained. Except for Junggi, the other men were all unfamiliar and indiscernible from one another. One of them, politeness ingrained in his professional mannerisms, handed her his business card. He was a lawyer with the last name Lee, not Jin.

"He is the lawyer who'll carry out Father's will. Father apparently left you this apartment," Junggi said indifferently, as if talking about the affairs of strangers.

"This apartment? Is this a joke?"

"No. It's true," said the lawyer who had handed her his card. There was a softness about him; he was much less businesslike than Junggi.

"Even if that was his wish, I'm sure they have no intention of carrying it out. I know these people."

"These people? I like that you're bold, but you're bordering on being rude. You're right. We're not happy about giving you anything, but our hands are tied, you see. He even notarized the will before his death."

Aran had addressed the lawyer, but Junggi answered her. She had spoken with venom, but he was smiling. It wasn't a forced smile but a suave, unctuous one. *They're playing with me, playing me for a fool.* Before she could recover from the insult, Junggi continued talking with a straight face.

"All matters of inheritance had already been settled before you became a member of our family. This place was Father's last asset he owned under his name. This is also where he passed away. That's why we feel that he left you the most valuable thing, even though it's nothing compared to what we received from him. It's hard for us to think just in terms of actual value. What he gave us, we split among ourselves; but what you got was everything, everything that mattered, all to yourself. So we feel a sense of betrayal. Especially Elder Sister. She almost passed out from shock at what he left you and was deeply hurt. Why wouldn't she be? When Father became ill, she moved into the same building and took charge of caring for him. That's not easy to do for someone with her own family to care for. But she knew that it would be harder for a daughter-in-law to care for Father, so she took on the burden herself. Five long years she tended to him. For the rest of us, we feel so indebted to her that we're willing to go along with her wishes. And she is so dead set against you living here. What can we do? Her only wish is for us to stop you from moving in. Considering everything she's done for us, it's the least we can do. But we also have to honor Father's will. That's why we've decided to buy the apartment from you. Do you understand everything I'm telling you?"

Aran didn't, so she turned her head sideways. Her eyes met those of the lawyer, who nodded to her with a reassuring look.

"The market value of this apartment as of last year was at least four hundred and fifty million won, but after the 1997 financial crisis—I'm sure you know all about that—it isn't sellable now, even at three fifty. Those desperate to sell are getting much less than that. If you don't believe me, you can stop by a realtor's office on your way out. Mr. Lee here is doing everything he can on your behalf. He's essentially your proxy looking out for your best interests, not so much ours. He and our party have reached an agreement to give you three hundred and fifty million won after various expenses. In actuality, we're buying this apartment way above the market value. With that money, you can buy a much better place. Or if you prefer, you can keep the money in cash, which is worth more with the current market interest rate than what four hundred and fifty would have been before the crisis. Do you get it? Since I'm obligated to give you this apartment, I wouldn't dream of ripping you off in any way. That would be like robbing from the blind. We came to this decision only because we don't want you living here. Not only does Elder Sister live a few stories upstairs, but most of us also live in or near the same apartment complex."

"You should take this offer."

Nodding his head in approval like a kibitzer at a chess game, the lawyer took out a bundle of documents. Aran was dumbstruck. Obediently, she stamped her seal page after page in the places that the lawyer pointed to. Whenever her eyes met his eyes, she felt relieved, as if exchanging silent communication with an ally in enemy territory. The money was to be paid in its entirety in a week without any deposit or down payment, and Junggi asked the lawyer to tie up all the loose ends in a week. A silver-haired woman barged out of the bedroom, practically foaming at the mouth.

"Sister, please get ahold of yourself. It's all over now." The other women rushed after her like a school of flickering fish.

"Get your filthy name off our family register, you, you, bitch! Two generations of money-grubbers who seduced our father!"

Mr. Lee quickly got Aran on her feet and, guarding her with his back, took her outside. While they were waiting for the elevator, Junggi followed them out and told her not to worry. He said he would make sure things went as planned. Outside, Mr. Lee hailed a cab for Aran. Watching him walk toward the parking garage, Aran thought that he looked just like the hotel waiter at the seventieth birthday party. Chairman Jin Hyukboo. He sure did live a long time. His firstborn, Junggi's older sister, appeared to be almost seventy years old herself.

A week passed from that fateful day. During the week, Aran still could not get a realistic grasp of her three hundred and fifty million won. She didn't question or fret over whether or not she'd actually see that much money in her hands. Even without such worries, the past week had been hell. She was just like her mother. Her mother did not believe in easy money or strokes of luck. There's no such thing as a free lunch, she used to say. That was a principle she lived her life by. Greater than the awe over the three hundred and fifty million was Aran's dread of the people who'd rather part with that much money than include her in their family. How disgusting and wretched she must be in their eyes. The one thing Aran's mother hated the most while raising her was her cruel blame: *Why did you have me?* It was a good thing that her mother was not there. Aran felt a murderous hatred toward her already-dead mother. *Aran, how disgusting and wretched are you?* She could forgive her mother for being a mistress, but not a mother who brought her into this world to live like this. She wanted to kill her for that.

On the morning of the day exactly one week from their meeting, Mr. Lee called. He asked Aran to come not to the apartment but to Junggi's office. In the presence of the two men, she received thirty-five certified checks each in the amount of ten million won. It suddenly occurred to Aran during this transaction that Junggi bore a striking resemblance to her father as she remembered him on the day of his seventieth birthday. Junggi looked as old as his father did then, but more importantly, he no longer felt like the complete stranger he had seemed during their previous meeting. Because she was ashamed by this sense of familiarity that flowed so naturally, Aran tried to appear nonchalant when receiving the checks. Apparently amused by her feigned indifference, Junggi grinned peculiarly, by moving only one corner of his lips.

"I'm not sure if you researched housing prices, but you can be sure that we're giving you a fair amount based on the current market price. Mr. Lee here is in complete agreement with me. In terms of interest, you can get more now than you would have with four hundred and fifty million won before the financial crisis. With this money, you can buy a property or keep it in cash.

It's all up to you. If you want, I can help you to invest the money with low risks and high returns. I'm sure you can easily net four or five million won per month from these investments. Given that you're single, I'm of the opinion that it would be better for you to invest rather than to buy a property. You can do a lot with four or five million by yourself. Since you seem to have put off marriage, you should consider studying abroad. Become a successful professional. That won't be so hard for you now. Instead of a house, I hope you invest that money in yourself so that you can live the life you want. But that's just my opinion. Of course, you're free to do what you want with the money. If you invest, the principal of three hundred and fifty will remain untouched while bringing in four or five hundred per month in interest. That's nothing to sneeze at."

Aran, who was unfazed by the big sum of three hundred and fifty million won, was deeply shaken by the notion of a monthly income of four or five million. A pleasant shudder ran through her spine when she understood her windfall. Was there such a thing as a free lunch? And wasn't it what she and her mother had secretly been after for all these years?

"Well, you can even study abroad," Aran addressed the white ball bouncing around her feet. Then she kicked it hard with the intent of sending it far away. She must have lacked the strength or the ball must have been too deflated, for it dropped to the ground not too far away and rolled back toward her like a loyal puppy. *Ah, you stupid ball.* Aran lightly shoved the ball back into its original hole.

When she came home, Aran suppressed her excitement and called her office. She said in a feeble voice that she wouldn't be able to work for a few days due to a severe flu. Since this was the first time that she had ever called in sick, the department manager treated her graciously enough. But a close colleague called her back after a few minutes, fretting that it was no time to play hooky over a little cold, given the many recent layoffs.

"I don't know why I'm feeling like this. I just want to sleep in all day," Aran said. Her friend was genuinely concerned, but Aran brushed her off casually. Miss Kim, who left for work earlier than Aran and came home later, saw Aran in bed until late the next day and immediately assumed that she had been fired. Aran didn't deny it, smiling ambiguously. Almost envious of Aran's indifference to being jobless, Miss Kim again whined about money.

"You have some money saved up, right? You're so lucky. You have a home and no needy family members bugging you for handouts. I can't afford to get fired. At least not until I pay off the installments on my ten-million-won savings plan. After I get that money, then I can quit or be laid off. You'll see."

Aran wondered how much money Miss Kim thought that she had saved up. She felt bad for Miss Kim, whose meager imagination could certainly not have exceeded a guess of ten million won.

For the next three days, three hundred and fifty million made Aran full without eating and alert without sleeping. She couldn't sleep the first night because of her excitement; she lost her appetite the next day thinking about the wad of checks overburdening her shabby five-hundred-square-foot apartment. She dithered around all day, having lost not only her appetite but also the ability to concentrate on anything else other than the money. She didn't have the courage to take the checks outside of her home, let alone leave them there unattended. So she had no choice but to guard them. One time, she stood on the street corner looking at her house. Even the home's façade looked different to her, knowing that it was holding assets many times its own worth. Aran got scared, thinking that if it looked different to her untrained eye, professional thieves and con artists could spot it a mile away. People strolling down the street all seemed like shady characters ready to rob her of her newfound wealth. It wasn't only the home that felt strange because of its sudden increase in value. She felt that way about herself, as if she had grown golden scales all over her body.

She spent all day bundling the checks, counting them one by one, or sorting them into separate piles; she stored them together, and then she changed her mind and stored them separately in smaller amounts. She was so exhausted from her fickle handling of the money that she had no energy left for other chores. Even at night, she was so busy hiding the checks inside leaves of books, between layers of clothing, and under the bed that she had no time to plan what she could actually do with her money. She knew she was being a pathetic basket case, but safeguarding three hundred and fifty million won was hardly a chore. Perhaps touching, handling, and fretting over that much money was what she dreamed about all along. She even thought about cashing in the checks so that she could spend all night counting the small bills. Just when Aran was making herself ill from trying to get used to her three hundred and fifty million, she got a call from Junggi. The first thing he asked about was the money.

"I have it just as you gave it to me," Aran replied.

"Good. I've been waiting for you to consult with me but you haven't called. I know that you have worked all these years so that you're savvy about money and other matters. But I'm still concerned about you. Too often I see even the people who've been professionals all their lives get duped out of their savings. Father would not have wanted me to just hand you a onetime payment and leave you on your own; he would have wanted me to make sure that you're taken care of. So I've been thinking. It's true that real estate values have hit rock bottom and it's also true that experts don't expect them to recover anytime soon. Interest rates will fall eventually, but for now, they're quite high. People like us in business have been hit hard, but it has been sweet for those with money to invest. Before the rates go back down, I recommend that you lock your money into sound investments. I think that's your best bet for now. An investment trust company has been courting me to try their various packages so I thought of you. What do you think? I've told you this before, but depending on the investment options you choose, you can easily net four or five million won in interest income."

The down-to-earth sum of several million still held a greater appeal to Aran than several hundred million. At least for now. Junggi said that he'd send an investment specialist over to her home. The specialist who showed up at her doorstep bearing a gift a couple of hours later was none other than the branch manager. As soon as he arrived, Junggi called again to reassure her that he was a trustworthy and knowledgeable professional. The branch manager gently chastised Aran for missing out on interest income by leaving her cash in the closet for so many days. He suggested that she diversify her investment portfolio by choosing four options: a tax-break savings plan, a six-month and a one-year fixed income plan, and an annuity plan. Once she accepted his recommendations, the branch manager promised to make the investments effective as of that day lest she lose another day's worth of interest. Then he wrote her a receipt for the deposit and took the certified checks with him. Aran was elated just thinking that she could sit around and earn more than a hundred thousand won a day. And to be rid of such a burden! Why didn't she think of doing this before? Like a fool, she had already lost out on several hundred thousand won by doing nothing with the money. But it was smart of her to have left the money untouched until Junggi called. Surely, she had demonstrated her naïveté instead of imprudence and greed. Most of all, the branch manager coming in person to collect the money had given her a taste of her new social status. Sipping the orange juice from the beverage set he had brought for her, Aran basked in self-satisfaction.

She must have fallen asleep. Waking up from a restless nap, she wondered if it was common for bank branch managers to make personal visits to clients even within the upper echelons of society. She had never heard of such a thing. Her pre-nap self-importance quickly turned into suspicion. She must have been under some kind of spell. Innocent souls bamboozled by con artists maintain that they were temporarily shortsighted by greed. Aran must have been similarly tempted by one day's interest income. Giving in to self-doubt, she nearly drove herself mad. The sleepless nights spent hiding the checks were nothing compared to the torture she was experiencing now. *Junggi would never . . .* Her belief in him was undermined by her distrust of the members of his clan who would have no qualms about giving just to take away. She could just see the smug smile on their lips and hear their mocking sneers buzzing in her ears. It did occur to her that they had absolutely no reason to be so cruel to someone who had made no demands. This thought, however, was overpowered by the suspicion that she had fallen prey to their perverted scheme. Despite her fears, she did not have the courage to call Junggi and find out the truth. Calling him would only prove that she was a poor ignoramus who didn't know what to do now that she had gone from rags to riches. The manager had told her that he would send someone or come personally tomorrow to bring her the paperwork for her new accounts. Telling herself that waiting was the proper thing to do, Aran barely made it through the night, trying to soothe her tormented soul. Even if the manager did come, how could she trust the bank books he brought with him when she didn't trust him as a person anymore? Aran, empowered by this fresh new doubt, resolved to never again be taken for a gullible fool. With a beating heart, she took out the branch manager's business card and dialed his phone number. She half expected to get a stranger or a disconnected number. But she was transferred directly to the branch manager. Before he could say anything, Aran told him that she would stop by his office that day since she planned to be in the area on other business. His office building, located downtown, was grand and impressive.

As soon as she entered the building, she received VIP treatment from the bank staff. She was immediately led into his office and while sitting cross-legged on a plush couch, fragrant green tea was brought to her. An assistant brought the papers to the office, and the branch manager once again explained in detail the different interest rates, features, and benefits according to the account type.

"I hear that you're going to study abroad. Well, best of luck to you," he said with a smile when they parted. Then he walked her to the lobby.

Walking out politely and gracefully as someone worthy of such VIP treatment, Aran turned around and stared at the bank building. *Unless that majestic building vanishes like a mirage, my three hundred and fifty million is a sure thing*, she thought. Once the nightmare disappeared, the whole world became beautiful. Like a foreigner charmed by the perfume of an unfamiliar city, Aran strolled down the street lined with clean-cut buildings and then stepped into a hip café playing rap music. She thought of her mother who dreamed about skipping work on a rainy day to listen to French pop songs. Her foolish mother, a fastidious housekeeper who dreamed such dreams. Although Aran was in possession of the same amount of money as before, she was now completely freed of her burden, her anxiety gone without a trace. She felt like someone who had undergone a difficult rite of passage or someone who had just recovered from a disease. At any rate, she thought that she'd never again experience that kind of angst in her lifetime. Up until now, she had lived her life like a barnacle desperately clinging to things, but now, she was able to take a step back and look at the world in a whole new way. Aran headed toward her home. Now that she could leave this hellhole anytime she wanted, the neighborhood amused her like a charming scene from a movie set. With money acting as a lubricant between her and the world, everything was good and beautiful.

When she saw the sculpture park, she thought of the ball in the ground. It was cruel to leave it in dark confinement when it had already tasted the freedom of rolling on grass. My poor ball, thought Aran, and she turned toward the park. She meant to kick the ball far away after retrieving it, but instead, she began juggling it with her feet. Happiness began bubbling inside her like a refreshing carbonated beverage. She must call Hun first when she got home. How long had it been since she last slept with him? She wanted to make love as soon as possible. She wanted to have fun with him, to make him do the same humiliating things he made her do many times over. A complete role reversal. Who knew that roles could be reversed this easily? She could watch the flesh burn on his flaccid arms, force him to crawl around the floor, or make him lick her body all over like a panting dog. Aran laughed out loud like a mad woman.

Sleeping with Hun was not the only reason she wanted to see him. She had something to tell him. That her dream was no longer to wait for him to crawl out of his cocoon and spread his wings so that she could become his good housewife. Aside from her, he had eight other family members clinging to that same dream, patiently waiting for his metamorphosis. She'd lighten his load by removing herself from that group. It wasn't that Hun had totally outlived his usefulness. Even without his wings, he could serve as her lapdog anytime she needed one, only to be discarded like an old shoe when she grew tired of him. *From now on, the one who has to live in fear of being dumped is you, Hun. Not me. The person who can do as she pleases is me. Not you. You must know that the haves have power over the have-nots for the same reason that men have power over women.*

What Aran was juggling with her feet was not a white ball

but Hun. Toying with him was so much more fun than becoming one with the ball. She kicked the ball with all her might. It flew far, far away and disappeared as soon as it touched the ground, in the vicinity of the "Pain of Existence" signpost. Not bad. Could this be a hole-in-one? She muttered under her breath, casually recalling the sports lingo she'd picked up somewhere. She turned around, with absolutely no intention of retrieving the ball from its hole.

Who knew that she'd come to such a reconciliation with the Jins? Only after tasting the power of money or the greed for it was she able to forgive them for the hardship she'd endured. Realizing this about herself suddenly brought her a sense of loss. The sorrow that she felt was vague and fleeting, like a waft of hillside grass or farmland fertilizer gently breezing past city dwellers.

J-1 Visa

Teaching was becoming exhausting. His wife was always cautious with him when he came home from work completely drained, but she was especially so today. He could tell even in his weary state that she was walking on eggshells. It was in the middle of cleaning up the dinner table that she finally opened her mouth. She probably figured his mood had improved after a hearty home-cooked meal.

"Dong Min has set the wedding date. The fourth of August. It's at the height of the summer heat wave over there as well. I asked my parents why he's getting married when it's so hot and they said they wanted it to be during your summer vacation. The bride's family wanted a May wedding at first but gave in to our side. You know how my parents go out of their way to accommodate you. Not that you should feel pressured."

Having said this as casually as possible, she swung around and dunked her rubber-gloved hands in the sink to resume the dishwashing. Dong Min was her youngest brother. She was the oldest of her siblings, and after she married, her parents immigrated to the United States. Her family now lived scattered throughout California. When it came to her family matters, his wife was always meek and unassertive. He felt bad that she had to approach him so gingerly about something as important to her as her brother's wedding, so he replied cheerfully.

"Oh, good. We haven't gone anywhere in a long time, so let's enjoy the trip. Let's take the kids, too. I'm sure your mother set the date in August hoping to see her grandkids, not so much me."

"Really, honey? You think you can go to the States without getting an apology from the American ambassador?"

His wife hurriedly peeled off her rubber gloves and asked in a serious tone. She had an incredulous expression on her face. Oh! That's when he realized his blunder and understood why she was behaving so strangely. In all probability, his wife had not waited all this time hoping and believing that he could actually get an apology from the ambassador. Despite her outward excitement, she clearly seemed to be disappointed in him. How could he have forgotten what she hadn't? If she were disappointed in him, then he should have rightly been disappointed in himself. It was a promise he had made to himself, but she was just an innocent bystander who had gotten dragged into the mess. As if caught having a meaningless affair with a woman far less beautiful than his wife, he was angry with her and disgusted with himself. He felt horrible. He made it worse by muttering, "We bring it upon ourselves to be ignored like this, us Koreans . . ." He was trying to brush off his forgetfulness and the insult he had endured by blaming the rest of his fellow countrymen.

Lee Chang Gu had received a phone call from Kim Hye Sook in mid-March the year before last. When the phone rang, he was in the school staff room thinking that teaching was getting tougher every day. That was a recurring thought, not one spurred by a recent difficult event.

"Teacher? This is Mr. Lee Chang Gu, right? Hello! This is Kim Hye Sook from the twenty-third class. I hope you're doing well." It was a cheerful, friendly voice.

"Oh, hi. What a pleasant surprise . . ." He mumbled hesitantly, pretending to know her, but he couldn't conjure up a face to go with the voice. He had been a Korean language arts teacher for over twenty years at a private girls' high school. If he were to look up the name Kim Hye Sook among the alumnae who had been through the school system during his tenure, he'd no doubt end up with a list of a few dozen people. She must have detected the uncertainty in his voice.

"I'm calling from the States. Los Angeles. Remember I stopped by to say goodbye before going abroad? I graduated at the top of my class and received an award from the Board of Education at the graduation ceremony. That Kim Hye Sook. Do you remember?"

Of course he did. She was the first and the last valedictorian to have emerged from his homeroom class. Clean-cut in appearance and from a good home, she was a gifted student. Her innate intellect was complemented by a predilection for studying, and in fact, she was a downright bookworm. In her senior year, she had no trouble gaining acceptance into Seoul University. No special care or attention had been required of him as her homeroom teacher. Once Kim Hye Sook's identity became clear, he felt more embarrassed than pleased to hear her voice. That was because he recalled the events leading up to the twenty-third graduation ceremony, something he'd prefer to permanently banish from memory. His colleagues as well as the principal had insisted that he take everyone out to celebrate. The valedictorian's homeroom teacher usually did, but they were pressuring him to give an especially big feast because the valedictorian was also bound for Seoul University. That year was the first time he had taught a senior homeroom class, but he vaguely remembered being treated to such an occasion previously. He had no idea what was expected of him. Get-togethers like these were unusually frequent at that school. Once, a female teacher wore a swanky new outfit to school and everyone admired how good it looked on her, fussing over what brand it was and how much it cost. Someone nagged her about celebrating her new outfit, and marinated beef slices appeared on that day's lunch menu. Apparently, you could hand money to the kitchen staff to buy a special food item, and as a favor they included it in the meal at no extra cost. At first, he had something similar in mind, but their clamoring for a double celebration made him think twice. So he decided on beef short ribs at a modest restaurant. From the beginning, his colleagues thought it odd that the gathering wasn't at a hotel buffet. When they found out during the meal that it wasn't Kim Hye Sook's parents who were treating them, they stopped chomping on the ribs and exchanged glances. Then everyone began treating him like a naïve fool. Some of his colleagues were openly indignant, as though they were about to storm out of their seats at any moment, while others tried to lecture him on how to handle parents of students who were exceptionally bright or came from wealthy homes. He was being chewed out instead of the short ribs and he endured it silently like someone guilty as charged. But inside, a part of him burned with shame and anger for belonging to such an organization.

He hadn't become an educator because of any ideals, but he wasn't doing it just for the paycheck either. He had been a college student in the 1970s, when widespread student demonstrations on campuses caused constant school closures. He was never arrested or expelled, but he knew what it was like to sing songs of the movement until his voice turned hoarse in protest against social injustices. He was in complete solidarity with the movement, in theory at least, and was preoccupied with its ideals throughout his college years. He lacked, however, the guts and the passion to do anything drastic. Other comrades were seemingly more zealous and would rather have died standing up than kneel in defeat. But even they eventually turned mainstream, their burning passion proving to be nothing more than a passing phase. A few diehard activists did carry on the cause beyond the campus, infiltrating the job market to organize labor movements against big corporations. He had mixed feelings about them, respect on the one hand for their unwavering principles and skepticism on the other for their radical actions. He chose a career that suited his wishy-washy stance. It was noble to sacrifice oneself for the good of the masses, but he thought it was just as honorable to live as a member of the masses. Teaching, in that respect, appeared to be one of the most people- and service-oriented occupations for a college student courting idealistic views. This belief was further validated by the scorn and pity he received when taking education classes, which were heavily favored by female students. An unmanly and unprofitable career choice meant that he wasn't selling out to mainstream society.

The nickname he earned on his first day of teaching was "girlie." For a man, he had a rather soft, effeminate face, and it turned beet red in front of the students. His nervous eyes didn't know where to fix their gaze. The girls got such a kick out of this bachelor teacher that they clapped and laughed, triumphant that they'd found the perfect object of amusement in the bashful young man. According to his own recollection, the girls meant nothing to him. What made his face burn was a sense of failure, the yearning for freedom that remained unfulfilled and the acute realization that he didn't know anything. The nickname "girlie" did not last long. He soon turned into a boring, stoic teacher and lost the bachelor title as well. But a part of him always remained as timid and insecure as a girlie. It was just that he no longer blushed so much. Only he could feel how much his insides still burned, instead of his face. The guilt that he had escaped the social conflicts facing his generation by finding refuge in the school system reddened his heart more than his face.

"It's been a long time. How can I help you?" he asked in a blasé voice, not caring whether she was calling from Los Angeles or the moon.

"I wanted to invite you here. What's your schedule like around May twenty-sixth?"

"Thank you for the offer but I've been to the States enough times. My in-laws live there."

"I'm not asking you to come for sightseeing. I'm officially inviting you to a seminar hosted by my department, the Department of East Asian Studies at the University. For the past three years, we've been holding a seminar with the theme, "The Experience of Colonialism and Modernity: the Cases of Korea, Japan, and China." We usually invite speakers from these countries, and this year's focus is Korea. I'm presenting on the topic."

"Are you saying you want me to come and listen?"

"Of course not. My thesis paper analyzes Korea's colonial period through your novel, *The Satgatjae Village*. I bet you had no idea that I was such an ardent fan and a researcher of your novel."

"So what are you saying?"

The irritation in his voice was obvious even to himself. Because he was often brusque and aloof with his students and even with his own children, he had been at times accused of being uncaring and irresponsible. When it came to his writing, however, he had a tendency to be overprotective.

"Teacher, please don't be angry. I feel like I'm being interrogated for something I did wrong. Anyway, let me get to the point. I wanted to invite you as the author of the original work. Before the conference, I plan to send out a translated version of *The Satgatjae Village* and an abstract of my thesis so that the participants can come prepared and use the materials for discussion. On the day of the conference, you will be introduced first—of course not as my high school teacher but as the author Lee Chang Gu—and then I will present my paper. Afterward, there will be a question and answer session on my presentation, but I suspect most of the questions will be directed at you. At this stage, I perceive my role as coming up with the discussion topics before the conference and moderating the discussion during the conference. For me to fulfill this role and to interpret effectively, I need to know even in general terms your views on the colonial period and its rippling effects on our modern society. One thing we can do is to have you present your views in a twenty-to-thirty-minute speech, but translation is again an issue. You can send me a draft of your presentation or I guess you can come here a couple of days early to brief me. I really want to do a good job. You'll see that there is growing interest in East Asian studies here in America, especially in California."

"Then perhaps there'll be a few people who can read and understand my book in our language?"

"No, most people aren't quite that proficient, although there are a few who can understand some Korean . . . Don't worry about the language barrier. I know I can do a good job of interpreting."

"Did you translate *The Satgatjae Village* into English?"

"No, I didn't have to. It's included in the collection of Korean short stories that Helen Kang translated with the grant from the Korean Literature Foundation. You didn't know about this?"

"Helen Kang . . . Yes, I know her. Do you think she's a reliable translator?"

"First rate. She immigrated here when she was in elementary school, and maybe because she grew up with a grandmother, she understands even the highly culture-specific aspects of the Korean language. Her command of English is, of course, just as good as that of a native speaker. She's my age and is married to an American. She's really smart and ambitious—very dedicated to raising awareness of Korean literature abroad."

Having listened up to that point, he told her that he would do his best to go when he received the official invitation and hung up hastily. He was irritated because of the mention of Helen Kang and the fact that her translation would be used.

He knew with certainty that he was an ordinary teacher with twenty years of experience. As a writer, however, he had no idea whether he was successful, popular, or recognized. He had absolutely no multitasking skills. He couldn't even read while listening to music. Still, he had tried his hand at both teaching and writing, neither of which was an easy discipline by anyone's standards. It was a mystery to him how he graduated from college having studied so little during those chaotic times, but the little that he did learn enabled him to earn a living. The ideals, to which he had devoted so much more of his time and energy than studying, couldn't just be abandoned. To do so would be an act of betrayal against his value system, and he didn't want to end up hating himself. Thus, teaching and writing were the two pillars that upheld his livelihood and his pride. He had resolved to write one or two pieces per year, for self-gratification if not for anything else. The problem was not that he didn't have enough time; it was that he couldn't write a word without completely transforming his mindset from that of a teacher to a writer. That meant that he could only write during his vacations, but this so-called transformation often lasted only days or weeks, so that it left even less time for writing. Always nervous and crabby, he was quite unpleasant to be around during these periods of transition. This writing process of his had become something of a bad habit with him. Usually he was never like that at school, and he was surprised to find himself now showing symptoms of anxiety reserved only for writing. He half-regretted consenting so quickly to the invitation when school would be in session in May, but he felt he had to attend. It wasn't that Kim Hye Sook had begged him to the point where he couldn't refuse. His decision was based on Helen Kang. Although he had never met this woman, he had spoken with her over the phone a couple of times. It was, of course, laudable for a translator to take the time to consult the author on tricky sections of the original text. But she had not called to discuss easily misunderstood passages or to share views on the subtle use of symbolism and metaphors. She called to ask the meanings of "rafters" on traditional roofs or "paying off someone else's debt," words or phrases in Korean that one could easily look up in a dictionary. She had tested his patience then. But when she asked him who comfort women were, he was at a complete loss for words. This was not simply a matter of searching the dictionary. No matter how fluent she was in English, she was simply not the right person to translate work dealing with such topics.

His story didn't deal directly with the experiences of the comfort women, but the story's setting was based on the devastation of a poor farming town toward the end of the Japanese occupation in Korea. His mother was born into poverty in such a town and was only eighteen when her parents essentially sold her off to a widower in his mid-thirties who'd been left with a bunch of kids. She had three more kids of her own before becoming a widow herself at twenty-three when her husband died in the Korean War. Her parents showed no remorse for how her life had turned out; they claimed that they had no choice but to marry her off in a hurry if they didn't want her to be dragged off as a comfort woman.

He was born after the liberation so he didn't even have a vague memory of the oppression, but he had come into this world through the body of a victim of that time. He had wrestled with the story, pouring all of his mother's bleeding sorrows onto the paper. He didn't want anyone reading it lightly. Helen Kang remained unapologetic, believing that her English proficiency more than made up for her shortcomings in Korean. What frustrated him more than her ignorance or audacity was his patience in putting up with her to the end. In getting one or two of his stories translated into English, was he hoping for his writing to break through the language barrier and step into the international arena? Or was he simply complying with someone fluent in English because of his inferiority complex? Either way, his heart ached with shame.

His English was probably worse than that of a typical high school student, owing to the fact that he was a Korean lit major in college in the seventies. Student demonstrations on campus and constant school closures did not make for a very conducive environment for academic learning. It was only after he became a writer that he began feeling inadequate about his English. Once he had published and joined a couple of trade organizations, he discovered that there were many opportunities for attending seminars overseas as long as he paid his way. At first he felt a certain pride in globetrotting not for the purpose of sightseeing but for sharing literary viewpoints. He was certainly not new to international travel. His wife's family was a large, tight-knit group. As the eldest son-in-law, he was constantly invited to their family events, and attending one every now and then had him frequenting the international airport. The different nature of his work-related travel from attending such family events was what was so appealing at first. His wife also encouraged him to travel for work, more pleased with the tickets she had to pay out of their meager savings than the prepaid tickets sent by her family. He soon learned, however, that these work trips didn't amount to much more than impressing his family and colleagues. From the very beginning, he, of course, was not deluded enough to think that he'd stand tall in front of foreigners and express his views. He was timid by nature and unsociable, so mingling with foreigners in his broken English was quite beyond his imagination. He had just wanted to see other people with different physical traits and cultural backgrounds working in the same field, to get a glimpse of their world. That desire to keep open a thin line of communication with the outside world was not unrelated to his suspicion that his writing was somehow crude by global standards. But these occasional strolls into the open world of literature always left him feeling ostracized. It was more than his inability to communicate in a universal language or the lack of opportunity to express his views. It was an odd feeling different from those frustrations. He and his countrymen were somehow invisible, even if they were to show up en masse and occupy all the seats. Maybe it was only he who felt that they never belonged. Once, a renowned colleague conversant in English made a presentation, insistent on speaking in Korean with a foreigner translating for him. The gist of his impassioned speech was that a Korean writer must be awarded the Nobel Prize in Literature within the next decade. He was ill at ease the whole time he was listening, feeling goose bumps spread on his skin. He must have been the only one to feel this way because the other participants, including the foreigners, all nodded in respectful agreement. Feelings felt only by him—they were always the problem.

There was a line from an old movie that he could never forget. A Jew living among Europeans summed up his experience this way: you can get close to the stream, but you can't drink. That line from the movie expressed so precisely the feeling that he could never be a meaningful part of English-speaking or otherwise white-dominated language circles. That particular scene from the movie was the only thing he remembered. For all he knew, that scene could be completely unrelated to the movie's main theme or the movie itself could be a forgettable, third-rate flick. Never mind the plot or the main characters; he couldn't even remember whether or not he had enjoyed the movie. For him to have zeroed in on that scene for no reason was probably due to his own antenna. Or probe. That was the thing about these feelings. What others accepted so naturally as the norm, he alone wavered and hesitated over, unable to go with the flow. Just as others could tell by looking at his outward appearance that he was none other than Lee Chang Gu, these hypersensitive feelings had always made him stand apart from others.

Knowing full well the type of person he was, he had still accepted Kim Hye Sook's invitation. It wasn't because he wanted to help her or because he thought the conference was important enough for him to attend despite his shortcomings. In fact, he supposed that the gathering was not much more than a study group held by a bunch of graduate students. This, he came to suspect much later. What made him accept so quickly was his lack of trust in Helen Kang. Even if she could convey the main gist of his writing, he highly doubted that she could tease out the subtleties woven into the story. The poignant intricacies of his native language that permeated his work would be almost impossible to transplant into another language. For someone like Helen Kang to volunteer to translate this kind of work was a testament to her lack of judgment and literary understanding. Overconfident in her bilingualism, she obviously took on work that did not move her. That was more than an insult; it was a butchering of the text for which he had sweat blood, and that he could not allow. He had to explain, to show the life he had breathed into every word. This sense of responsibility and passion for his work was strong enough to override his shamefully narrow-minded ways.

After he had spoken to Hye Sook on the phone, he received a letter from her university on April 30th. The letter was dated April 18th and was signed by Donna White, the director of the Humanities Research Center of the University. As is often the case with official correspondence, the letter was, fortunately for him, easy enough to understand given his high school level proficiency in English. She began with a greeting and extended an invitation to him on behalf of the organizers of the conference "The Experience of Colonialism and Modernity: the Cases of Korea, Japan, and China." She also included the schedule and the terms of the invitation. In addition to airfare and miscellaneous expenses, an honorarium of $500 was offered. "Humph, they want me to go all the way to America to make $500," he complained to his wife. He could indulge in this kind of complaint only because an honorarium, however small, had been offered. He had no idea what others received in these situations, but an honorarium was never a consideration in his decision to attend. He figured they would pay for his travel, lodging, and meals, but money was not the deciding factor in attending the conference. It wasn't a matter of wanting to attend. He had to. Five hundred dollars was certainly not much, but it was a nice icing on the cake. Attached to the letter was a form requiring him to fill in his birth date and other personal information, which they needed to include in application papers for the J-1 visa that is issued for cultural exchange programs. They also wanted his itinerary and a credit card number for reserving a hotel and transportation.

Before responding, he needed to get permission from the principal for a leave of absence during the school session. He had never made an overseas trip during the semester. Fortunately, he didn't have a homeroom this semester, so as long as someone covered his lectures, his students would not be terribly inconvenienced. He could have planned to do some sightseeing before or after the day of the conference on May 26th, but he didn't want to seem opportunistic. The East Coast, maybe, but he'd been to California many times. His wife might get upset if he went all the way over there and did not see her parents, so he planned to stay one night at their place after the conference. He was tentatively working out a five-night stay when Kim Hye Sook called him at his home. East Asian Studies departments from a couple of other universities were interested in meeting with him, so she wanted him to factor extra time into his schedule. In addition, a poet he was not acquainted with contacted him, claiming to be the general secretary of a literary organization.

"Mr. Lee, I understand that you were invited by the university? That's wonderful news for us here at the Western Chapter of the Korean-American Literature Society. We are always looking for ways to invite renowned authors from Korea, but our funds are very limited. What a stroke of luck it is for us that we have this opportunity to piggyback on their invitation. Please do not say no. We know that your schedule is tight and we don't want to burden you, so we're planning an informal round-table discussion. We'd be honored if you'd meet with us. One of our members is a reporter for a Korean newspaper branch here, and he's hoping to meet with you, too. I hope you won't refuse an interview with him either."

The man certainly was polite, perhaps overly so, but there was a pushiness to him that exerted plenty of pressure. Was it really him they wanted to invite? He was confused and pleased at the same time. *Hey, am I really who I am?* he joked to himself. Imagine being dragged from one place to another to meet people. He might just be too busy to sit down for a meal with his in-laws. Just thinking about it made him chuckle. His wife's family never looked down on him, but it thrilled him to think that they might look at him in a whole new way. Kim Hye Sook insisted on taking him sightseeing for a day, so even an eight-day trip might prove to be too short. Although that itinerary included a Sunday, he would have to miss a full week of school, for which he needed permission. The principal was a self-proclaimed dilettante of literature who didn't mind sharing with the world that he had entered, without success, the annual spring literature contest for three years straight. He apparently hadn't read any of Lee Chang Gu's work, but always feigned interest. When he entered the office, the first thing the principal asked him was, "Do you not write these days, Mr. Lee? It's never easy for writers to debut, and now that you have, you must continue to publish. How else will you win anything?"

The principal habitually lamented the omission of Lee Chang Gu's name whenever big and small literary awards were announced. So here he was again harping on about winning awards. Normally he would have ignored him, but considering that he had a request to make, he replied politely.

"I may not win any awards, but I am writing diligently. Just last month, I published a novella in a literary magazine."

"Tut tut. How can any writer be this cold and indifferent? If my story got published in a magazine, I'd bring multiple copies to leave here in the principal's office and the staff room. I'd also promote it among the students. I'm not saying this because I want a free copy. In this day and age, you have to toot your own horn. There are all kinds of literature awards out there and you haven't won a single one. That, in my opinion, has more to do with your lack of marketing skills than your writing skills. Others who don't know you might think that you're stuck up because you're proud and stubborn. You come across like that here in school, too, you know."

"Me, stuck up? Oh, no. I'm the opposite, actually. I'm so insecure that I cringe when someone claims to have read my work."

"Then why become a writer and publish? That makes no sense to me."

The conversation was headed nowhere, so he made a blanket apology to end further argument. Then he informed the principal about the conference and requested to take leave, adding that he tried to make the trip as short as possible so as not to inconvenience the students.

"Is this true? Does this mean that your work is recognized overseas? When was it translated? I take back what I said about your lack of marketing skills. Forget the small awards and go straight for the Nobel Prize, eh? I envy and commend you for your grand ambition in this age of globalization! Well, well. Good for you!"

The principal, easily excitable by nature, jumped at the news with his eyes bulging out of their sockets. He squirmed, afraid that someone outside might hear them and snigger. It would be a mistake not to mention that the invitation came from Kim Hye Sook.

"Please calm down. Nobel Prize? You misunderstand. Do you remember Kim Hye Sook? The valedictorian of the twenty-third class?"

"'Course I do. The best student we've ever had since the school opened. How could I forget?"

The principal's exaggerated speech sounded like the lines in a popular television comedy, and he almost laughed. He tried to explain in a more serious tone what Kim Hye Sook was doing in America and why she wanted to invite him. But the mention of her name excited the principal even more, and he viewed the two of them as international celebrities.

"That Kim Hye Sook. She sails into Seoul University bringing honor to her alma mater and now she's trying to promote Korean literature on the world stage. She did research on her mentor's book and is now inviting you as the author of the original work. Well, there's a former student worth her weight in gold! It must be times like these that you reap the rewards of being both a teacher and a writer. You are so blessed."

As if that song and dance weren't enough, he continued to hanker after the Nobel Prize, commenting that such-and-such a writer in Japan was able to nab the coveted award after partnering with a capable translator and that there was no law against the pair of Kim Hye Sook and Lee Chang Gu doing the same. During the staff meeting held the next morning, the principal made a big announcement on the subject. Fortunately, much of the time was devoted to applauding the illustrious alumna Kim Hye Sook, and the bell rang before the globalization of Lee Chag Gu's literary work could be discussed. One thing about the principal was that he considered keeping class time a top priority. So in that respect, the principal's grand illusions of his work served him well when he asked for a whole week away from school.

After obtaining his leave, he sent Donna White his travel itinerary and the personal information necessary for a J-1 visa application on May 2nd, which was two days after he received the invitation letter. He asked her to reserve a room for him and said he would buy the airplane ticket and bring the receipt to be reimbursed. With his own trip to America pending, he often spotted articles in the paper featuring the increased number of visa applications at the U.S. embassy and the difficulties experienced by applicants. Sometimes photographs of long lines in front of the embassy accompanied the article, warning that even after all that waiting and passing the interview, it could still take over a month for the visa to be issued. This was the peak season for visa requests with students and tourists trying to leave during the summer months. Complaints poured in that the embassy did nothing to meet the increased demand despite being aware of the problem. But he doubted that the embassy would budge to quell public outcry. He vividly remembered his own horrible experience of standing in line for hours in front of the embassy the first time he applied for a tourist visa. So he called up a travel agency to find out how long it would take for a J-1 visa and was told that it normally takes two or three days, but more than a week during busy periods. Fortunately, his tourist visa was still valid for another two years.

Despite having that tourist visa as a safety net, he began feeling nervous as almost two weeks had passed since he'd received the letter. Kim Hye Sook called often. Her fussing bugged him, but he knew that she was just trying to prepare him before the important event. She had sent him a summary of her thesis presentation in Korean, but he could not focus on reading it as he was too anxious about the visa. He wasn't sure that there was enough time after the papers arrived from the U.S. He hated to leave things up in the air, so he forwarded a letter to Donna White to this effect:

"I'm sure you sent the application papers upon receiving my information, but I have not yet received them. Even if I get them sometime this week, there might not be enough time considering how long it takes the U.S. embassy to issue a visa these days. I have a valid tourist visa that will enable me to enter your country, and I'm not sure why we have to go through this much trouble to obtain a J-1 visa."

Donna White responded immediately the next day. She explained that the university policy stipulated without exception that international participants come under the J-1 visa and that the five-hundred-dollar honorarium and reimbursement of other expenses would only be possible under that condition. She had already sent the original copies of the papers, so they should arrive shortly. He asked his travel agent to have the application ready for submission when the papers arrived from the U.S. and to make a flight reservation departing on May 25th. May 15th came and went, but still no papers arrived from the U.S. The travel agent called daily and nagged him about the papers. In his desperation, he contacted the university again, urging that unless the papers arrived by international express mail that it would be impossible to obtain a visa. When Kim Hye Sook heard the news, she immediately condemned the Korean postal service for its unreliability, assuming that it was the culprit for the delay. She also comforted him by saying that the U.S. embassy probably would not treat a respectable scholar such as himself like any other tourist. Considering that the invitation came from a major American university, he thought what she said could be possible. Donna White also wrote back saying that she had sent another set of papers by express mail. He didn't understand why original copies had to be submitted when today's technology allowed electronic communication to occur instantaneously. The express mail didn't arrive right away but three days later, at the same time as the papers sent by regular mail. It was Friday, May 19th, and no matter how much they rushed, the papers couldn't be submitted until Monday morning on the 22nd.

His hopes of receiving special treatment did not pan out. After sending him the papers by express mail, the conference organizers must have realized the unlikelihood of his obtaining a visa at this point. Kim Hye Sook sounded panic-stricken on the phone, and he could almost see her stamping her feet in anxiety. Donna White also wrote to him every day. He informed them that obtaining a visa by the 25th was not feasible at this point, secretly hoping that they would ask him to come on a tourist visa. Given all their fretting, he figured that it wouldn't be so difficult for them to bend the rules a bit if they truly wanted his participation. The honorarium and travel expenses were hardly grand sums, and they could pay him at a later date through other means. And if that weren't possible, heck, he supposed he could waive it altogether. But it was up to them to first suggest alternative means so that he could reluctantly accept. Equipped with both a valid visa and a flight reservation, there was nothing holding him back from going to the States. Nothing, that is, except the damn J-1 visa.

He was so desperate to go solely because of his reputation. Thanks to the principal, the whole student body and his colleagues knew about his pending trip to a major American university to make a presentation on his book in front of foreign scholars. His friends in literary and social circles naturally came to know about his plans because he had to reschedule meetings with them during his travel dates. News travels fast, and many of his friends and acquaintances had been telling him to look up so-and-so at the university or to say hello to so-and-so at another university. Now that he thought about it, it had already been two months since he'd received the invitation. Those two months had been so chaotic for him and he barely got any work done. And to think that he had endured so much anxiety and humiliation for nothing made him feel infinitely small and worthless. He was about to give up, almost relieved at not having to participate in a conference that would be conducted entirely in English. Obviously, he was still insecure about that. Then the university contacted him asking how much longer it would take for the visa to arrive. He consulted the travel agency and was told that another week should be sufficient time, to which the organizers suggested postponing the conference to June 8th. So he was going after all. Now that he was going, he kept thinking that it'd be far easier for him if he weren't. At any rate, he briefed the principal on all that had happened. The principal shook his head and said that he could have gotten him a visa in a day if he had consulted him sooner.

"Do you know what's so great about teaching? Our reach spans high and low places, every nook and cranny in this country. Our students, past and present, may appear to be all the same, but they come from all kinds of backgrounds—a kid with family connections all the way up to the president, a daughter of a gang boss who could dig up a stolen diamond ring, to name a few. People think that teaching is a dead-end occupation with neither money nor power. I beg to differ. No one has as many connections at every level of the social hierarchy as a teacher. You have no idea. Do you know Yoon Aera, a sophomore who speaks excellent English? Her father has immediate connections to the American embassy. He's now a congressman but he used to be a diplomat who once served as an ambassador to the U.S. Thanks to him, my son got issued a visa that had been rejected the first time. It's true. That man sure had some powerful connections."

Even while listening to him, he had no idea then that he'd resort to asking that student's parent for a favor. He thought he still had plenty of time. On the day that he expected the visa to come through, he got another disappointing call from the travel agency. The reason was that the conference date indicated on the invitation letter was May 26th, but the application was submitted after that date. Truly, this was ludicrous business, especially because the embassy was technically correct. Without anyone specific at fault, the process had taken too long and the visa was denied. Explaining how the conference had been postponed to the embassy staff would be futile because that person would be powerless to do anything about it. He was too weary to be roused to anger, so he simply informed Kim Hye Sook by phone and Donna White by fax of the situation. They did their best to help him, but he had no regrets because he was so fed up with anything associated with America at this point.

Because of this resolve, he was recovering surprisingly quickly from the debacle when Donna White contacted him again. It was too late to resend the papers even by express mail, so she said that the university administration would contact the embassy to explain how the conference had been postponed from May 26th to June 8th and to request for leniency given the unfortunate circumstances. He wanted to put the matter behind him but was caught up in it once again. With little time left and feeling more clueless than ever about the workings of the U.S. embassy, he consulted the principal. Of course, his intention was to secure the help of the powerful politician with connections. The principal exceeded his expectations by quickly and proactively making a request to Yoon Aera's father. Soon, word was received for them not to worry. The travel agent also suggested that things would go much more smoothly if the university contacted the embassy directly. One week of the two-week postponement had already passed, and only a week remained until the conference. That meant that he had to leave in five days, and in his anxiousness he made repeated visits to the principal, and continued to check if the university had contacted the embassy. According to his travel agent, the embassy had not heard from them yet, so he called

Kim Hye Sook and lashed out. She was an easy target for his anger and complaints. Donna White soon contacted him, saying that they had sent a fax to the embassy.

Again, he spent restless days in waiting, unable to do anything other than worry about the J-1 visa. In a dream, he dropped his passport on the street and instantly the ground turned into a slithering conveyor belt that whisked away his passport. Even in the dream, he shook from head to toe in deathly fear of losing his passport. He awoke from the nightmare in self-pity and scorn. Despite the ominous dream, happy news soon arrived from the connected politician. The principal called before school started on the morning of June 5th.

"The visa has been issued. You need to go in person to pick it up sometime this morning. Ask for Mr. Roberts. I've had the pleasure of meeting him already—a handsome, friendly guy who is quite conversant in our language. So don't worry. And don't wait in the long line by the back door, but go straight to the front door from Sejong Avenue. Okay? Mr. Roberts, don't forget."

Reminders from the principal were quite unnecessary because he had conjured up an image of a robot in connection with the name. There was a protest in front of the Korea Communications building, which was adjacent to the embassy. He suddenly felt guilty that he had tuned out important societal affairs because of petty personal concerns. One of the flyers thrown from the rooftop was coming at him, so he waited for it to hit the ground and picked it up. Without reading it, he shoved it into his pocket. He told the guard at the gate that he had an appointment with Mr. Roberts and was admitted upon producing identification. He had to pass through several heavy doors including revolving doors, which made him feel as though he was entering an impenetrable bunker. The hefty doors somehow made him feel intimidated and bullied. Soon after he reported the purpose of his visit at the lobby, Roberts came down, a passport proudly jutting out from his hand. It seemed ages ago that he had parted with his passport, and seeing it again brought him great relief. In his eagerness to be reunited with it, he first thanked Roberts. But what Roberts brought with him was only the passport and not the visa. Roberts whipped out an application form and said that if he filled it out right then and there, he'd try to issue a visa as soon as possible.

He took the form, but hands shaking from anger and humiliation prevented him from writing. Being farsighted, he could see only the top line in bold letters that read, "Please print or type in English in the blank spaces that appear below."

"This form has already been submitted. Why do you need me to fill this out now? Tomorrow is Memorial Day and the embassy will be closed, and I have to leave the country by June 7th, which is the day after tomorrow. I can't get ready for my trip expecting the visa to come through that morning. There isn't enough time for me to stop by here before going to the airport."

Roberts was flipping through the passport while he spoke. With innocent blue eyes, he asked, "Why are you so intent on traveling on a J-1 visa when you're obviously pressed for time? I see here that you have valid B-1 and B-2 visas. I simply don't understand."

Was it because Roberts was waving the open passport while he spoke? He couldn't put his finger on it, but he was deeply insulted.

"Then please let me have my passport back. I'll figure something out, so don't concern yourself with what visa I use."

Roberts willingly handed him the passport and shook his hand to wish him a safe trip. He seemed relieved to be freed from further responsibility.

The principal, when told what had happened, reacted heatedly and was about to run off to Yoon Aera's father. He held him back.

"This can't be true, Mr. Lee. I bet you didn't act quite right at the embassy. By that I mean you don't always know when to appear humble and when to be proud. No doubt, you were making stiff demands."

The principal concluded the matter by blaming him for the plans gone awry. He bore no hard feelings, however, because the principal had been the single most helpful person throughout this ordeal. He had confided in a few of his teacher or writer friends who sometimes traveled abroad on business. Of course, what he wanted from his friends was not practical advice but consolation by collectively denouncing the American embassy. But they disappointed him by taking the opportunity to brag about themselves instead: so-and-so was demeaned during the interview but *I* was shown respect; most people get a one-year visa at most but *I* was able to get a five-year one, and so on. He suffered through countless examples of insincere condolences that could be summed up as "too bad for you, but I got the royal treatment." Fools made petty comparisons, and idiots bickered over who was better. As the biggest idiot of them all, he felt like he had fallen to rock bottom, crawling on all fours and licking the dirt off the ground. He didn't ever want to think about it again.

Kim Hye Sook was understandably upset, almost weepy in her distress, and needed to be consoled. He then spent the night summarizing his presentation and organizing the thoughts spinning in his head, addressing the questions that were likely to have been raised. Before faxing over his work, he attached a note to Hye Sook urging her not to be discouraged by his absence and wishing her a successful conference. He was not quite ready to put matters to rest, however, or dismiss the nightmare he suffered as mere bad luck. Even an earthworm thrashes about when stepped on. After calming his nerves over the course of a few days, he wrote a letter to the organizers of the East Asian Studies conference as follows:

"After much deliberation, I am writing to share my experiences in the hopes that you'll have an easier time inviting other speakers from overseas in the future given the nature of your seminars."

He then explained from beginning to end all that had occurred.

"What infuriates me is what happened afterward. After nine days without any response, the U.S. embassy turned down my application because the conference date indicated on the original invitation had already passed. They wanted me to provide further evidence that the conference had been postponed. I was scheduled to leave in two days, but I could not tell if they would issue me a visa the next day even if I were to produce the necessary documentation. For all I knew, they could have made me wait another ten days before asking for something else. There never have been any standards in the American embassy's dealings with Korean nationals requiring their services. Thus, it is quite impossible for us to make travel plans to the U.S., not knowing if it will take a day, a week, or a month to secure a visa. I'm not sure if you have any idea what it is like for a busy person like me to make international travel plans, cancel them, and repeat the whole process again all to no avail. I was not sure if I needed to buy a plane ticket until the day before I was scheduled to leave. Although I was greatly inconvenienced by the U.S. embassy's practices, I have no means of protesting because the embassy does not accept civil complaints. That is why I am writing to you. I doubt that it is in the national interest of the U.S. to mistreat people to whom official invitations have been extended by reputable organizations. Thus, it is my wish that you will make an appeal to the U.S. embassy in Seoul on my behalf as the organizers of the conference who have requested my participation. Another matter I'd like to address is your university policy requiring a J-1 visa for conference participants. Without this requirement, I would have been able to attend on the given date without any difficulties."

Soon, he received a reply from the organizers. Everyone regretted his absence, and the discussion of his literary work had been very enlightening, with the summaries and notes he'd sent playing a crucial role in shedding light on the topic. In addition to this formal greeting, his concerns had been addressed as follows:

"We deeply regret that our plan to have you present at the conference failed to take place due to forces beyond our control. We understand that you are frustrated and angry with the U.S. government. This experience confirms our belief that colonialism is still alive and well on the Korean peninsula."

He hadn't blushed in a while, but what followed burned his heart as well as his face. A copy of the letter sent to the U.S. embassy in Korea was attached. This letter of protest was signed by the organizing scholars of the conference, "The Experience of Colonialism and Modernity" sponsored by the Humanities Research Center of the university. There were also signatures of scholars from other universities.

The letter outlined the course of events from the time he was first contacted by the university to the changes that both parties had made to accommodate his travel, leading to the ultimate disappointment of his not being able to attend. With exact dates and clear explanations given, the letter provided a more comprehensive account than his own memory of what had transpired. The conclusion of the letter was as follows:

"We are angered by the American government's abuse of power in dealing with persons of intellectual distinction in Korean society. In addition to unreasonable delays in processing paperwork, Mr. Lee Chang Gu was questioned for having ulterior motives for obtaining a J-1 visa. The staff member responsible for this kind of behavior must have assumed that he'd seek employment in the U.S. solely because that particular visa permits it. Mr. Lee was treated with the same oppressive attitude rendered toward Koreans by Americans in general, exposing our ignorance of the cultural frontrunners who shape that society. For instance, we couldn't imagine Nadine Gordimer of South Africa being treated in the same manner. As persons in academia researching topics pertaining to East Asia, we are in constant need of sharing cultural and literary ideas with relevant countries. The quality of our written work and teaching is intimately tied to our ability to make such exchanges. Your disregard and disrespect have resulted in the deterioration of international relations and the hindrance of academic endeavors. A prominent Korean literary personage has been affronted and the participants of the conference sponsored by those of us at this university have been greatly inconvenienced. With East Asian relations becoming increasingly important in the U.S., we have lost out on an important opportunity to further our efforts. This kind of incident can lead to a bigger social issue, arousing anger and hostility among the leaders of Korean society. If that happens, it will in no way be beneficial to the U.S. As the first step in preventing future incidents like this, we ask that a formal apology and explanation be given to Mr. Chang Gu Lee. In addition, we ask that you reimburse him for the expenses incurred in applying for a visa twice and in cancelling his flight reservation. We, the members whose signatures appear below, look forward to hearing from you soon."

He was with his wife when he read the letter. Feeling embarrassed and awkward, Lee Chang Gu blurted out, "These people think less of us than South Africans!"

His wife gave him a penetrating look and retorted, "Why, what do you have against South Africans?"

He became even more flustered and bluffed to his wife that he'd never again set foot on American soil without a formal apology from the U.S. embassy.

An Anecdote:
The Bane of My Existence

My computer was acting up again. This time, the problem was senility. Less than a year had passed since it devoured thirty A4-sized pages of my document. I wanted to take this opportunity to update the 386 model to the newer 586, but the thought of having two sets of computers in the house was repugnant to me. Of course, the logical thing would have been to throw away the old computer or donate it to a worthy cause. But I didn't think I could do that. It was because of the missing thirty pages. They were equivalent to three hundred handwritten pages on standard manuscript paper, but it was more than the sheer number of pages that concerned me. The missing portion made up a quarter of the novel I'd set out to write. Whether I'm writing a full-length novel or a short story, the first half is always the most difficult. In terms of time also, that part takes me forever. After writing the first quarter, writing the second quarter is infinitely easier. Finishing off the remaining half is like skipping downhill humming and whistling after a difficult climb to the top.

It was that precious first quarter that my computer had swallowed up. I called the manufacturer but all I got from the maintenance technician was a lecture about not backing up my work. I asked around and was referred to several computer gurus, but all they could retrieve was less than ten lines. At first, I was grateful even for that. My hope was to bring back the file little by little in that fashion. But no one was able to recover anything beyond that initial amount. I suppose one thing I gained from that experience was overcoming my dependence on that magical machine and adopting a more wary attitude. Sometimes I do miss the good old days of computer-free writing. It's not easy to constantly back up my work, not to mention how tiring it is to distrust a partner—even if it is a machine—with which I spend countless working hours. But I know well that there is no turning back.

After the gurus made every attempt and came up empty-handed, I thought of bringing in torture experts. Torture presented a neat prospect for me, because what could not be teased or coaxed out could perhaps be wrung out. I remember distinctly the time I inadvertently kicked a broken radio and recovered its sound. So I pounded the computer with my fist, tapped on it here and there with my knuckles, cursed it as the bane of my existence, and threatened it with a heavy club. Still, it refused to budge, disclosing only the file name and not its contents. I wrestled with it for days, making myself sick. By the time I recovered, the bits of my writing stored in my short-term memory had also vanished. Thus, what might have been the greatest novel of my career was completely gone. Still, I couldn't just trash the bane of my existence. For one thing, its word-processing capability was unaffected despite the abuse inflicted upon it. For another, I still maintained a relationship with it in the form of anger and resentment for having swallowed up the fruits of my labor, the pages begotten from my sweat, blood and tears. I am one of the few remaining writers from the old school who can claim with a straight face that the inspiration for writing comes from a hot-blooded heart and a noble conscience. That same person was now in a relationship from hell with a scrap of machine.

For the machine, it must have been the most human-like treatment it ever received. The latest problem I was having with the computer could only be explained by senility. That was the very human-like response I got for treating it like a person. After a few lines, the consonants and the vowels would refuse to come together, or the consonants would bounce off. For example, I'd type "go" but I would only see the letter "g." Thinking I didn't press down hard enough, I would retype the letter "o" several times to no avail. A closer inspection would reveal that the o's had scattered randomly, latching onto other words and crippling them. In another instance, I'd type the word "river" and the second "r" would run off elsewhere. This kind of misbehavior occurred at unpredictable times and showed no detectable patterns, with the vowels and the consonants flying off in all directions. If you spit on your palm and slap on it, you never know which way it will splatter. My computer spewed out gibberish in the same manner. I began calling my gurus again. But these so-called gurus didn't quite understand what I was saying, claiming never to have heard of such a problem. The diagnosis of senility was probably first suggested by one of them because it certainly didn't come from me. Senility is said to be a nightmare of a disease for humans, and it proved to be just as maddening for computers. I was fed up with anything computer-related, but as luck would have it, I had a deadline to meet. A friend took pity and lent me a notebook.

The notebook proved to be far less satisfactory than the computer I had grown attached to. Yeah, right. Attached to a darn machine. An ancient machine that I couldn't give away even if I tried. But as long as my next great masterpiece was hiding in that thing, it was for me an oyster containing a pearl. I couldn't give it up. I called the manufacturer one last time and requested a house call. The young technician who showed up didn't understand my explanation of senility, so I had to show him what I meant by typing. But the wretched machine refused to cooperate. It had always acted up every two or three lines, but with the technician over my shoulder, I typed a whole page without any glitches. I began to sweat. My typing was so clumsy and slow, and at that speed, it was impossible to tell whether I or the machine was at fault. After watching painfully, the technician spoke up.

"Who used this computer before you?"

"It's not used. It's been mine from the beginning."

"So, you're chatting on this thing with *your* computer skills?"

His face, which had been full of peeved derision suddenly assumed a brief and impish curiosity. Maybe it was a good thing that he hadn't caught on to the fact that I was a writer whose work required the regular use of a computer. I always thought I had made a name for myself as a writer, but perhaps I was mistaken.

"I don't do any chatting, whatever that is."

"Then you must be into gaming."

He became even more brazen, slimy in his insolence. Then he took over the keyboard. After his fingers danced adroitly over the keys, he declared that the computer was hopelessly infected by a virus.

I hurriedly grabbed the notebook sitting next to it and took it to another room.

"What are you doing? Why did you take that away?"

"Didn't you say the computer had a virus? I don't want it spreading . . ."

"Ma'am, are you sure you're the one using this computer?" The young man asked me in disbelief. Oh . . . I smiled sheepishly when I realized my mistake. Granted, I was technically challenged, but I wasn't so ignorant to think that a computer virus could be transferred by air or by touch. My blunder was due to a reflex action to the word virus, an instinctive response to protect someone else.

"So is the virus responsible for jumbling my letters?"

"I'll fix what I can now. You can find out for yourself when you use it later." Shoving the diskette he had brought with him into the computer, he replied brusquely. At my age, why had I given up the simple beauty of a pen in favor of this newfangled machine and thus made myself vulnerable to this kind of insolence? It was so frustrating. The technician said that he had finished repairing the computer and asked once again if I was the main user. The third time was not the charm in this case. I felt compelled to reveal what I did for a living.

"Young man, as it is your job is to repair this machine, mine is to type on it to write."

He nodded his head in understanding, his face full of compassion.

"Ma'am, you live in a nice apartment like this. Why make life so difficult for yourself? With your typing skills, how much can you make a day? My mother is much younger than you. She gets a monthly allowance from us children, travels, and is enjoying her golden years. You should do the same."

"So I should," I sighed. Before I knew it, I was agreeing with him. One mistake after another with this guy.

"There are so many typists out there who can run circles around you. It's a wonder that you even get jobs."

The young man mumbled in a concerned voice and handed me a bill for seven dollars for the repair. Yes, it was a wonder for me as well.

Park Wan-suh (1931–2011) was one of the most beloved and recognized authors in Korean literature. In 1970, at age thirty-nine, when not many women would dare dream about a new career, Park debuted as an author with her first novel *The Naked Tree*. Her works went on to be best-sellers, and have been published widely around the world.

Elizabeth Haejin Yoon was born in Korea and immigrated to the US at age eleven. She attended Cornell University before working in various nonprofit organizations in the US, Korea, and Japan. *Lonesome You* is her first full-length translation of Korean fiction into English.

The Library of Korean Literature

The Library of Korean Literature, published by Dalkey Archive Press in collaboration with the Literature Translation Institute of Korea, presents modern classics of Korean literature in translation, featuring the best Korean authors from the late modern period through to the present day. The Library aims to introduce the intellectual and aesthetic diversity of contemporary Korean writing to English-language readers. The Library of Korean Literature is unprecedented in its scope, with Dalkey Archive Press publishing 25 Korean novels and short story collections in a single year.

The series is published in cooperation with the Literature Translation Institute of Korea, a center that promotes the cultural translation and worldwide dissemination of Korean language and culture.

SELECTED DALKEY ARCHIVE TITLES

MICHAL AJVAZ, *The Golden Age.*
The Other City.
PIERRE ALBERT-BIROT, *Grabinoulor.*
YUZ ALESHKOVSKY, *Kangaroo.*
FELIPE ALFAU, *Chromos.*
Locos.
IVAN ÂNGELO, *The Celebration.*
The Tower of Glass.
ANTÓNIO LOBO ANTUNES, *Knowledge of Hell.*
The Splendor of Portugal.
ALAIN ARIAS-MISSON, *Theatre of Incest.*
JOHN ASHBERY AND JAMES SCHUYLER,
A Nest of Ninnies.
ROBERT ASHLEY, *Perfect Lives.*
GABRIELA AVIGUR-ROTEM, *Heatwave and Crazy Birds.*
DJUNA BARNES, *Ladies Almanack.*
Ryder.
JOHN BARTH, *LETTERS.*
Sabbatical.
DONALD BARTHELME, *The King.*
Paradise.
SVETISLAV BASARA, *Chinese Letter.*
MIQUEL BAUÇÀ, *The Siege in the Room.*
RENÉ BELLETTO, *Dying.*
MAREK BIEŃCZYK, *Transparency.*
ANDREI BITOV, *Pushkin House.*
ANDREJ BLATNIK, *You Do Understand.*
LOUIS PAUL BOON, *Chapel Road.*
My Little War.
Summer in Termuren.
ROGER BOYLAN, *Killoyle.*
IGNÁCIO DE LOYOLA BRANDÃO,
Anonymous Celebrity.
Zero.
BONNIE BREMSER, *Troia: Mexican Memoirs.*
CHRISTINE BROOKE-ROSE, *Amalgamemnon.*
BRIGID BROPHY, *In Transit.*
GERALD L. BRUNS, *Modern Poetry and the Idea of Language.*
GABRIELLE BURTON, *Heartbreak Hotel.*
MICHEL BUTOR, *Degrees.*
Mobile.
G. CABRERA INFANTE, *Infante's Inferno.*
Three Trapped Tigers.
JULIETA CAMPOS,
The Fear of Losing Eurydice.
ANNE CARSON, *Eros the Bittersweet.*
ORLY CASTEL-BLOOM, *Dolly City.*
LOUIS-FERDINAND CÉLINE, *Castle to Castle.*
Conversations with Professor Y.
London Bridge.
Normance.
North.
Rigadoon.
MARIE CHAIX, *The Laurels of Lake Constance.*
HUGO CHARTERIS, *The Tide Is Right.*
ERIC CHEVILLARD, *Demolishing Nisard.*

MARC CHOLODENKO, *Mordechai Schamz.*
JOSHUA COHEN, *Witz.*
EMILY HOLMES COLEMAN, *The Shutter of Snow.*
ROBERT COOVER, *A Night at the Movies.*
STANLEY CRAWFORD, *Log of the S.S. The Mrs Unguentine.*
Some Instructions to My Wife.
RENÉ CREVEL, *Putting My Foot in It.*
RALPH CUSACK, *Cadenza.*
NICHOLAS DELBANCO, *The Count of Concord.*
Sherbrookes.
NIGEL DENNIS, *Cards of Identity.*
PETER DIMOCK, *A Short Rhetoric for Leaving the Family.*
ARIEL DORFMAN, *Konfidenz.*
COLEMAN DOWELL,
Island People.
Too Much Flesh and Jabez.
ARKADII DRAGOMOSHCHENKO, *Dust.*
RIKKI DUCORNET, *The Complete Butcher's Tales.*
The Fountains of Neptune.
The Jade Cabinet.
Phosphor in Dreamland.
WILLIAM EASTLAKE, *The Bamboo Bed.*
Castle Keep.
Lyric of the Circle Heart.
JEAN ECHENOZ, *Chopin's Move.*
STANLEY ELKIN, *A Bad Man.*
Criers and Kibitzers, Kibitzers and Criers.
The Dick Gibson Show.
The Franchiser.
The Living End.
Mrs. Ted Bliss.
FRANÇOIS EMMANUEL, *Invitation to a Voyage.*
SALVADOR ESPRIU, *Ariadne in the Grotesque Labyrinth.*
LESLIE A. FIEDLER, *Love and Death in the American Novel.*
JUAN FILLOY, *Op Oloop.*
ANDY FITCH, *Pop Poetics.*
GUSTAVE FLAUBERT, *Bouvard and Pécuchet.*
KASS FLEISHER, *Talking out of School.*
FORD MADOX FORD,
The March of Literature.
JON FOSSE, *Aliss at the Fire.*
Melancholy.
MAX FRISCH, *I'm Not Stiller.*
Man in the Holocene.
CARLOS FUENTES, *Christopher Unborn.*
Distant Relations.
Terra Nostra.
Where the Air Is Clear.
TAKEHIKO FUKUNAGA, *Flowers of Grass.*
WILLIAM GADDIS, *J R.*
The Recognitions.

JANICE GALLOWAY, *Foreign Parts*.
  The Trick Is to Keep Breathing.
WILLIAM H. GASS, *Cartesian Sonata
  and Other Novellas*.
  Finding a Form.
  A Temple of Texts.
  The Tunnel.
  Willie Masters' Lonesome Wife.
GÉRARD GAVARRY, *Hoppla! 1 2 3*.
ETIENNE GILSON,
  The Arts of the Beautiful.
  Forms and Substances in the Arts.
C. S. GISCOMBE, *Giscome Road*.
  Here.
DOUGLAS GLOVER, *Bad News of the Heart*.
WITOLD GOMBROWICZ,
  A Kind of Testament.
PAULO EMÍLIO SALES GOMES, *P's Three
  Women*.
GEORGI GOSPODINOV, *Natural Novel*.
JUAN GOYTISOLO, *Count Julian*.
  Juan the Landless.
  Makbara.
  Marks of Identity.
HENRY GREEN, *Back*.
  Blindness.
  Concluding.
  Doting.
  Nothing.
JACK GREEN, *Fire the Bastards!*
JIŘÍ GRUŠA, *The Questionnaire*.
MELA HARTWIG, *Am I a Redundant
  Human Being?*
JOHN HAWKES, *The Passion Artist*.
  Whistlejacket.
ELIZABETH HEIGHWAY, ED., *Contemporary
  Georgian Fiction*.
ALEKSANDAR HEMON, ED.,
  Best European Fiction.
AIDAN HIGGINS, *Balcony of Europe*.
  Blind Man's Bluff
  Bornholm Night-Ferry.
  Flotsam and Jetsam.
  Langrishe, Go Down.
  Scenes from a Receding Past.
KEIZO HINO, *Isle of Dreams*.
KAZUSHI HOSAKA, *Plainsong*.
ALDOUS HUXLEY, *Antic Hay*.
  Crome Yellow.
  Point Counter Point.
  Those Barren Leaves.
  Time Must Have a Stop.
NAOYUKI II, *The Shadow of a Blue Cat*.
GERT JONKE, *The Distant Sound*.
  Geometric Regional Novel.
  Homage to Czerny.
  The System of Vienna.
JACQUES JOUET, *Mountain R*.
  Savage.
  Upstaged.

MIEKO KANAI, *The Word Book*.
YORAM KANIUK, *Life on Sandpaper*.
HUGH KENNER, *Flaubert*.
  Joyce and Beckett: The Stoic Comedians.
  Joyce's Voices.
DANILO KIŠ, *The Attic*.
  Garden, Ashes.
  The Lute and the Scars
  Psalm 44.
  A Tomb for Boris Davidovich.
ANITA KONKKA, *A Fool's Paradise*.
GEORGE KONRÁD, *The City Builder*.
TADEUSZ KONWICKI, *A Minor Apocalypse*.
  The Polish Complex.
MENIS KOUMANDAREAS, *Koula*.
ELAINE KRAF, *The Princess of 72nd Street*.
JIM KRUSOE, *Iceland*.
AYŞE KULIN, *Farewell: A Mansion in
  Occupied Istanbul*.
EMILIO LASCANO TEGUI, *On Elegance
  While Sleeping*.
ERIC LAURRENT, *Do Not Touch*.
VIOLETTE LEDUC, *La Bâtarde*.
EDOUARD LEVÉ, *Autoportrait*.
  Suicide.
MARIO LEVI, *Istanbul Was a Fairy Tale*.
DEBORAH LEVY, *Billy and Girl*.
JOSÉ LEZAMA LIMA, *Paradiso*.
ROSA LIKSOM, *Dark Paradise*.
OSMAN LINS, *Avalovara*.
  The Queen of the Prisons of Greece.
ALF MAC LOCHLAINN,
  The Corpus in the Library.
  Out of Focus.
RON LOEWINSOHN, *Magnetic Field(s)*.
MINA LOY, *Stories and Essays of Mina Loy*.
D. KEITH MANO, *Take Five*.
MICHELINE AHARONIAN MARCOM,
  The Mirror in the Well.
BEN MARCUS,
  The Age of Wire and String.
WALLACE MARKFIELD,
  Teitlebaum's Window.
  To an Early Grave.
DAVID MARKSON, *Reader's Block*.
  Wittgenstein's Mistress.
CAROLE MASO, *AVA*.
LADISLAV MATEJKA AND KRYSTYNA
  POMORSKA, EDS.,
  *Readings in Russian Poetics:
    Formalist and Structuralist Views*.
HARRY MATHEWS, *Cigarettes*.
  The Conversions.
  *The Human Country: New and
    Collected Stories*.
  The Journalist.
  My Life in CIA.
  Singular Pleasures.
  *The Sinking of the Odradek
    Stadium*.
  Tlooth.

JOSEPH MCELROY,
   Night Soul and Other Stories.
ABDELWAHAB MEDDEB, *Talismano.*
GERHARD MEIER, *Isle of the Dead.*
HERMAN MELVILLE, *The Confidence-Man.*
AMANDA MICHALOPOULOU, *I'd Like.*
STEVEN MILLHAUSER, *The Barnum Museum.*
   In the Penny Arcade.
RALPH J. MILLS, JR., *Essays on Poetry.*
MOMUS, *The Book of Jokes.*
CHRISTINE MONTALBETTI, *The Origin of Man.*
   Western.
OLIVE MOORE, *Spleen.*
NICHOLAS MOSLEY, *Accident.*
   Assassins.
   Catastrophe Practice.
   Experience and Religion.
   A Garden of Trees.
   Hopeful Monsters.
   Imago Bird.
   Impossible Object.
   Inventing God.
   Judith.
   Look at the Dark.
   Natalie Natalia.
   Serpent.
   Time at War.
WARREN MOTTE,
   *Fables of the Novel: French Fiction
      since 1990.*
   *Fiction Now: The French Novel in
      the 21st Century.*
   *Oulipo: A Primer of Potential
      Literature.*
GERALD MURNANE, *Barley Patch.*
   Inland.
YVES NAVARRE, *Our Share of Time.*
   Sweet Tooth.
DOROTHY NELSON, *In Night's City.*
   Tar and Feathers.
ESHKOL NEVO, *Homesick.*
WILFRIDO D. NOLLEDO, *But for the Lovers.*
FLANN O'BRIEN, *At Swim-Two-Birds.*
   The Best of Myles.
   The Dalkey Archive.
   The Hard Life.
   The Poor Mouth.
   The Third Policeman.
CLAUDE OLLIER, *The Mise-en-Scène.*
   Wert and the Life Without End.
GIOVANNI ORELLI, *Walaschek's Dream.*
PATRIK OUŘEDNÍK, *Europeana.*
   The Opportune Moment, 1855.
BORIS PAHOR, *Necropolis.*
FERNANDO DEL PASO, *News from the
   Empire.*
   Palinuro of Mexico.
ROBERT PINGET, *The Inquisitory.*
   Mahu or The Material.
   Trio.
MANUEL PUIG, *Betrayed by Rita Hayworth.*

The Buenos Aires Affair.
Heartbreak Tango.
RAYMOND QUENEAU, *The Last Days.*
   Odile.
   Pierrot Mon Ami.
   Saint Glinglin.
ANN QUIN, *Berg.*
   Passages.
   Three.
   Tripticks.
ISHMAEL REED, *The Free-Lance Pallbearers.*
   The Last Days of Louisiana Red.
   Ishmael Reed: The Plays.
   Juice!
   Reckless Eyeballing.
   The Terrible Threes.
   The Terrible Twos.
   Yellow Back Radio Broke-Down.
JASIA REICHARDT, *15 Journeys Warsaw
   to London.*
NOËLLE REVAZ, *With the Animals.*
JOÃO UBALDO RIBEIRO, *House of the
   Fortunate Buddhas.*
JEAN RICARDOU, *Place Names.*
RAINER MARIA RILKE, *The Notebooks of
   Malte Laurids Brigge.*
JULIÁN RÍOS, *The House of Ulysses.*
   Larva: A Midsummer Night's Babel.
   Poundemonium.
   Procession of Shadows.
AUGUSTO ROA BASTOS, *I the Supreme.*
DANIËL ROBBERECHTS, *Arriving in Avignon.*
JEAN ROLIN, *The Explosion of the
   Radiator Hose.*
OLIVIER ROLIN, *Hotel Crystal.*
ALIX CLEO ROUBAUD, *Alix's Journal.*
JACQUES ROUBAUD, *The Form of a
   City Changes Faster, Alas, Than
   the Human Heart.*
   The Great Fire of London.
   Hortense in Exile.
   Hortense Is Abducted.
   The Loop.
   Mathematics:
   The Plurality of Worlds of Lewis.
   The Princess Hoppy.
   Some Thing Black.
RAYMOND ROUSSEL, *Impressions of Africa.*
VEDRANA RUDAN, *Night.*
STIG SÆTERBAKKEN, *Siamese.*
   Self Control.
LYDIE SALVAYRE, *The Company of Ghosts.*
   The Lecture.
   The Power of Flies.
LUIS RAFAEL SÁNCHEZ,
   Macho Camacho's Beat.
SEVERO SARDUY, *Cobra & Maitreya.*
NATHALIE SARRAUTE,
   Do You Hear Them?
   Martereau.
   The Planetarium.

SELECTED DALKEY ARCHIVE TITLES

ARNO SCHMIDT, *Collected Novellas.*
Collected Stories.
Nobodaddy's Children.
Two Novels.
ASAF SCHURR, *Motti.*
GAIL SCOTT, *My Paris.*
DAMION SEARLS, *What We Were Doing and Where We Were Going.*
JUNE AKERS SEESE,
Is This What Other Women Feel Too?
What Waiting Really Means.
BERNARD SHARE, *Inish.*
Transit.
VIKTOR SHKLOVSKY, *Bowstring.*
Knight's Move.
A Sentimental Journey: Memoirs 1917–1922.
Energy of Delusion: A Book on Plot.
Literature and Cinematography.
Theory of Prose.
Third Factory.
Zoo, or Letters Not about Love.
PIERRE SINIAC, *The Collaborators.*
KJERSTI A. SKOMSVOLD, *The Faster I Walk, the Smaller I Am.*
JOSEF ŠKVORECKÝ, *The Engineer of Human Souls.*
GILBERT SORRENTINO,
Aberration of Starlight.
Blue Pastoral.
Crystal Vision.
Imaginative Qualities of Actual Things.
Mulligan Stew.
Pack of Lies.
Red the Fiend.
The Sky Changes.
Something Said.
Splendide-Hôtel.
Steelwork.
Under the Shadow.
W. M. SPACKMAN, *The Complete Fiction.*
ANDRZEJ STASIUK, *Dukla.*
Fado.
GERTRUDE STEIN, *The Making of Americans.*
A Novel of Thank You.
LARS SVENDSEN, *A Philosophy of Evil.*
PIOTR SZEWC, *Annihilation.*
GONÇALO M. TAVARES, *Jerusalem.*
Joseph Walser's Machine.
Learning to Pray in the Age of Technique.
LUCIAN DAN TEODOROVICI,
Our Circus Presents . . .
NIKANOR TERATOLOGEN, *Assisted Living.*
STEFAN THEMERSON, *Hobson's Island.*
The Mystery of the Sardine.
Tom Harris.
TAEKO TOMIOKA, *Building Waves.*

JOHN TOOMEY, *Sleepwalker.*
JEAN-PHILIPPE TOUSSAINT, *The Bathroom.*
Camera.
Monsieur.
Reticence.
Running Away.
Self-Portrait Abroad.
Television.
The Truth about Marie.
DUMITRU TSEPENEAG, *Hotel Europa.*
The Necessary Marriage.
Pigeon Post.
Vain Art of the Fugue.
ESTHER TUSQUETS, *Stranded.*
DUBRAVKA UGRESIC, *Lend Me Your Character.*
Thank You for Not Reading.
TOR ULVEN, *Replacement.*
MATI UNT, *Brecht at Night.*
Diary of a Blood Donor.
Things in the Night.
ÁLVARO URIBE AND OLIVIA SEARS, EDS.,
Best of Contemporary Mexican Fiction.
ELOY URROZ, *Friction.*
The Obstacles.
LUISA VALENZUELA, *Dark Desires and the Others.*
He Who Searches.
PAUL VERHAEGHEN, *Omega Minor.*
AGLAJA VETERANYI, *Why the Child Is Cooking in the Polenta.*
BORIS VIAN, *Heartsnatcher.*
LLORENÇ VILLALONGA, *The Dolls' Room.*
TOOMAS VINT, *An Unending Landscape.*
ORNELA VORPSI, *The Country Where No One Ever Dies.*
AUSTRYN WAINHOUSE, *Hedyphagetica.*
CURTIS WHITE, *America's Magic Mountain.*
The Idea of Home.
Memories of My Father Watching TV.
Requiem.
DIANE WILLIAMS, *Excitability: Selected Stories.*
Romancer Erector.
DOUGLAS WOOLF, *Wall to Wall.*
Ya! & John-Juan.
JAY WRIGHT, *Polynomials and Pollen.*
The Presentable Art of Reading Absence.
PHILIP WYLIE, *Generation of Vipers.*
MARGUERITE YOUNG, *Angel in the Forest.*
Miss MacIntosh, My Darling.
REYOUNG, *Unbabbling.*
VLADO ŽABOT, *The Succubus.*
ZORAN ŽIVKOVIĆ, *Hidden Camera.*
LOUIS ZUKOFSKY, *Collected Fiction.*
VITOMIL ZUPAN, *Minuet for Guitar.*
SCOTT ZWIREN, *God Head.*

FOR A FULL LIST OF PUBLICATIONS, VISIT:
www.dalkeyarchive.com